# Rescue Nightfall

Leah Hermann

This book is a work of fiction. Names, characters, places, and incidents are the product of the author's imagination or are used fictitiously. Any resemblance to actual events, locales, or persons, living or dead, is coincidental.

Dedicated to Jason and Trinity, my two goofy kiddos. The world may not be ideal, but as long as you set your eyes above and love one another, you will find life can be beautiful.

## Acknowledgments

As always, thank you to my beta readers for taking the time out of their busy schedules to help read over my manuscript. I love that you all are so willing to continue to stick by my side for as long as I write.

Thank you, Dad, for always letting me watch R-rated movies, especially the vampire ones, when most parents wouldn't allow it. You should get most of the credit for the vampire novels I write.

Liane Larocque, thanks for always doing such a phenomenal job editing my manuscript. More so, thank you for always being there whenever I'm in need of your advice. You always look out for me, and I appreciate you for that!

Hypercat Creative, you produce the most outstanding covers. You never disappoint and exceed my expectations every time. I'm thankful for everything you do and all your support.

Alexia Lardinais, you have been nothing but supportive from the very start of my journey as an author. You always encourage me with genuinely kind words, and it means so much to me. You are the type of person that is rare to come by, and I thank you for choosing to be a part of my life.

# Chapter One

## Too Many Questions

"The van needs gas, Delilah," my grandpa shouted from the basement where he slaved away all day, every day.

"But it's only a couple of hours until dusk," Ben answered since I was preoccupied with chomping down on the last bite of canned beans left in my bowl.

When Ben shot me a glance for approval, I nodded, agreeing. Grandpa never had us leave the house when it was that close to sunset. But as soon as I stood from the kitchen dining table and brought my bowl to the sink, we heard Grandpa's footsteps coming up the stairs—one foot dragging at a time accompanied by the squeaking of his knee brace that he never kept lubricated.

Grandpa was approaching his ninety-first birthday, and he hadn't been getting around too well the last few years. It didn't help that he injured his knee when he was in the military and had to wear a metal brace to keep his leg from buckling underneath him.

"Uh-oh," Ben whispered across the kitchen to me. "I guess that was the wrong answer."

Grandpa took a seat at the table next to Ben. After Grandpa caught his breath, he began to explain himself, "You kiddos know I hate asking you to run errands for me, but as you both know, I've been working on a large order this past week. I lost track of time. I meant to have you fill up the van sooner."

"You mean, you're finally done?" I asked excitedly.

Grandpa became an engineer in the military just as vampires began to emerge. He gained a lot of useful knowledge by choosing the military as a career path, but after a few short years, the military became practically nonexistent due to the losses that came with the endless battles against an unfamiliar species. When the military collapsed, Grandpa made his way back home and to the basement under our house, which became his new base.

Grandpa was one of the lucky ones. Thank goodness because he continued to save countless lives by slaving away for the last seventy years of his life. Everyone assumed he would spend less time working once Ben and I were born, but that wasn't the case. Grandpa would never sacrifice innocent lives to spend more time with his grandchildren. As sad as it made me to admit such a thing, it was the truth.

Ten years after the war began, Grandpa started producing UV lights of various sorts. He played an important role in the fight against the vampires, and Ben and I provided a helping hand. Grandpa had us tag along on scrapping missions as well as set up perimeters, and as much as I complained about not being Grandpa's number one priority, I knew I shouldn't since our work was what kept us and others alive.

Once vampires came into existence, it felt as if it was a simultaneous occurrence that more than half the population was wiped out. No one knew how many of us were left, but we did know Grandpa's work was one of our last lines of defense. With garlic, holy water, and wooden stakes being myths, we were left with only a couple of options—weapons forged of silver and sunlight, and unless you knew how to fight, which most didn't, weapons weren't as useful as a good ol' ray of sunshine.

Living in a small town also helped us survive. The larger cities were the first to become infested by bloodsuckers. The news described them as rodents, breeding uncontrollably. Except these rodents had sharp fangs and craved human blood. Grandpa used to talk about how he hated growing up in a small town. That's why he joined the military—anything to get out of Hope, Idaho. However, Grandpa's opinion about his home eventually changed.

Many factors played in our survival, but Grandpa deserved almost all the credit. He kept us fed by selling and trading lights to nearby survivors. So, although Ben and I didn't get to spend much quality time with Grandpa, we knew we'd be lost without him, or rather sucked dry, rotting away in an alley, or even worse, turned into one of the blood-sucking creatures.

I also assumed Grandpa's work saved *him,* too, since his daughter-in-law died when we were born. It wasn't easy to find the proper medical care, especially during a birth after the sun went down. And as if things couldn't get any harder, our dad went out to help Grandpa make a delivery one day and never returned. When Grandpa went looking for his son, he found his truck broken down on the side of the road. The hood was propped open as if my dad was trying to get it running again. Grandpa assumed the monsters who owned the night took him since there wasn't a body in sight, and he had yet to return.

Without Grandpa's work to keep him busy, he'd probably be in the darkest of places. I knew I reminded him of his son, and it made it hard for him to look at me for a prolonged period. Ben didn't have that effect on Grandpa since he didn't look like a part of the family with his freckles and blinding red hair. Ben hated being a ginger and wished he had gotten the brunette hair I was gifted from our parents. The only thing Ben and I had in common was our brown eyes and fair skin. Other than that, no one would ever guess we were twins, let alone related. And although I wanted to spend more quality time with my grandpa, I did my best not to hold onto any hard feelings.

"Yes, I'm finally finished," Grandpa answered as he lowered his chin to look at Ben over the frame of his glasses. "Could've used some help, though. Would've gotten things done a lot faster if I had an extra set of hands."

"Delilah has two hands," Ben pointed out.

Grandpa ignored Ben's comment and continued, "I was up all night after getting word from the buyers that they want their order by tomorrow or they aren't going to pay us what they agreed. I will admit, the lights did take me a bit longer than usual to complete this time." Grandpa stretched his fingers, extending them, and then curled them in a ball, over and over again, releasing the tension built up in his hands. "Joints aren't greased up like they used to be. Just glad I was able to get things done this time. Anyway, as I'd mentioned, I didn't realize how late it was getting. More frequently, I find myself wondering where the time went. Must be getting old," he joked.

"No way," I countered. "You aren't allowed to get old. You know that."

My comment made Grandpa smile.

Immediately after Ben finished eating, he began playing on his Game Boy which used to belong to Dad. "Sorry, Gramps, you should've asked," Ben added, his eyes fixated on the screen. "You know I would've helped you out."

"Hmm," Grandpa hummed. "I'm not too sure about that. I know you kiddos would rather be playing those video games than doing manual labor... or anything else, for that matter. When I was a kid, we used to beg to go outside and roll in the dirt."

I chuckled. "Grandpa, why would anyone want to roll in the dirt?"

"It's just a saying," Grandpa smirked.

"Can't exactly run around outside like you said *kids* used to, you know… with the danger and all," Ben countered, always looking for an excuse to be a slug.

Ben also didn't like Grandpa calling us kids. For whatever reason, he'd get super offended.

"You can when the suns up!" Grandpa said, annoyed, as if Ben didn't have any common sense.

Sometimes, I believed the video games Ben played really did rot his brain.

"Can't be too safe," Ben said, his eyes still glued to the Game Boy.

"That's Ben," I clarified. "I've never touched Dad's old video games, which I'm glad because it seems addicting."

"I could be addicted to worse things," Ben scowled.

Ben had Dad's video games and the memories of staying up late and playing them together. I had Mom's necklace that I never took off, and the three of us had photos of them that hung on the walls of the house, but that was all that was left of our parents, that and the stories Grandpa told us.

"It's all right," Grandpa continued. "I know it's been difficult not being able to grow up like children used to before the vampires took over the night."

"We just turned eighteen, Gramps. We're not *kids*," Ben replied.

"Oh, I know, I know," Grandpa answered. "Both of you grew up too fast, right before my very own eyes. You kids have helped keep me young for the last eighteen years. I don't know how these old bones of mine lasted this long, but God willing, they have. Although you both know I can't keep living forever."

Grandpa raised us, taught us, and saved us. Ben and I never imagined our lives without him. We couldn't picture a life without him and didn't want to.

"Don't talk like that, Grandpa," I countered. "You're going to live another eighty years. I heard you have your twenty-first birthday coming up."

Grandpa chuckled loudly, "Yes, that's right, young and in my prime." His laughter died off, knowing a good sense of humor wouldn't deliver the lights. "Anyway, I need you two to get the van filled up for tomorrow. The delivery is up north, a little past Shiloh."

"What?" I asked, surprised, "but that's over an hour away. We've never traveled that far."

"Yes, well, desperate times call for desperate measures," Grandpa explained. "I've provided almost all the survivors nearby with lights. I couldn't turn down these folks on their offer. They have what you'd call a mansion and need a ton of lights for protection. It was equivalent to three or four orders we normally get. They are going to give us an entire month's supply of food."

"Why would they stay there? Wouldn't it be safer in a smaller home?" I wondered. "There'd be less property to monitor."

"You'd think so, but one would assume it's not that easy leaving your home. Plus, I think their land provides for them," Grandpa answered. "Can you imagine having to leave the home your father, and now you and Ben, grew up in?"

Grandpa had a point, but at the same time, I thought about what it would be like to see the rest of the world like Grandpa did when the military gave him that opportunity. The house we were confined to often felt like a prison. Although in my right mind, I knew it was for our own safety, even though humans weren't meant to be locked away. We couldn't experience life at its fullest, but we weren't meant to *live.* We were meant to *survive.*

"Anyway, kiddos. I better get things ready to load up for tomorrow morning since we should leave early in case we run into any problems along the way. All three of us are going to go, and that includes you too, Ben."

Ben took a brief moment to look up from his game. "Seriously, Gramps?" he asked, still annoyed by Grandpa calling us children and even more so from being told what to do.

"Yes," Grandpa responded firmly. "It's a long drive. It's a lot for us to do. It'll take us all afternoon to get the perimeter set up around the place."

Ben paused from his game to dramatically roll his eyes and let out a sigh of disappointment. "I hate getting up early in the morning," he grumbled under his breath, quiet enough so Grandpa didn't hear his endless complaining.

"Come on, let's go, Ben," I urged.

I grabbed the car keys, and as a precaution, the oversized UV light that was too heavy to carry for a prolonged time. Like Grandpa would always say, "Better to be safe than dead."

"Stay safe," Grandpa told us before retreating toward the basement.

"We always do," I replied. "Ben, let's go!" I repeated, and he finally stood from his seat.

The gas station we always filled up at was only a few blocks away from our home, and for us, the gas was free since we provided the business with a light perimeter and repairs.

"Don't you ever get off that thing?" I scolded Ben as we drove.

"Dad left these *for me.* That means he *wanted* me to play them."

"Well, I think you use that as an excuse to bury your head," I pointed out.

"Just because Mom didn't leave you stuff nearly as cool doesn't mean you have to get your panties in a twist."

"Shut up, Ben. Don't talk about panties!"

"You've never heard that saying?" he laughed.

"Of course I have. But hearing the word panties leave your mouth is… *it's just wrong,*" I explained.

"Okay, whatever. You're so dramatic," he said under his breath in a mocking tone.

"I heard that," I scoffed and glared at him as we pulled up to the pump, not like he noticed. "Get out and pump after I tell Chad we're here," I ordered, thinking Ben ought to make himself useful like Grandpa mentioned.

"Huh?" Ben scoffed. "Why? You always pump the gas. It's like… *your job.*"

"I'm not your mother," I jabbed back. "You can help me once in a while."

"I do help," Ben mentioned, offended.

"You could help out *a lot* more," I added. "Grandpa's right, you have been spending a lot less time down in the basement with him and more time with your games."

Ben eventually set down his Game Boy but not without hostility. "I told you I don't like that kind of work."

"Come on, Grandpa needs you. He's getting to the point where he won't be able to work as hard anymore. He's old, Ben!" I yelled, becoming angry. "We can't keep thinking we can rely on him forever. He's getting tired. Can't you tell?"

"I know…" Ben said, finally showing some sympathy. "But you heard what he said. Our childhood was basically taken from us."

"So, what does that mean?"

"It means I should find enjoyment when I can. I don't want to be working all the time like him."

"I don't understand how you can sound so ungrateful. I'm starting to think it's not the type of work you don't like but rather that you don't like *any* kind of work," I reminded him. "You don't do anything these days besides play your dumb games."

"That's not true. I've been working hard the past eighteen years," Ben said, exaggerating.

"Oh, yeah?" I asked in disbelief. "And what job have you had the past eighteen years?"

"Keeping you safe," he answered as if he truly believed what he was saying. "And it's not like I try to make it sound like I take everything Gramps does for granted. I know what he's done for us, all the sacrifices he's made."

I shook my head before turning the engine off, knowing Ben was full of it. "Yeah, right," I murmured, but then Ben stopped me.

"Wait! I like this song. Leave the engine running."

"Grandpa said to always turn off the engine when pumping gas," I reminded him.

"Don't worry. I'll turn it off before I start pumping," Ben assured me.

"You're ridiculous, and you should probably get it out of your big, bloated head that you've been protecting me the past eighteen years," I said before leaving him to listen to the same song that played over and over again on the one surviving station.

If anyone asked Ben who had done the better job of taking care of the other, Ben would say he was my protector because that was what he believed. I was sure it had to do with him being born five minutes before me, and technically being the "older" sibling automatically gave him that role.

"Evenin', Delilah," Chad greeted me as the metal bell hanging above the gas station door swung, alerting him that a customer had entered the store. "You're here later than usual."

"I know. Our grandpa sprung a gas run on us last minute. I think he originally planned on us coming later in the week and earlier in the day, but his buyers pressured him to finish their lights earlier than expected. He lost track of time like he normally does and forgot to tell us to come earlier today. We need to load up and leave tomorrow morning."

"Where ya guys headed?" Chad asked, tugging on the bill of his grease-stained baseball cap.

"Some place just past Shiloh," I answered.

"Oh, that's farther than usual."

"That's what I said. Business is getting harder to find," I explained. "Big order, though. It's going to take some time to set up the perimeter."

"At least ya guys are staying fed," Chad mentioned. "It's been a struggle to get fuel deliveries these last few months. Really, the past few decades have been a struggle, seeing as we can't transport gas or anything during the night anymore."

"I can imagine. Well, my family appreciates your generosity," I reminded him.

"Hey," Chad began hesitantly. He took a moment to scratch his scruffy chin. "If… if it's not too much to ask, do you think your grandpa would be willing to make me a handheld light? Ya know, just in case of an emergency?"

I turned back and smiled. "I'm sure it wouldn't be a problem."

"Thanks, Delilah," Chad replied.

"No, thank *you* for the fuel."

"You do more for me than I could ever do for your family," Chad mentioned. "Anyway, I see where you're parked. I'll get the pump flowing for you."

I walked out of the store and saw that Ben decided to get out of the van to help pump the gas, but instead of reaching for the gas nozzle, he walked around the van toward me with worry strewn across his face.

"What's wrong?" I asked.

"I, uh— the…" Ben looked over his shoulder and pointed to the van, or rather to the black puddle underneath it.

"What happened?" I exclaimed. "Did you try to start it up again?"

"No, not yet."

I quickly hopped into the van and turned the key, starting the ignition. A sense of relief washed over me since nothing seemed wrong, but then suddenly, the oil light came on, and any relief I felt instantly vanished.

Ben knocked on the passenger window. I rolled my eyes at Ben but leaned over and cranked the window down.

"What?" I asked, annoyed. "You couldn't just open the door?"

Ben ignored my question and peeked his head in through the window. "So, are we good?" he asked, hopeful.

"I don't know," I admitted. "Let me get Chad. He might know what's going on."

Chad not only ran a gas station but also had a small garage on the side of the building where he worked on cars. It was convenient to have someone close to home with knowledge we didn't have.

"Looks like you have a cracked oil pan," Chad explained.

"Can we drive it home?" Ben asked, hopeful.

"Uh…" Chad stammered, scratching his chin again, unsure if it was a good idea. "I mean, I don't know."

"We're only a few blocks away," I reminded Chad.

"Yeah, ya guys might be able to make it, but weren't you saying you have to make that delivery tomorrow?"

"Damnit!" I screamed. "You're right. Shit! You're right. What are we going to do?" I asked, becoming panicked.

"Well," Chad continued, "It's not all that bad. There could be a lot worse things."

"So, are you saying that you can fix it?" I asked.

"I can, but it'll take me a little while," Chad explained.

I looked up at the sun which would be gone soon.

"We should have just enough time before I need to lock up and hit the lights," Chad mentioned. "Thankfully, the oil pan in your ride is pretty easy to get to." Then he pointed to himself like pride had washed over him. "And I'm awesome at my job."

I didn't see how we had any other choice. A month's supply of food was hard to come by. Grandpa usually only got a week's worth from one normal-sized order, if that, or maybe a day or two from a repair job. Sometimes, people paid in cash, but it was more common for customers to trade supplies or sustenance. A month's supply of food would allow Grandpa to relax for a little while, that is if he could bring himself to do so. If anything, it would give all of us peace of mind that food would be on the table.

"Can we use your phone?" I asked Chad.

"Course," he replied.

"Ben, go call Grandpa and let him know what's going on and that we will be home late, but don't worry him. Tell him we will be home before the sun goes down."

Ben nodded and did as I instructed.

Almost three hours later, Chad wiped his greasy hands along the side of his pants. "All right, Delilah. I think she's good to go. Sorry, took me a little longer than I had anticipated, but I know you don't have too far to go."

"We owe you. I'll tell Grandpa we need to bring you some cans of food next time we see you," I mentioned. "And, yes, we just live— oh, shoot! We never filled up."

"Oh, yeah," Ben chimed in and jogged over to the pump, waiting to gas up.

"No worries. I'll go in and reset it," Chad said. "But I'm going to lock up and turn the perimeter lights on. So, I'll have to catch ya next time. Don't take too long out here. Gangs like to stop by to hang out in the parking lot fairly often these days."

"L-like vampire gangs?" Ben stuttered.

"No, not exactly. Actually, I'm not sure. Maybe I shouldn't have called them gangs, but I'm certain they aren't vampires. They like to duke it out in front of my store. Don't know how long their presence will last, but I can't contest, and they don't do any harm, so I guess it's fine. And who knows, maybe they might ward off vampires."

"Vampires are scared of them?" I asked, more confused than ever.

Chad shrugged, "It's just a theory I have. They do get a bit rowdy, though, and keep me up at night. You'd think vampires would be attracted to the sound, but I haven't seen any." Chad chuckled like it couldn't have been more ironic they picked his parking lot, and then he glanced at his watch. "Anyway, if they do show up, they will start arriving any minute. So, hurry and fill up your tank. I can't say for sure that they are the friendliest bunch."

I nodded at Chad. He gathered his tools and placed them in the toolbox, and then he retreated to the shop where he also called home.

"You're probably good to start pumping now," I told Ben a moment after I watched Chad lock the doors, frustrated Ben hadn't already started pumping.

I guess I shouldn't have been too surprised when it took Ben forever to remove the gas cap. He didn't have much practice.

"What's taking you so long?" I asked Ben while keeping an eye out for unwanted company. "Grandpa's probably worried about us."

The sun was hardly visible, and the van was just out of range from Chad's light perimeter. I grabbed the bulky UV light from the back seat just in case.

"I— I, um," Ben stuttered as I walked around to see what was going on. His hand shook slightly as he fumbled putting the nozzle in the opening.

"Geez, get a grip, Ben!" I murmured hotly under my breath.

"Can you blame me? Chad freaked me out. He said gangs come at night, but they aren't vampires? Wh-who comes out at night? Wh-who's crazy enough t-to come out at night?" Ben's voice shook just as badly as his hands.

"I don't know. Let's not think about that and focus on getting back home. I don't want to be here when the sun goes down any more than you do."

"Too late," Ben mentioned, and I tilted my head back to see the sky filled with darkness.

"Of course," I breathed anxiously. "Here, you hold this," I told Ben after turning on the light and handed it to him. "Let me finish pumping the gas."

But just as I put the nozzle back and closed the cap on the van, a car pulled into the parking lot.

"Get in the van, Ben," I ordered, but he was frozen.

The car pulled up next to us and rolled down its window. Two guys sat in the front, and the driver smiled at us. They seemed to be around the same age as us, or maybe a couple of years older.

"What's that you got there?" the guy asked Ben, nodding toward the UV light.

Ben quickly raised the light, blinding both the driver and the passenger.

"What the hell, man? I'm not a vampire!" he laughed, raising his hand to block the light from his eyes.

Ben lowered it, his arms fatigued from the weight of the oversized light. We were both relieved the people in the car weren't vampires, although, the light would've easily turned them to ash.

"Sorry," I responded for Ben. "We can never be too sure."

"Was that supposed to disintegrate me?" the guy in the driver's seat asked mockingly.

"I— it would've if y-you were a vampire," Ben explained nervously.

The two in the car laughed hard at Ben's answer. "Well, I don't see it ending the war anytime soon," the passenger murmured under his breath.

"No one said anything about ending the war," I said defensively, "but it does the job when needed."

Chad mentioned that these people might ward off vampires. I wasn't so sure Chad was right, but one thing I was certain of was that they were dicks! The driver looked sketchy with his spiked mohawk and dark eyeliner. Grandpa said people who had tattoos and piercings in odd places were bad news, and that was the first time in my life that I had to agree with him.

"If you say so, *sweetheart*," the driver cooed affectionately. "I didn't mean to come off the wrong way." His demeanor completely changed as if he were trying to win me over. "Are you two sticking around for the fight?"

I would've taken more time to wallow in disgust if I wasn't so curious about what the guy meant and if it wasn't dark out, so I ignored his appalling term of endearment.

"Fight?" I asked, curiosity bubbling to the brim. "What do you mean… *fight*?"

The two guys exchanged glances with one another and smirked while whispering something that I couldn't quite make out.

"We'd better go," I told them. "We've been out too long as it is."

"You worried about the vamps coming around?" the passenger asked and pointed to his friend. "Frankie will keep you safe," he joked.

"Huh?" I asked, confused.

"You heard him," Frankie added. "I'll watch out for you, baby. I won't let any vampires touch you."

"Sorry, but my sister isn't fond of *assholes*," Ben said, surprisingly confident. However, when I looked down at Ben's hands, they were still shaking.

"What was that?" Frankie scoffed. Frankie and his friend didn't particularly enjoy being talked to that way and swung open their doors to confront Ben.

"Ben!" I yelled, shocked he'd put us in such an uncomfortable situation.

"What? It's true," he said innocently. "B-but m-maybe I shouldn't have said…"

"Get in the van now!" I screamed, and we scampered off to safety before the guys got nearer. "*I have an idiot for a brother*," I said angrily under my breath, quiet enough so Ben couldn't hear.

I started the engine and slammed on the button to lock the doors. Ben used both hands to crank up the window faster than ever as more vehicles came rolling into the parking lot.

"Do some of those look like military vehicles to you?" I asked Ben.

"Does it even matter?" he snapped.

I suppose Ben was right. It didn't matter, but thankfully, Frankie and his friend got back into their car when they realized we were out of their reach and safely in the van. I could hear them laughing loudly and mocking Ben.

A sense of relief washed over me now that we weren't within reach of harm's grasp, but my heart was beating a thousand miles a minute as I pictured Ben getting a beating.

"Why did you do that?" I asked Ben, frustrated.

"What'd I do?" he shrugged, playing dumb. "I was just trying to defend you."

"Defend me?" I scoffed. "I don't need you to *defend* me!"

"I was just trying to be a good brother."

"You're in no shape to be poking grizzly bears," I said, eyeing his scrawny arms.

"They weren't *vampires*," he countered.

"Yeah, I know, but they don't have to be vampires to kick your ass," I reminded him.

"Whatever," Ben replied, crossing his arms at my insults that were one hundred percent true. "Let's just go home."

But did I really want to go home? Were we safe? Chad said it was a possibility, and a part of me wanted to believe his theory. Also, I couldn't help but wonder what Frankie meant about a fight, and it didn't make sense how vampires stayed away when these people were around. I had so many questions and curiosity was violently clawing at my back.

I peered out the side of the van through the window, double-checking to see if our new acquaintances were going to come back and harass us a second time after parking their car. Luckily, Frankie found interest elsewhere with a guy dismounting his motorcycle. The motorcyclist removed his full-face helmet, revealing his blonde hair and eyes that reminded me of the sky before it turned to darkness.

Frankie excitedly greeted the guy who had just arrived as if he was his brother, grasping his hand while pulling him in tightly to pat him on the back. It seemed a bit odd that they were so chummy with one another since the guy who rode the motorcycle didn't look anything like Frankie or the guy who was in the passenger seat. The guy didn't have a crazy mohawk or any facial piercings.

I stared, watching the interaction between the three guys, and more specifically, I watched as the breeze caught the blonde hair of the motorcyclist. His body looked perfect—the type of build my brother probably envied. He looked strong like he could withstand a storm, like he would be the last person someone like Frankie would think of challenging.

"What are you looking at?" Ben asked, annoyed I hadn't started driving home yet.

I ignored him and continued to watch what was unfolding in the parking lot.

The guy unzipped his leather jacket and placed it on the top of his bike, but he didn't stop there. He removed his white T-shirt as well, leaving him clothed in only his jeans which revealed a tattoo of a phoenix on his back from shoulder to shoulder.

I could see every defined muscle, every striation. His body looked as if it had been made to be like that intentionally, almost unnatural, but at the same time… perfect. Being locked away from the world definitely had its disadvantages, and that was the first time I'd ever seen a man like him. It felt wrong to stare for so long, but it felt impossible to turn away.

Ben leaned over to look out the window, curious about what had caught my eye.

"You have got to be kidding me," Ben scowled, and as he spoke, a group of girls pulled up to join the guys.

The girls instantly flocked to the shirtless man, but one girl in particular was overly fond of him, running her hand down his chest. She was also attractive in her revealing outfit and long black hair, and at that moment, I was glad no one else had seen me in my raggedy overalls and worn shirt.

"What are they doing?" Ben asked, less hostile probably because the group not only consisted of guys anymore.

"I don't know," I answered. "Some kind of fight? That's what that one guy was saying… I think?"

"Maybe it would be best if we didn't stick around," Ben reminded me.

"Yeah," I nodded, slightly disappointed we couldn't stay. "Grandpa will come looking for us any minute."

"That's what I've been trying to say!" Ben said, hurrying me along.

I took the van off park and began driving out of the parking lot, but to do so, we had to pass the group that was gathering. I couldn't help but peer out the window one last time, and as I did, my gaze caught the eyes of the guy who everyone was rallying around. Everything seemed in slow motion as he smiled at me, his eyes as entrancing as the blue Idaho sky, beautiful and mysterious.

"Keep your eyes on the road!" Ben screamed when I began to veer off the road, almost running into the curb.

I gasped and pulled my gaze away to focus on the road while quickly jerking the steering wheel in the right direction. "Sorry," I mumbled.

"Goodness! Are you trying to kill us?" Ben continued, annoyed. "All we need is for you to crash our only means of transportation."

"Just shut up already," I said under my breath. "It's not like you're a better driver."

We returned home just as Grandpa was putting on his jacket.

"We're home, Grandpa," I said, throwing down the keys. "Sorry we're late."

Grandpa sighed and sat in the living room chair, relieved we were home. He didn't bother removing his jacket, exhausted from worrying.

"You told me you were going to be home before the sun went down," Grandpa added frustratedly. "What was the hold-up?"

"Nothing!" I answered a bit too loudly.

"Nothing?" Grandpa squinted, and I quickly looked over at Ben to make sure he wasn't going to open his big mouth.

"Yeah," Ben chimed in. "Just took Chad a bit longer than he thought to fix the van."

"Hmm," Grandpa thought for a moment, debating if he should dig deeper. "You should've called again to let me know it was going to take longer than expected."

"We should've," I admitted, hoping to ease any suspicion Grandpa might've had. "We just kept thinking Chad was going to be done any minute. The last thing we wanted to do was to worry you."

"You guys cut it close is all. I worry about you kiddos," Grandpa added.

"We know," I replied apologetically and went over to remove his coat. Grandpa willingly let me help him, and when he leaned forward, I noticed the shotgun propped against the wall beside his chair. "What were you going to do? Walk all the way to the gas station?"

"If that's what it came down to," Grandpa replied.

"You're in no condition to do such a thing," I mentioned.

"I'm not as fragile as you think," Grandpa reminded me. "I'm strong for an old man."

Grandpa was right. Minus that his walk wasn't steady, the rest of his body was strong for his age, and his mind and reflexes were still sharp. But even a younger man half his age shouldn't be out walking after nightfall. It was too dangerous.

"You could've been attacked on your way to the gas station," I reminded him, feeling terrible for lingering in Chad's parking lot a few more minutes than necessary.

A minute longer, Grandpa would've been out after the sun went down.

"That's better than sitting at home and worrying myself to death, wondering what happened to you two kids," Grandpa countered.

"We're sorry we worried you," I told Grandpa again.

Grandpa let out a long sigh, "I suppose I have to stop worrying at some point." Then he kicked back in the recliner and closed his eyes. "Like I said, I won't be here to keep you from the dangers forever. You two will have to learn to make your own decisions and protect one another."

I walked back over to my grandpa after hanging his jacket on the coat rack. I placed a blanket over him and kissed him gently on his forehead. "We know, Grandpa. Now, get some rest. We have a long trip tomorrow."

"That's right, we sure do," he replied. "And to be clear, I was going to bring my shotgun when I went looking for you two. Everyone knows I'm still the best shot." Grandpa smirked, his eyes still shut.

"We know, Grandpa," I chuckled. "We know…"

# Chapter Two

## Memories to Keep

That night, after returning home from Chad's gas station, I couldn't fall asleep. I lay awake in bed, tossing and turning, unable to stop my mind from thinking and trying to solve the hundreds of questions I didn't have an answer to. No matter how hard I tried to turn my mind off, it was impossible. I couldn't stop picturing the guy on the motorcycle. No one ever smiled at me like that before. No one ever looked at me the way he did.

He was clearly someone of importance. It was obvious by the way the girls as well as the guys reacted toward him. Everyone was drawn to him, dying for his attention. I wondered if I knew who he was, would I want to be around him just as much as everyone else?

I suppose it was silly to think someone like him would give me the time of day since I didn't look like those girls in the parking lot. I didn't have a mother to teach me how to be a girl or, rather, a woman. Although maybe it was a good thing that I didn't have memories of my mom since it would only make me miss her that much more. It was easier to live without someone who I hadn't grown attached to. I knew this was true because I had memories of my dad that reminded me of how much my heart ached without him.

Our dad went missing when Ben and I were eleven. I always felt I should remember more from my childhood, but I'd kept enough memories to remember that when he was alive, our hearts were fuller, they weren't as broken. A lifetime spent with Dad wouldn't have been enough time together, but he was around enough years for me to know that I missed every moment I had with him, the good and the bad. I wished he'd never left that day on that repair run, and more often than I should've, I asked God why he had to go so soon. Why did it have to be *him*? Why did he have to take more from us? What was the point of our dad leaving two children in a world infested with vampires?

My eyes began filling with pools of water, so I rolled onto my side to empty them. Once my tears seeped into my pillowcase, I could see more clearly, able to gaze out my bedroom window at the moon that was full that night, but my heart still hurt thinking about what I'd lost.

I hated how my mind wandered. I despised how I couldn't turn off my brain. Even though the emotions that overcame me felt familiar, I didn't want to cry myself to sleep again. I reached for the stuffed teddy bear across my bed and held him tightly against my chest. Ben always made fun of me for keeping such a juvenile thing, but I wouldn't ever be able to let it go, especially since it reminded me of one of the times I had with my dad.

Dad returned home from repairing a perimeter, and I rushed over to greet him, wrapping my arms around his leg.

"Hey, sugar bear," he said, rubbing the top of my head before kissing my cheek.

One of his hands stayed behind his back as if he was hiding something.

"Hi, Dad. You're back late," I mentioned.

"I know. I had to make a detour," he explained.

"For food?" I asked, curious.

"No," he replied.

"For tools?" I continued to guess.

"Nope," he answered as a smile began to form.

"For, um, for something Grandpa needed?"

"Not this time."

I tried to look behind his back to see what he was holding. I was all out of guesses. But then I had a hunch, and I hoped my last assumption would be right.

"I'll give you a hint," Dad added. "I wanted to get you and Ben something for your birthday. You guys will only turn six once, you know."

"My birthday is today?" I asked excitedly.

"No, it's next week, but I wanted to make sure I found something extra special for the two of you."

"Oh! Oh! I know. It's a dress," I said, hopeful, and began to jump up and down. "Is it like the one Mommy's wearing?" I wondered, pointing to one of the pictures hanging on the wall.

"Sorry, sugar bear, it's not. Not sure they make too many dresses anymore, remember? And I told you, it's better that you wear outfits like this," he reminded me, tugging on the sleeve of my shirt.

Textile factories, for the most part, stopped making girly clothing. They had to choose wisely when deciding what clothing to make, considering everything became scarce when the war started. Most people picked practical over fashionable. Survival was above all else, and if one ran into a predicament then the heels and dresses my mother wore in many of her pictures weren't the best choice to defend yourself in.

My excitement vanished, and I pushed out my bottom lip while staring at my faded jeans that were two sizes too small. "Darn," I murmured to myself.

With my dad's free hand, he tilted my chin and smiled at me. "You know, you're just as beautiful as your mother."

My pouty face ceased from hearing my dad say something so flattering. "Really?" I asked.

"I wouldn't lie, sugar bear."

"Thanks, Daddy."

"Of course, but you should know, even though she was the most beautiful woman I'd ever seen, that wasn't why I fell in love with her."

"Did she bring you yummy food?" I asked, beginning to make guesses again.

"No," he laughed.

"Hmm… Did she—"

"It was because of her personality," he explained.

I folded my arms across my chest, frustrated my dad didn't let me get all my guesses out. "Hey, you didn't let me finish," I said crossly.

"Oh, I'm sorry. I didn't mean to do that. I'm sure you would've gotten it right eventually."

I liked that my dad thought I was a smart kid, so I let my arms relax at my sides. "Yeah, you're right. So, what does personality mean?"

He pointed to my chest. "It means what's inside of you."

I looked down to where he was pointing, still confused. "Like my heart?"

"Exactly," my dad said while smirking. "She was more beautiful inside than out. She loved everyone she met with a full heart. I don't think there was a bad bone in her body. Your mom lived, loved, and forgave like people are supposed to. Oh, and I can't forget to mention her humor. She always kept me laughing. It was one of the best things about her."

"So, you are saying that I should work on being funnier?" I asked, confused.

My dad laughed even harder. "Only if you want to. I think you're quite the comedian already," he mentioned.

"What's a comedian?"

But before Dad could answer, Ben ran up to him, pushing me out of the way. "Hi, Dad!" he yelled.

"Ben!" I screamed angrily. "You aren't supposed to do that! I was talking to Dad first!"

"Okay, you two, let's calm down," he said and stuck his hand into his pocket, still making me wait for my present. "Ben, I got this for you." In Dad's palm was a gray plastic square-looking thing.

"No way!" Ben squealed excitedly. "Where did you find this?"

It must have been a game.

"I went to the town's toy store that had been abandoned since it was vandalized. It was on the floor under one of the shelves. Almost missed it while walking by. Wasn't sure I'd find anything."

Ben grabbed the game from Dad's palm and ran off while yelling, "Thanks, Dad! You're the best!"

My pouty lip decided to make another appearance. "Ben always gets to go first because he was born first," I grumbled.

"Not always," Dad mentioned.

"Most of the time," I countered.

He took a knee to meet my gaze. "You're right. Sorry that I always keep you waiting, but I like to save the best for last."

I couldn't help but grin and tried to look behind his back again. Just as I thought I was about to sneak a peek, he let me see what he was hiding. He held out a teddy bear with a bright red bow tied around his neck.

"For my sugar bear," he said. "Do you like him?"

I nodded, smiled, and quicker than Ben, I grabbed him out of Dad's hand. "Yes, Daddy, I love him! He's perfect."

"I'm glad you like him."

"He's so soft and cuddly," I cooed while pressing the bear close to my chest.

"That's not the best part," my dad added while slowly pulling the stuffed animal away from me, undoing the Velcro that lined the back of the bear.

"What are you doing?" I asked.

He pulled out a heart from inside the bear and showed it to me.

"Aw, he has a heart," I cooed.

"He sure does, and it happens to be a big one," Dad said.

"I love you, Daddy," I said, hugging him tightly.

"I love you too, sugar bear."

# Chapter Three

## The Perfect Delivery

"This is a farm," Ben stated as we pulled into a paved driveway. "I thought you said we were going to a mansion."

"Huge ranch house, mansion—same thing," Grandpa replied. "Did business over the phone, and now it makes sense why they have so much food for payment."

The farmhouse was painted a beautiful sky blue with white shutters that were slightly tattered due to time. There was a large wooden sign with the words "Bryer Farm" painted on it. Surrounding the house were fields that extended as far as the eye could see, some that were recently harvested and others with wheat just starting to sprout out of the dirt. The land was full of life and thriving, and the fluffiest of clouds hovered above. A pair of chestnut-colored horses ran wildly in a circle in a corral next to the farmhouse, and a large chicken coop was on the opposite side. It looked as if the war hadn't impacted the farm in the slightest bit, untouched by monsters. It didn't seem like a perimeter was necessary, but as I stood in awe, I realized why such a large piece of land was worth holding on to.

Before I could put the van in park, a lady dressed in a long ivory skirt walked out of the house, and I wondered where she got her outfit. Her wavy brunette hair flowed freely down to her hips. She waved at us like she'd been waiting all morning for our arrival.

"Hi there," she greeted us warmly as we hopped out of the van.

"Good morning. You must be Joseline?" Grandpa said while holding out his hand.

She gave him a firm shake. I could tell she was trying not to stare at his knee brace.

"Yes, it's nice to finally meet you in person," she replied, "and sorry to put so much pressure on you to get things done. I didn't mean to sound rude over the phone or seem like I was threatening not to pay you. Sincerely, I d-didn't..."

"It's all right," Grandpa replied. "There's no need for an apology. I can see you have a lot to be concerned about. How have you maintained so much land? Vampires don't come around here?"

"We've put up a barrier around our land using barbed wire as a precaution," Joseline said.

"Barbed wire?" Ben asked, skeptical.

"Melted all the jewelry passed down from my great grandma. The silverware, too, and whatever we came across over the years," she explained. "What neighbors we have nearby were kind enough to trade what they had for some of our food."

"Oh, *fancy* barbed wire," Grandpa joked.

"Guess you could say that," Joseline laughed as if she was trying to make light of a serious situation.

"And the vampires?" Grandpa asked again.

"Well, for the most part, while I was growing up, they stayed away. I only remember hearing of one encounter during my childhood when my dad went about a mile out to hunt for meat. My son just turned nineteen last month, and for nineteen years of his life, he's had the luxury of being sheltered from what's really out there. I hoped for at least another generation of peace, but I guess that was too much to ask for. That's why I called you to see what you could do to ensure our safety." Joseline crossed her arms as the breeze rustled across the farm, causing the tree branches to sway. She looked into the wind like there was something toxic sweeping by. "The horses have been uneasy the past few weeks… like something is coming. When we went into town, we heard the townsfolk talking about your work. I don't know if it made me more worried or less worried when I heard about how you set up perimeters. I felt a sense of relief knowing there was a solution, but I was also concerned that the chatter about such necessities finally reached our doorstep."

"Like I always say, *better to be safe than dead*," Grandpa laughed.

"That is very true," Joseline agreed, joining in with an uncomfortable chuckle. Not everyone was used to Grandpa's dry humor. "And that's exactly why I called you. My husband kept telling me to be patient, but I'm the worrywart of the two of us." She looked ashamed for rushing my grandpa to finish sooner. "I-I would like to apologize again for—"

"And I already told you, an apology isn't necessary," Grandpa countered.

"Right…" Joseline smiled warmly.

"Well, we better get to work," Grandpa said with no hard feelings. "It's going to take us all afternoon to get things set up."

"My husband will be back any minute now. He's finishing repairing a hole in the chicken coop, and then he can give you a hand. Don't want you and your kids to get home too late."

"That would be appreciated," Grandpa said, thankful. "Although my grandkids will get the job done nonetheless."

"I'll bring out some ice-cold lemonade in a little," she said before heading back inside.

"Lemonade?" Ben asked, confused. "What's that?"

I chuckled and nudged his shoulder. "An indulgence we could never afford. I wouldn't say it's as expensive as ice cream, but still up there."

"Guess we're in for a treat," Grandpa added.

And with that, we began unloading the van and got to work.

Hours ticked by, probably slower than they should've, but eventually, I finished mounting the last light to the house. "Catch," I told Ben as I stood on the ladder and tossed him the drill.

He frantically looked up while throwing his hands in the air, awkwardly catching it.

"Why do you do that?" he asked annoyed.

"Do what?"

"Such dangerous stuff. What if it hit me in the head?" He fumbled the drill before grasping it by the handle to shake angrily in my direction. "This is heavy, you know."

"It didn't knock you unconscious, so calm down."

"Well, what if it fell on the ground and broke? Grandpa would be so pissed."

I rolled my eyes at Ben and climbed down. "If it did happen to break, then you'd be at fault because you didn't catch it."

"How does that make any sense at all?"

"Just stop, Ben. You're always thinking of the worst possible situation, and you're too dramatic."

"I just like to be prepared. I know my actions have consequences… *unlike someone.*"

I was exhausted from a long day's work. Not like Ben who, on every job, simply handed me what I needed. I had to do all the heavy lifting, so I didn't have the energy to continue our argument.

"Get the ladder, and let's get going," Ben ordered. "I forgot my Game Boy at the house."

"Really?" I scoffed, but why was I surprised that Ben didn't want to help me load up the ladder?

"I'm tired too, you know!" he yelled as he stomped off toward the van.

I sighed loudly, frustrated by Ben's laziness, and then a voice from behind startled me, causing me to jump.

"I can help with that," a guy said.

I held my hand over my chest while breathing heavily and turned around to see who was behind me.

"Goodness! A little warning would be nice," I snapped.

It was Joseline's son. He was wearing a button-up shirt and pants that were covered in dirt. I would've normally looked into a person's eyes when meeting him for the first time, but his shirt was completely unbuttoned. His skin was tan from working on the farm, and his chest glistened with sweat from working in the fields.

"Sorry, didn't mean to startle you," he said. "Name's Nick."

"I, uh, I," I stuttered, still unaware of what his face looked like.

"My mom told me to come check on you and see if you needed any help."

"Mhmm," I managed to murmur. I stood there awkwardly due to my lack of social interaction over the past eighteen years and because a single droplet of sweat was making its way down the center of Nick's abdomen.

"So…?" he asked, bending down to meet my gaze, which caused me to return to planet Earth.

"Huh? Wh-what?" I asked, realizing I didn't fully take in what he'd said.

"Can I help you with anything?" Nick asked again.

The next thing I noticed about Nick was his hazel eyes. They were kind and gentle, ones that hadn't experienced tragic death or struggle. He also met me with a sincere smile, the kind of smile only men who were too willing to lend a hand had. I'm sure his brunette hair would've been perfectly swept to the side if it weren't drenched in sweat and covered by a cowboy hat. He must've been thankful I'd stopped by to add a little spice to his daily routine.

"Oh, yeah, sorry. I— my name is Delilah," I said, regaining my composure as best as I could, and held out my hand.

After Nick shook my hand, I looked at mine. It was even more grimy than before he introduced himself.

"Ah, my bad," he chuckled while rubbing his neck. "I should've washed my hands before coming to say hi."

I wiped my hand on the side of my jeans. "It's fine."

"Uh, so, can I give you a hand with the ladder?" Nick asked.

"Yeah, that would be nice. Thanks."

Grandpa had been waiting in the passenger seat for things to get wrapped up, and Ben had been in the back seat even longer. I was glad our workday had ended and was ready to head back home, but just as I was about to get into the driver's side, Nick abruptly ran out of the farmhouse.

"Hold up," he shouted, holding a jar in his hand as he jogged nearer.

"What's going on?" I wondered.

"Hey, I wanted to give you this," Nick said while handing me the jar. "It's the last of the pickled asparagus. My dad didn't want to give it up since it's one of his favorites, but it's amazing, and you have to try it."

"But you gave us so much already," I insisted, trying to give him back the asparagus. "I-I couldn't, especially if it's your dad's favorite."

Nick stuck his hands in his pockets, refusing to take no for an answer. "He's had enough, trust me. Plus, I pickled this batch, and I can say that this is the best I've done so far. You would regret passing up something so tasty."

"All right, I guess you twisted my arm," I smirked. "We appreciate it."

"Yeah, no problem. Call me!" he shouted before heading inside.

I stood there confused. *Call him?* Then, I looked at the mason jar filled with pickled asparagus. Nick had written his phone number on the lid.

As I got into the van, I was instantly annoyed at Ben laughing at me, and he'd been doing so since Nick ran out of the farmhouse to say bye.

"Did that guy seriously give you his number?" Ben mocked.

"Uh, yeah, maybe… I guess so," I stammered, embarrassed.

"I always thought the guy was supposed to ask for the girl's number," Ben chuckled.

"I think the world's past that, Benjamin," Grandpa mentioned.

"Yeah, what Grandpa said," I agreed.

"That's lame," Ben added. "That's not gentleman-like at all."

"And what would you know about being a gentleman?" I asked while looking in the rearview mirror, so I could glare at my ridiculous brother.

I wasn't surprised when Ben didn't have an answer.

"Seemed like a nice family," Grandpa mentioned.

"Yeah, I guess so," I shrugged.

"You know, Delilah, your grandma and I met when we were just sixteen," he added while smirking. "Then we married after six months."

"I barely know the guy, Grandpa. If anything, we'd just be friends," I explained.

"That's good. Friendship should come before love," Grandpa replied.

"Don't encourage it, Gramps," Ben chimed in.

"Well, like I said before, I won't be around to take care of you two forever," Grandpa reminded us.

"I think I can take care of us just fine when the time comes," Ben added.

"You're delusional," I jabbed at Ben. "The only thing you're good at is staying up late and playing video games, and for the thousandth time, I've told you both that I can take care of myself. I don't need anyone to look out for me."

"I don't doubt that," Grandpa agreed. "But it's nice to have a life partner, someone to have your back… someone to start a family with."

"I'm only eighteen, Grandpa!" I shouted. Grandpa's absurd planning for my future was too much. "Plus, I couldn't even imagine having children in the world we live in, not with the war going on."

"I know, I know," Grandpa chuckled to himself. "You are a very capable young woman, but as for children, they will forever be a blessing, no matter what the world looks like."

Once Ben and I finally became tired of bickering during the drive home, Grandpa fell asleep. When we returned home, the sun had begun sinking below the horizon. We'd made it back just in time.

I gently nudged Grandpa's shoulder. "Grandpa, we made it home."

He slowly awoke and groggily dragged himself inside.

I unloaded the food from the van to the pantry. Then I turned on the perimeter lights and bathed, but instead of crawling into bed, I wandered back into the pantry to retrieve the jar of asparagus with Nick's number. I considered calling him tomorrow… or maybe the next day? Was I supposed to wait a few days? I didn't know how things worked. It didn't matter, though, because like I told Grandpa, it would only be a friendly relationship. I changed my mind and set the jar back on the shelf. Maybe I would avoid calling him altogether.

# Chapter Four

## The Unexpected Run-in

The following afternoon, I paid Chad another visit. The van's tank was empty from the drive to Bryer's Farm, and I thought it would be a good idea to fill up ahead of time for our next trip. I also owed Chad some food for the repair work he did on the van.

"Hey, Delilah," Chad said as I entered the store. "I'd figured you'd be back soon since ya had a long drive. Delivery go okay?"

I held up a jar of food in each of my hands, showing everything went smoothly. "Brought some vegetables. Turns out they live on a farm."

"Oh, fresh food!" Chad beamed.

"Well, *fresher*. I'm not sure how long they've been preserved for," I explained.

"Yeah, it'll be good," he said happily, taking the jars from my hands. "I remember my dad talking about fresh meat, fresh vegetables, *fresh* everything before the war started. Only on special occasions did my dad save up for a good cut of steak."

"You're lucky. I only know what the canned stuff tastes like," I added.

"These days, one has to know the right people or run a town to afford delicacies such as those," Chad said. "Anyway, you haven't picked up any supplies besides gas in a while. Ya guys need some other stuff?"

"Yeah, we do need a couple of things," I said and pulled out cash from my pocket that Grandpa gave me from a job last month. "Would you happen to have some cream for rashes?" I asked.

Chad kept the first aid items and alcohol behind the counter—the good stuff people liked to steal. He looked behind him. "You're in luck. I just got in a couple of hydrocortisone tubes."

"That's good. Grandpa's been complaining about his Eczema," I explained.

"I need to grab some toilet paper too. Will forty be enough?"

Chad nodded. "Whatever you need, Delilah."

I shot Chad a smile full of gratitude. He was too kind. I walked down the toiletry aisle. The shelves weren't fully stocked, but they weren't completely bare either. Grandpa said they were always full once upon a time. I wondered what it was like to be able to afford more amenities. What was it like to be in a world that wasn't constantly struggling? There were a lot of "what ifs," but at least the world could still function somewhat normally as long as the sun was up.

After I grabbed what I needed, I turned to make my way toward the checkstand, but when I heard someone entering the shop, I paused. I looked at the mirror mounted on the corner of the ceiling to see who had come in.

Once I realized who it was, I felt a wave of shock run through my entire body, and the package of toilet paper seemed to slip out of my hands. It was the girl from the other night, the one from the group that congregated outside of Chad's place. I felt my heart race as I watched her pick up one of the hand baskets by the door. She looked even more perfect in daylight, and she walked around the shop, filling her basket like everything was free. I didn't want to run into her because I knew I would act awkward like I always did, especially around intimidating people. The last thing I wanted was to make a fool of myself. In my baggy shirt and ripped jeans, I would look like a sack of potatoes if I stood next to someone like that. I knew I shouldn't have cared so much since no one else was in the store besides the two of us and Chad, but I couldn't help that I felt insecure.

The girl eventually began to make her way closer, and quicker than a gazelle running from a predator, I recovered the toilet paper and rushed to check out, hoping to go unnoticed. But in my frantic state to avoid the girl, I didn't realize another person had walked through the door, which caused me to bump into him and drop the toilet paper again.

"S-sorry," I managed to say. "Excuse—" But just as I was about to finish my apology, my throat seized up, and I couldn't speak.

I should've assumed the girl wasn't alone. The shirtless guy with blue eyes who drove the motorcycle was with her.

"Whoa," he laughed as if I didn't do anything wrong. Rather, he found my clumsiness amusing. He bent over to pick up the toilet paper and set it on the counter as I stood frozen, unsure how to respond.

I knew it would be worse to stand there in silence, so I conjured what courage I had and spoke, "You— you're that one guy from the other night."

He moved his sunglasses to the top of his head so he could meet my gaze, revealing a black eye. I wanted to run out of the store and get as far away as possible before I said something I would regret, but the guy's presence was magnetic, and without saying a word, it was as if he was demanding that I look him in the eyes. They were even bluer up close, bluer than the feathers on a Barn Swallow, and the longer I stared, the more curious I became. There was sadness that lingered within them, a rare type of pain that few people had.

To prolong answering my question, he grinned at me in a mysterious way. I couldn't help but wonder what his story was. My heart started to race even faster, and I wasn't sure how that was possible. It felt like I was going to have a heart attack and keel over right there in Chad's gas station. And although I felt like I was going to pass out, I still had a hundred more questions running through my head, one being, where did he come from? Anyone could tell he wasn't from around here.

"I thought I recognized that van," the guy said.

"Are you one of the people who's been meeting in my parking lot at night?" Chad asked, interrupting.

I wasn't upset by Chad chiming in. I needed someone to remind me that I didn't *always* act like a weirdo. I could have a normal conversation with Chad. In fact, I've had many perfectly normal conversations with him.

"Yeah, thanks for letting us come by," the guy told Chad as if the owner of the gas station invited him for the late-night gatherings.

"Shoot! I should be thanking you," Chad said. "Nothing's been vandalized since you guys showed up."

"That's good to hear," he replied.

"I heard the city to the east of us has been having a lot of trouble after nightfall," Chad added.

Then, the guy rested his elbow on the counter and leaned closer to Chad. "But nothing in this city? You haven't noticed any changes in activity with—"

But before he could finish, the girl pushed her way between who I assumed was her boyfriend and me to set her basket on the counter. She looked annoyed that I was standing in her way. I was sure she intentionally brushed her shoulder against my chest while making it known she was ready to check out. I couldn't help but become angry at her for touching me in such a hostile way.

"Excuse me would've sufficed," I said under my breath.

She turned to glare at me with disgust, probably because I dared say something. I was surprised that her perfect face, which was covered so intricately with makeup could make such an ugly expression.

"What did you say?" she sneered.

Where does one find makeup these days? I never saw it during shopping trips. Chad sure didn't carry any in his store. The only time I'd seen makeup was in my mom's vanity. It went untouched because one, I didn't know how to use it, and two, it felt sacred like it was meant only for her. Everything had stayed in its original place for the past eighteen years.

I pursed my lips and shook my head, denying speaking. "Nothing. I didn't say anything." Then I turned to Chad. "Chad? Did you say something?" I asked, redirecting the girl's focus.

"Uh," Chad murmured awkwardly, trying to think of how to de-escalate the situation. "Yeah, I— will this be all for you?" he asked the girl.

She rolled her eyes at the both of us. "Okay, whatever," she said, annoyed, but took the bait. "Yeah, ring us up," she ordered, but then she was confused as to why there were additional items on the counter. "Babe, why are you buying toilet paper and itch cream?"

"Oh, those aren't mine," he told her.

"I see…" she said and turned to look at me. "For a minute, I thought you might have had an itchy butt rash."

"I-I don't have a rash. It's for my grandpa," I said quietly, embarrassed.

"Come on, Veronica, that's a stretch. It doesn't even make sense. You don't need toilet paper for a rash. The two items don't play hand-in-hand," the guy countered.

Chad looked at Veronica like she was beamed here from another planet. Everyone in our town was friendly and kind. They thought before they spoke and were considerate of other's feelings. Chad handed Veronica the groceries he had bagged up for her.

"That'll be $288.00," Chad said.

Veronica took the groceries and, while walking out, said, "Phoenix, pay the man, would you?"

It seemed like the guy was used to being ordered around by Veronica and reached into his pocket. "I'll get hers too," he told Chad, pointing to my items.

"What?" I asked, shocked at such an offer. "No, you don't need…"

"It's the least I can do for having to put up with Veronica. She's a different kind of species, that one," he chuckled.

"Please, I couldn't let you do that," I replied. "I already gave him the money."

But he didn't want to take no for an answer, and he asked Chad, "How much did she have to pay for those?"

"Uh—" Chad stuttered while being put in an awkward position.

"I'm at the same pump as usual," I told Chad, and I took my things off the counter and went on my way. "Thank you for the offer though," I told Phoenix before walking out the door.

Veronica was sitting impatiently inside a nice car, waiting for Phoenix. She did her best to pass the time by inspecting her manicured nails and exquisite hair in the fold-down mirror. I assumed Phoenix would get into the car, they would take off, and I would never see them again, but I was mistaken.

I tossed the toiletries into the passenger seat, walked around the van, and popped the gas cap. As I began to fill the tank, I was startled by someone who had snuck up on me.

"Hey," Phoenix said, standing inches away from me.

Thankfully, the hose from the pump acted like a barrier between us. I could pretend someone as beautiful as him wasn't standing in arms reach of me, yet again.

"Um… hi," I replied, looking around as if he might not have been talking to me.

"I didn't get your name," he mentioned.

"Oh, uh, my name…" I stammered, taken by surprise that Phoenix wanted to continue to talk to me, and even more so that he wanted to know my name. "It-it's Delilah."

"*Delilah…*" Phoenix repeated in a whisper as if my name was something sacred.

"Yup," I answered.

"Like Samson and Delilah?" he asked.

"Um, yeah. You know that story?"

"It's one of my favorites," he answered, catching my full attention.

For a moment, I wasn't thinking about my strange mannerisms. I didn't have to worry about the cat clawing at my tongue. For a moment, I was intrigued by what Phoenix knew, and my heart managed to beat at a normal speed. I wasn't completely intimidated by the gorgeous man who stood in front of me.

"It was my mom's favorite. My dad always said she must've liked that a woman could be the reason for a man's undoing," I explained.

Phoenix laughed, "Oh, is that why?"

I shrugged. "My dad liked to joke and give my mom a hard time."

Then Phoenix squinted hard at me like I needed his sympathy. "I noticed you're talking about your parents in the past tense."

I tucked my hair behind my ear, stalling. "Uh, I—"

"Phoenix!" Veronica yelled from the car. She was no longer sitting but stood by the open door, annoyed. "What the hell are you doing?"

"Coming," he said while shaking his head, but his feet didn't move. Instead, he smirked at me while feeling the need to introduce himself. "Well, Delilah, it was nice to meet you. My name's Phoenix White."

"I know," I said.

"You know?" Phoenix asked, confused.

"Oh— I mean, yeah, I heard," I said, pointing in Veronica's direction. "Uh, well, your first name… I, um, heard your first name was Phoenix," I went on awkwardly.

"Right…" Phoenix chuckled.

I wanted to believe that his laughter wasn't a product of how I was acting, but I couldn't quite convince myself and could feel my cheeks becoming warm.

"Anyway, I'm assuming you live close by?" Phoenix wondered.

"Uh, not too far," I answered.

"Then you should come and hang out next Friday night. We meet here pretty much every Friday. That is, for as long as we're here."

"You mean after the sun goes down?"

"We head out as soon as nightfall approaches," he confirmed.

"Um, yeah… I-I don't know about all that."

"You don't know?" Phoenix asked, smirking as he leaned in a bit closer.

"W-well, as you know… it's dangerous," I explained.

"Trust me," he whispered swooningly. "You don't have to worry about vampires showing themselves. They stay away when my friends and I are around. I can guarantee you will be safe with me."

With those words and the touch of Phoenix's breath on my cheek, my heart was no longer calm, and my palms began to sweat worse than my underarms. I tucked my hands into my pants' pockets in hopes of calming my nerves.

"I heard, but why is that?" I managed to ask.

Phoenix didn't answer my question and instead grinned. "It was nice meeting you, Delilah," he said a second time while reaching for one of my hands that was still in my pocket. I stood frozen as Phoenix slightly bent over, keeping eye contact the entire time as he successfully retrieved one of my hands out of the side of my jeans. I felt the urge to pull away, but something kept me from doing so. As strange as it was, I simply let Phoenix pull my hand toward his lips so he could kiss the top of it.

"Oh, uh…" I replied. My cheeks felt hotter than the sun, and I prayed the sweat from my palm had soaked into the fabric of my jeans before Phoenix's hand touched mine. "Th-thanks— I mean you too…"

Phoenix walked away, but not without glancing over his shoulder one last time at me. "If you want to find out, come Friday," he shouted.

Veronica looked even more annoyed than before as Phoenix approached the car, and soon enough, she began laying into him, complaining about having to wait an eternity.

I watched as Phoenix and Veronica drove off, trying to sort out what had just happened. I kept replaying the conversation I had with Phoenix in my head as if I'd get answers to my questions by doing so.

I wanted to accept Phoenix's invitation. I wanted to find out more. Even more so, I wanted to do something else besides lie in darkness each night, waiting for the sun to rise.

But I knew I shouldn't. I knew what dangers enjoyed frolicking in the moonlight…

# Chapter Five

## Make the Call

"Mmm! This was worth the work," Grandpa said while pouring himself a second glass of milk. "I almost forgot what milk tastes like."

Ben dug in, too, filling his plate with a variety of vegetables.

"Kids these days can't say no to eating their veggies," Grandpa chuckled.

"What do you mean?" Ben asked.

"He's talking about when there was more to eat," I explained. "When people had more choices."

"Oh… right," Ben replied.

"So, did you give that nice boy a call?" Grandpa asked me. "What was his name?"

"Nick? No, I didn't call him," I said flatly.

I hadn't thought about calling Nick. Nothing had been on my mind besides the run-in with Veronica and Phoenix. I'd spent every waking moment trying to figure out why vampires stayed away from them.

"Why not?" Grandpa wondered, disappointed.

"I don't know," I said, thinking any excuse would suffice. "I didn't think it was a big deal if I didn't call Nick."

"It wouldn't hurt you to give him a quick ring," Grandpa mentioned.

"I know," I replied. "I just—"

"He has a lot to offer. If you two decide to be friends, I'm sure his family will make sure you and your brother are taken care of after I'm gone."

"Really, Grandpa?" I asked, bummed he wanted me to make friends with Nick so he could have peace of mind after he was gone.

"I know I worry more than I should, but I can't help it," Grandpa admitted. "Please, just call him. It can't hurt."

*"Yeah, Delilah, just call him,"* Ben said in an annoyingly squeaky voice and then puckered his lips to make kissy sounds, doing his best to push my buttons.

"Shut up, Ben!" I yelled. "What are you, five?"

*"What are you, five?"* he repeated.

"Why, I ought to reach over the table…" I said under a hot breath and stood, ready to silence Ben.

"Okay, okay!" Grandpa butted in, waving his hand at me to calm down.

"I'm just giving Delilah a hard time, Gramps," Ben admitted, speaking as if I wasn't sitting at the table with them. "She shouldn't be that upset."

"Remember that time when you really were five," I reminded Ben, "and Dad had to come and rescue you when you pushed me too far? Remember when you passed out due to me strangling you because you kept pushing my buttons?"

Ben gulped and brought his hand to his throat, and I was glad I had successfully shut him up.

"That's enough, Delilah," Grandpa sighed, tired from constantly playing referee. "Let me put it this way. Do you want to be stuck living in this house with Ben ten years from now?"

Grandpa had a good point, but I still knew I would be more than capable of taking care of myself after he was gone. Maybe I'd even continue the family business and buy a place of my own that was nowhere near Ben. But to satisfy Grandpa and put an end to the conversation, I agreed to make the call, "Yeah, you're right. I'll call Nick after dinner."

"Didn't you say you just wanted to be friends?" Ben reminded me. "There's no way Nick would want to date you anyway, and there's an even slimmer chance he'd ever ask you to move in with his family… not in a billion years. Such a farfetched idea. Don't let Gramps put radical thoughts in your head."

"I'm not! I don't plan on dating anyone! It's Grandpa who has this whole… *notion*," I replied, still peeved.

"Uh-huh," Ben murmured.

"You are a mighty fine catch, Delilah," Grandpa tried to reassure me. "You need to give yourself more credit."

"No need to lie to her, Gramps," Ben continued to mock.

"Can we please stop talking about Nick now?" I said, raising my voice in frustration. "Can we stop imagining my life ten years from now? Please, enough is enough!"

Then I heard Ben murmur something under his breath about panties getting in a twist again, and that's when I slammed my fists on the table, grabbed my plate, and left the room to finish eating in private.

Once things calmed down, I followed through with my word, but I thought about hanging up the phone after it rang one time. Although it didn't seem like the best idea since I had watchful eyes nearby. Grandpa sat in his chair while watching the news as I sat in the living room. The only phone we had was the one phone on the end table by the couch, and it wasn't one of those fancy ones that didn't have a chord.

"Hello?" Joseline answered.

"Uh… hi," I replied awkwardly. "It-it's Delilah. Is Nick free to talk?"

I was hoping Nick was busy, but I knew he wouldn't be out in the field or tending to the animals since the sun was about to go down, so he most likely would be able to chat.

"Oh, Delilah!" Joseline beamed. Apparently, she wanted things to work out between Nick and me just as badly as Grandpa. "We were hoping to hear from you soon. Let me grab him."

It felt strange to be forced into a relationship. Although, maybe, it could be a good thing in the long run. Not that I wanted to use Nick for his food or security or big house, which seemed beneficial the more I thought about it. But more so, the thought of having a companion other than Ben or Grandpa sounded nice, and maybe Nick needed someone to talk to more than I did. It wasn't like I had many friends anyway.

Vampires didn't stop relationships from forming, but homeschooling did. Dad thought Ben and I would benefit from learning at home. Our dad said that when the war started, homeschooling became more common, and homeschooled kids tended to be smarter. Grandpa wasn't the best at teaching after Dad disappeared, but Jenny, who lived half a mile down the road, would come over and help with the curriculum. She was good at spelling and reading, and she liked to read the Bible like my mom did. Jenny also had a daughter, Betsy, who I wasn't fond of. Betsy was close in age and attended our homeschooling sessions, and although I didn't care for her, I felt obligated to pretend that I liked her.

"Delilah?" Nick asked over the phone.

"Hi."

"Hey! I'm glad you called," he mentioned, even more enthusiastically than his mom. "I've been waiting to hear from you."

I guess I should've called sooner, but how was I supposed to know?

"Um, so… how are you doing?" I asked, realizing I should've written down topics to talk about beforehand so I could avoid unwanted silence. I hoped Nick would know what to chit-chat about so that responsibility wouldn't fall on me.

"Things have been good. My parents are happy to have the perimeter up. I think everyone's sleeping better at night."

"That's good…"

"Yeah."

"I… yeah…" I repeated, stumbling over my words. I had a feeling Nick wouldn't want me to call him a second time.

"My mom's worried something bad is going to happen," Nick replied, unfazed by my lack of social skills, which surprisingly made me feel less self-conscious.

"Nothing ever comes around our little town. Maybe it'll stay that way," I mentioned, hopeful. But then Veronica and Phoenix came to mind, and I wanted to take back what I said.

"Yeah, let's hope it stays that way. My mom is usually paranoid about those kinds of things. I doubt anything will happen."

"Mhmm… So, how do you like living on the farm?" I asked, finding it nice that Nick was so easy to talk to.

"I like it."

"Seems like hard work having to tend to the fields."

"I love working with my hands, but I guess I don't know anything else," Nick said. "You're the first person around the same age as me that I've had a chance to talk to in a long time. I don't get out much."

"Don't tell me…" I chuckled. "You were homeschooled, too?"

"How'd you guess?" he joked, laughing with me. "Also, I'm just so dang busy helping my family with the farm. I know they need me."

"You're lucky to have such a wonderful place. Seems like a lot of fun with all the animals… and the food."

"The farm does have its perks," Nick replied.

"The food you gave us really was amazing. Nothing like I'd ever had."

"It most definitely is," he agreed. "But hey, I was wondering if you'd want to hang out sometime? That is if you think Mr. Summers would be okay with it."

I wasn't expecting Nick to want to spend time with me, but I guess that's what friends do. Even more surprising was Nick calling my Grandpa Mr. Summers.

Maybe Grandpa liked that about Nick—seeming old-fashioned and whatnot.

"Oh, uh, yeah, sure. We can. Although we live so far from each other."

"I don't mind driving," Nick volunteered.

"So, you don't want to meet halfway or something?"

"Nah, we don't have to do that. I'm used to getting up early in the morning. I'll leave after breakfast and make it back before dark."

"You sure? It can be dangerous on the road if you don't get back home before nightfall."

"Yeah, I'm not worried."

I had a feeling Ben would approve of Nick and his "chivalrous" characteristics that were starting to show.

"As long as you're comfortable with doing that. Although there isn't much to do around here."

"Hanging out with you is everything I could ask for and more," Nick added.

Wow, such flattery. Flattery that I was not used to. I didn't know how to respond to that level of compliment.

Then Nick cleared his throat as if he thought he was being too forward. "I-I mean… you know, seeing as I spend most of my time with the farm animals. Gets kind of repetitive and a bit lonely."

"You're right. I can relate," I said sarcastically. "A lot of the time, the animals here are either napping or playing video games."

Nick chuckled at my lame joke. "Like I said, I'm glad you called. You made my day, Delilah. So, when's a good day for me to come and see you?"

"Uh, well, I'm free tomorrow," I said.

"Ah, dang, tomorrow I promised my dad I would help drive to get hay for the horses, and since I'll be gone all day, I'll have to take care of my chores the next day. I could visit on Saturday. I'm usually less busy on the weekends."

"Yeah!" I said excitedly, which came out unexpectedly.

I didn't think our conversation would end with plans to spend time with each other. I didn't think I would have such strong cravings regarding a friendship after talking to Nick.

"All right, well, as much as I don't want to, I'm going to have to let you go, Delilah," Nick said, disappointed. "I can hear my little sister screaming for me to read her a bedtime story. For some reason, it's just not the same if my mom or dad read to her," he chuckled.

"I'll see you Saturday," I said, but surprisingly, I didn't want to say goodbye either.

# Chapter Six

## Out the Window

I had just finished eating dinner with Grandpa and Ben, and I did what I normally did as the sun began to slip past the horizon—I washed up and sat on my bed, staring out the window at the old oak tree.

It was pointless to try and fall asleep that early in the evening, so I used the time to wind down and allow my thoughts to escape before attempting to shut my eyes. However, the thoughts continuously running through my head often followed me to bed and kept me awake.

Unlike me, Grandpa would conk out in his recliner any minute. I suppose if I ever lived to Grandpa's age, sleep would come easier, and I'd be thankful for that. I assumed Ben would have his eyes glued to his Game Boy until midnight or later. I often wondered if he'd ever grow out of playing video games. At least he had something to take his mind off of what was going on in the world.

The old oak tree had been fully grown as far back as I was able to remember. Its roots were strong, unwavering. It flourished where it grew and seemed content with the soil it was stuck in. Its leaves were just starting to change to autumn colors, and in the weeks to come, they would fall to the ground. Many would find themselves being swept away by the Idaho breeze—taken someplace else… maybe somewhere better.

I wondered where the wind would transport them. What else would they see? What more would they discover? As I thought about the leaves falling from the tree and being taken elsewhere, my heart was filled with envy. I wanted to live how people were intended to live. I wanted to take Phoenix up on his invite. I didn't want nightfall to continue to imprison me. I yearned to be free, whether the sun or moon ruled the sky. I wanted to be as light as the leaves on the old oak tree, so the breeze could sweep me away and show me what I was missing.

I knew Phoenix and his crew would be heading toward Chad's. I had been trying to convince myself it was too dangerous to meet him after nightfall. I reminded myself *we never leave the house after dark under any circumstances.* Those were the words Grandpa had instilled in us. "Leaving our haven after the sun goes down is like playing a game of roulette, and taking that risk enough times will eventually get you killed," he'd say.

I shouldn't have needed any other reminders of how dangerous it was to go out at night since I almost got myself killed when I was younger. That reminder should've been enough, but even with my near-death experience, my desire to do anything else besides sit in front of my window, staring at the oak tree, fought against my better judgment. I wanted nothing else than to know more… *live more.*

I pushed Grandpa's advice to the back of my mind and grabbed my necklace, which had a silver cross on the chain. I draped it over my neck and tucked it under the collar of my shirt. I picked up the small flashlight that had a UV bulb and held it in my hand for a few seconds, deciding if I needed to take it for protection. Phoenix said I didn't need to worry about vampires when he was around, but I felt safer knowing the light could turn a bloodsucker to ash. I tossed it in a bag as well as a larger silver cross that hung on my wall. I convinced myself if I was smart and prepared, I would be fine.

"Shoes, I need shoes," I said to myself, becoming excited as I thought about meeting up with Phoenix. My chest began to pound from the adrenaline. "And clothes… real clothes, not pajamas."

I couldn't recall a time when I'd been more excited. I wanted to sprint as fast as I could to Chad's, not wasting another minute. But just as soon as I went to pick up the bag after getting dressed, it slipped out of my hand when I was startled by a knock at my bedroom door.

"Who is it?" I asked, hoping it wasn't Grandpa.

I quickly recovered the bag and frantically searched for a place to hide it. I thought underneath the covers on my bed was as good of a hiding spot as any other, considering I was in a pinch.

"What are you doing in there?" Ben asked casually. "There's a lot of restlessness coming from your room."

"Go away! It's none of your business!" I growled in annoyance.

Shouldn't he have been playing his dumb video games? It truly was a shame that I never had any locks on my bedroom door or any real privacy. I quickly kicked off my shoes and shoved them underneath my bed, just in case Ben decided to barge in.

"It's Friday night," Ben mentioned. "So, it makes sense."

"What are you talking about? I don't need a reminder of what day it is. Just leave me alone!" I snapped.

But Ben didn't listen. He never did, so I wasn't too surprised when he entered the room without permission.

"I know what you're planning on doing," Ben said as I rushed to sit in front of the lump under my comforter, realizing there were a dozen better places I could've picked to conceal the bag.

"What the hell, Ben!" I scoffed. "You'd be so pissed if I went into your room without your permission."

"Ah-ha! I knew it!" he said with arrogance tainting his voice.

"Knew what?" I asked innocently.

"You are in regular clothes, and I know you just took your shoes off before I came in. I can see your sneakers sticking out from under the bed. You're up to something."

"No, I'm not," I said firmly.

"You're going to go check out what's going on at the gas station, aren't you?"

"Nope."

"Yeah, you are. I can see right through you," Ben said, his eyes narrow with suspicion.

It was no use. My shoulders slouched in defeat. "Fine! You're right. I was going to see what was going on at Chad's."

"Are you crazy?" Ben scoffed. "You don't know those people. What if they're serial killers?"

I sighed at Ben's absurd ideas. "That would be a heck of a lot of serial killers, don't you think?"

"You know what I mean. They could be dangerous."

"Some aren't," I countered.

"And how would you know that?"

"Um…" I trailed off. I didn't want to tell Ben everything.

"Spit it out!" Ben demanded.

"It's nothing."

"You know I'll find out one way or another. I always do," Ben said.

I sighed deeply, disappointed I was pressured into sharing more information. "I ran into a couple of them at Chad's while picking up some supplies."

"And?"

"*And*… I talked to one of them," I explained. "His name is Phoenix."

"This wouldn't happen to be the guy you were ogling over when you almost ran us off the road, would it?"

"Uh, I don't know what you're talking about," I replied, doing my best to play dumb.

"The guy on the motorcycle?" Ben clarified.

"Yeah, that's the one…" I admitted, wishing Ben would end his interrogation. "He's actually really nice."

"So, you talk to a guy one time… *at a gas station.* I'm assuming the conversation couldn't have been more than a few minutes."

"Yeah, and what's your point?" I replied in a snooty tone. I wanted Ben to be aware that he was pushing my buttons, and that he'd better tread lightly.

"And therefore, you automatically know he's a nice guy?"

"Yup."

I glared at Ben, waiting for him to say something else or walk out of the room, but he stood there with his arms folded across his chest, meeting my stare like it was a contest to see who would blink first.

"Whatever," I said, breaking the silence. "You aren't Dad or Mom, and you sure as hell aren't Grandpa. You need to stop telling me what to do. I don't need your permission."

"You're right… I'm not Mom or Dad," Ben said, becoming angry. "They're *dead*, and you know why they're dead?"

"Seriously, Ben? Do we have to do this right now?" I said while putting my shoes back on.

"Dad was killed by vampires, and if you think about it, those bloodsuckers are to blame for our mom's death, too. If Mom could've been driven to a hospital to receive the care she needed, she could've pulled through," Ben reminded me. "I can't believe you're stupid enough to go out at night. Haven't you learned anything?"

Surprisingly, Ben sounded smarter than he usually did. I could see through his anger that he was more concerned rather than frustrated.

"I'll be fine," I assured him. "I'm going to bring my bag of… *stuff*, and even Chad said vampires don't like to be near that group of people."

"That is just a theory! And have you thought about *why vampires stay away from them*? Maybe they're worse than the bloodsuckers!"

"It's not a theory. Phoenix confirmed it's true, and I doubt anything could be worse than vampires."

"Well, I can see my opinion doesn't mean anything to you!" Ben snapped.

"Nope, it sure doesn't," I replied, jabbing back while standing to leave.

"Nice, real nice, Delilah," Ben whispered to himself as if I genuinely hurt his feelings.

"Go back to playing your dumb video games, Ben. I'll be back in a few hours," I said while opening the window to make my escape.

"Wait," Ben said, and I looked over my shoulder, expecting him to try and convince me to stay one last time. "I'm coming with you."

"What?" I scoffed in disbelief. No way Ben was serious.

But he was. He practically pushed me out of the window so he could climb out after me.

"I'm coming too. It's not fair you get to have all the fun around here."

"Fun? We both know what your idea of fun is. It starts with video and ends with games."

"Okay, well, I just want to make sure you get home safely," Ben admitted.

"I don't need you to look after me," I reminded him as I began walking toward the gas station, but unfortunately, Ben still followed.

"Two is always better than one," Ben went on.

"Can we please keep things quiet?" I asked, annoyed. "At least until we get where we need to be?" I was done listening to Ben's nonsense, and he often rambled when he was frightened.

"Yeah, good idea," Ben said. "Then we can hear if a bloodsucker is trying to sneak up on us. Because you know, you n-never know… Although vampires are supposed to be stealthy unless they are running super-duper fast to rip out your throat. Oh, gosh…" Ben held his hand to his neck and gulped loudly, becoming nervous while thinking about getting his neck torn open. "Y-you don't think my throat is going to get—"

"We're going to be fine, Ben," I sighed. "It's just a couple of blocks away."

"Mhmm," Ben murmured, looking around frantically like something would attack us at any moment.

# Chapter Seven

## Fight Fright Night

The moon was full and bright, and as we walked to Chad's, I was distracted by the twinkling night sky. I should've been as frightened as Ben, but it was like the stars took away all my fear. It was as if the moonlight gave me courage.

"See, we made it, and your throat is still intact," I whispered to Ben once the gas station came into view.

"A-are you sure you want to do this?" Ben stammered nervously. "It-it's not too late to turn around and go home."

"We're already here. I didn't walk all this way to go back home. I told you there's nothing to worry about," I assured Ben. "You don't need to be scared."

"You keep saying there's nothing to worry about, but you don't even know who these people are!" Ben said, frustrated that I continued to refuse to acknowledge his warnings. "And— and who said anything about being scared?"

I rolled my eyes, annoyed that Ben was wasting my time, and continued walking toward the crowd of people. Ben didn't follow me at first, but after a few moments, he sighed loudly in defeat and ran to catch up with me.

The parking lot was filled with the same guys and girls we had seen the other night plus many others I didn't recognize. Hundreds of people in one place, but I guess that was a good thing because more of them meant less vampires… supposedly.

"Uh-oh," Ben murmured with cowardice.

"What? What is it?" I asked, worried, and began to reach into the bag that was slung over my shoulder.

"It's those guys again," Ben pointed out.

Frankie and his friend were making their way toward us, putting off creepy vibes more so than the last time I saw them. Maybe it was because I was able to get a better look at them and the copious amounts of facial piercings they both had. Also, Frankie's mohawk spikes looked like they could've impaled a bird if it fell from the sky.

I had plenty of deterrents to keep vampires at bay, but it would've been perfect if I had something in my bag to keep *jerks* from getting too close to us.

"Maybe they will walk past us," I added, hopeful.

"No, it looks like they're coming over to finish what they started the other night," Ben said, cowering.

"Stop!" I yelled and yanked on Ben's arm so he'd stand up straight. "You'll only make things worse by acting like a scared little baby."

By the time the two guys made their way over, Ben regained his composure, but I could tell from his pursed lips he wanted to run away.

"Well, well, well," Frankie said as his sidekick chuckled weirdly to himself. "Fancy seeing you here."

His eyes trailed from my neck and then slowly to my hips. Then up and down again, violating whatever he thought was worth a glance. I tried not to make eye contact and folded my arms across my chest to discourage his gaze. Maybe if I pretended I didn't remember him, he'd get bored and move on. There were plenty of other people Frankie and his friend could entertain themselves with. Why did it have to be us?

"Couldn't resist coming to see me again?" Frankie cooed and slowly raised his hand to brush my hair to the back of my shoulder.

"Don't touch me," I growled while slapping his hand away.

Frankie held his hands up like he didn't mean any harm. "Sorry, I didn't know you like to take things so slow," he chuckled.

"Leave her alone!" Ben yelled, and once again... I wish he hadn't tried to say anything.

"Ohhh. I almost forgot, Marko," Frankie said, amused as he glanced over his shoulder at his friend. "This one here is Mr. Tough Guy."

"Yeah," Marko laughed, "doesn't know when to keep his mouth shut."

"Sorry," Ben said sarcastically and raised his voice again. "What I really wanted to ask you was… do you wear your hair like that for a reason? Why are the spikes so long? Are you trying to compensate for something? And what's with all the metal on your face? You *actually* think the ladies like that?"

With a murderous gaze, Frankie slowly turned toward Ben. "You got a death wish, punk?" he gritted through his teeth and shoved Ben, sending him to the ground.

Frankie lunged at Ben, placing a firm hand along his collarbone to pin him in place.

"G-get off of me," Ben squealed helplessly.

"My hair is sick, and just so you know… all the *metal* on my face is for when vampires get too close, and then I can burn the shit out of them," Frankie spat.

"Uh… wh-what?" Ben managed to ask, confused.

"Nothin'. A weakling like you wouldn't understand," Frankie mocked.

Marko's laughter became uncontrollable as he watched Frankie pick on Ben.

"Stop!" I yelled, trying to push Frankie off my brother.

Surprisingly, with a second shove, Frankie released Ben, but Frankie still knelt beside his plaything, laughing at him. Ben did his best to try and get away, but he couldn't stand on two feet. Instead, he scooted on the ground like an injured animal. I was sure Frankie didn't hurt Ben physically, at least not to the extent that Ben couldn't stand. Rather, Ben's pride was smashed to pieces, and that's what kept him from getting up.

Then Frankie stood. I couldn't tell if he was done messing with Ben, so I thought it best to step in. I couldn't just watch as Frankie harassed my brother.

"Leave him alone!" I screamed and positioned myself between the jerk and Ben.

My actions resulted in Frankie smirking at me in silence, which made me even more furious.

"You're such a bully!" I said as harshly as possible and pushed against Frankie's chest with all my might as if it would keep him from pursuing Ben. "Why don't you just leave us alone?"

I hoped he would give up, but my actions resulted in Frankie grabbing my hand with both of his. "I'll leave him alone if you come with me," he said gently.

I yanked my hand away. "Get away from us, creep!"

Then Frankie forcefully grabbed my arm like he was going to drag me someplace I would dread.

"This… *creep* knows how to show you a good time," Frankie said, offended by my name-calling. "You should be flattered."

"Get off of me!" I yelled, trying to break free from Frankie's hold. "Someone help me!"

I didn't expect anyone to hear my struggle because it was so loud with all the chatter in the parking lot, and everyone seemed preoccupied with their own groups of people. I didn't think it mattered how loudly I shouted, and if someone did notice, this type of thing might've been normal to them. No one knew us, so I doubted anyone would care my brother and I were being mistreated.

Or so I thought…

"Hey!" I heard an authoritative voice from behind me yell.

Frankie instantly released his grip on my arm as soon as he looked past me, and his eyes widened with concern. I turned around to see what Frankie was so worried about, and I noticed Ben running toward us. With all the craziness, I didn't realize Ben had left my side.

"I found him," Ben said, out of breath as if he'd run a marathon. "This is the guy, right?" He asked while pointing his thumb behind him at a guy following close behind.

I was speechless and nodded. I couldn't believe Ben found *him*...

"What's going on here?" Phoenix asked Frankie.

Frankie shrugged, pretending to be innocent. "Nothin', man."

"That's not what Ben told me," Phoenix countered.

Frankie shrugged a second time but didn't say anything. It was as if he was afraid to stand up to Phoenix.

Phoenix placed a gentle hand on my shoulder. "Are you okay?" he asked, concerned.

"I'm fine," I nodded, holding my arm where Frankie had grabbed me.

"Leave them alone," Phoenix told Frankie sternly. "They're here with me."

The expression on Frankie's face told everyone that his blood was turning to molten lava. It was obvious Frankie wasn't used to backing down from what he wanted, but for whatever reason, he didn't challenge Phoenix. He bit his tongue, nodded, and turned away while calling to his friend, "Come on, Marko, let's go."

Once Frankie and Marko retreated, Phoenix positioned himself in front of me to get a better look at my arm. I slowly lowered my hand, revealing red marks that I knew would eventually turn into a bruise.

Phoenix sighed, disappointed I had gotten hurt. "I'm sorry. I didn't think you would show."

"Yeah, me either," I laughed awkwardly, trying to shake off the terrible encounter with Frankie.

"Does it hurt?" Phoenix asked. His voice was gentle, not like when he was talking to Frankie.

My arm was in pain. "I'm okay," I lied.

"Frankie is all talk, no bite," Phoenix explained. "I don't think he would've done anything serious, and unfortunately, many of us don't know how to control our own strength."

"Or temper," Ben butted in after catching his breath.

"Ben!" I whispered angrily. He'd never learn to keep quiet.

"Look at her arm, dude," Ben snapped as he glared at Phoenix. "Maybe things shouldn't be put so lightly."

The entire time Phoenix was there, I had kept my gaze down. It wasn't until Phoenix began running his fingertips up and down the side of my arm that I looked up at him. He must've been trying to make eye contact ever since he stood in front of me because he was looking at me too intensely. His touch sent goosebumps trickling down my arm and to the tips of my fingers. The way he stared at me made me feel like he truly cared I had gotten hurt. His gaze was tainted with guilt, like he was to blame.

"Your brother is right. I'll have a private chat with Frankie later," Phoenix said. "I'll make sure nothing like this ever happens again."

"I'm surprised that Frankie listens to you. He doesn't seem like the type to do as others say," I mentioned.

"He knows his place," Phoenix explained as a half-hearted grin filled with smugness appeared.

Ben shook his head like he couldn't believe what had happened, like he couldn't believe I put him in another position that he couldn't fight his way out of.

"Why'd you invite Delilah here?" Ben asked defensively, as if it didn't matter that Phoenix had come to our rescue moments ago.

Phoenix didn't look at Ben when he spoke. He forever kept his eyes on me, and I did my best not to look away. I mean... *I didn't want to.* His blue eyes were beautiful. *He* was beautiful and mysterious in the most solemn way.

Phoenix tilted his head closer, causing a lock of hair on the front of his head to hang slightly over one of his eyes. I felt uneasy being even closer to him than the last time we ran into each other. Phoenix hovered over me, more than an entire foot taller, which also made me feel like I didn't have a choice but to keep my eyes locked in on his. His body language demanded attention. I could see why people did as he said.

Then I realized why he leaned in closer. "I wanted to talk to you more," Phoenix whispered, answering Ben's question, but so only I could hear.

"Oh, uh..." I stammered, confused. "You— you wanted to talk to me... *more*?"

He grinned and nodded. "Yeah."

Ben flapped his arms at his sides, becoming impatient, and let out an exaggerated sigh, annoyed by Phoenix's secrecy. "Really?"

Then Phoenix stood up straighter and spoke louder, "I'm glad you brought your little brother with you. He's funny."

"Oh, he's not—" I began to clarify.

"Seriously?" Ben scoffed, offended. "I'm her *older* brother."

Then Phoenix finally broke eye contact with me to give Ben a once-over. "My bad," he apologized with sincerity. "I guess I shouldn't judge a book by its cover."

"Don't worry about it," I told Phoenix. "He's only older than me by minutes."

"Ah, twins," Phoenix said. "That's cool."

"Yeah, twins… *So awesome!*" Ben repeated hotly, full of sarcasm.

"I think it is," Phoenix replied. "Twins are rare."

"Have you seen enough?" Ben asked me. "Can we go now?"

"I kind of want to stay a while longer," I told Ben, and out of the corner of my eye, I saw Phoenix smile.

Then Phoenix waved his finger toward a girl chatting in a group a few feet away from us. "Hey, Carmen," he called, and the girl walked over without a second thought.

"What's up, Phoenix?" she asked.

"I have a new friend here, Ben," he told her. "You think you can keep him company?"

Carmen was just as gorgeous as all the other girls there, and the way she presented herself made her seem kind and friendly. I could tell the revealing shirt she was wearing made Ben nervous, or maybe it was the short leather skirt that hugged her thighs.

Carmen smiled at my brother before entwining her arm in his. "Of course," she replied happily.

"Wait, no," Ben murmured uncomfortably.

"Come on," she encouraged, tugging on his arm. "I'll introduce you to some of my friends."

"Uh, I, um—" Ben stuttered.

"You'll have fun with me," Carmen assured him.

"I don't think I— I should probably stay with—" Ben protested with his words, but he allowed Carmen to drag him along as if he were a well-trained dog being pulled on a leash by his owner.

"Don't worry, I don't bite. I promise," Carmen giggled while giving her long blonde hair a twirl.

I watched as Carmen transitioned her hold on Ben's arm to his hand, and before I knew it, they disappeared. I stood on my tiptoes as they became lost in the sea of people, trying to keep an eye on Ben. I needed to make sure he was going to be safe.

"It's okay," Phoenix assured me. "Nothing's going to happen to him. Carmen has been a friend of mine for a long time. I would trust her with my life."

"Oh, okay," I replied, still unsure if *I* could trust someone I didn't know.

There had to have been over a hundred unfamiliar faces, but I was mostly concerned about one specific person. "That girl you were with at the gas station…" I mentioned hesitantly.

"You mean, Veronica?" Phoenix asked.

I nodded.

"What about her?"

"Uh, is she going to get upset that I'm here?" I wondered, worried about another unwanted encounter. "She didn't seem all too happy to bump into me while doing her shopping."

"She was needed at the base tonight," Phoenix said.

"The base?" I asked, confused.

"Yeah," Phoenix answered without further explanation.

"Uh, okay…" I replied, trying to figure out how to find out more without seeming too nosy. "Are you and your girlfriend a form of military or something?"

"I don't have a girlfriend," Phoenix laughed as if he was offended by my assumption.

I tried not to seem annoyed that Phoenix avoided answering the serious questions. "Oh, sorry, I just assumed you and Veronica were—"

"No," Phoenix shook his head like I had mentioned something ridiculous. "I wouldn't be caught dead with someone like that."

"Sorry, I just thought… She seemed—"

"Well, she and I had a thing, but that was a while back when I was dumb. She hasn't gotten over everything still."

"Oh…" I said, unsure how to respond.

I wondered why I was satisfied hearing Phoenix wasn't attached to anyone. Then, one of the girls walked past me while laughing at my outfit, reminding me that it didn't matter if he was single.

I glanced down at the clothes that I was wearing, becoming more self-conscious. "I guess I'm a little underdressed for the occasion," I tried to joke.

"You look great," Phoenix said, and it was strange that he sounded genuine. "You're probably the best-looking girl here."

I laughed aloud like he was making a joke. "Yeah, right," I said under my breath.

Before Phoenix could say anything else, the crowd of people began to gather in a large circle as booming rock music began to play, and I wondered if Chad had invested in a good set of earplugs. I looked around intently, trying to figure out what was going on. There was someone in the middle of the circle of people yelling something that I couldn't quite make out. Phoenix grabbed my hand to pull me to the front row of people so we could get a better view.

Across the circle, I saw Ben standing next to Carmen. He looked more content than when I saw him a few minutes ago, and I was relieved he was okay. Then, all eyes shot over to Frankie, who was removing his shirt, revealing even more tattoos. Frankie was violently nodding his head to the music and jumping around while Marko yelled something over and over to him.

Frankie seemed focused as he began to throw his fists in the air in front of him that were wrapped in some kind of bandages.

"What's going on?" I asked Phoenix. "What's Frankie doing?"

"He's getting pumped for the fight," Phoenix explained casually.

"Fight?" I asked, confused. Then I remembered Phoenix's black and blue eye, which he no longer had. "Is that why you had a—" Was it rude to ask such a question? I didn't know proper fight etiquette.

"Had a what?" Phoenix smirked while looking down at me.

I raised my hand slowly and pointed to my eye—my other hand, that is, the one that wasn't still in Phoenix's. Surprisingly, holding Phoenix's hand wasn't all that bad. It wasn't strange in any way. Oddly, it felt normal. *He* made me feel normal.

"Oh, yeah, you noticed that at the gas station?" he asked.

I nodded my head.

"Yeah," Phoenix explained, "my mind was distracted. Let Victor catch me with a right hook."

"So, you lost?" I wondered.

Phoenix laughed as if I cracked a joke. "Hell no. You should see Victor."

I didn't think I wanted to. Violence wasn't exactly at the top of my list of things that excited me. But there I was, waiting for a bloody knuckle fight as Frankie's opponent joined him in the inner circle. He looked about a foot shorter than Frankie but twice his weight. I wondered if Frankie would get what he deserved.

"How often do you have to fight?" I prodded.

"I wouldn't say *have* to. I usually *try* to participate once a month, if not more," Phoenix explained.

"Oh, I see…" I cringed and glanced around at the crowd. Everyone was shouting, impatient for the fight to start. Even the girls seemed pumped for the show… but not me.

"Not really your thing?" Phoenix asked.

"No," I shook my head, "not really."

"Me either," Phoenix said, which didn't make sense.

"What do you mean? You just told me you try and fight at least once a month."

"I know, but it's not because I *like* to fight."

"I don't understand," I said, becoming frustrated because nothing he was saying made any sense.

"I do it to stay alive," he explained.

Then suddenly, it was as if time stood still. Another person stood between the fighters who faced each other. The viewers froze, waiting for the countdown. The music was turned low, and the guy threw his hand down between the fighters three times, counting down with his fingers as he screamed the numbers aloud. When he clapped his hands together, the fight began, and Frankie and the other guy began circling one another.

"You mean like training?" I asked Phoenix.

"Yeah, exactly," he confirmed.

"What are you training for?"

"Ending the war."

"Huh?"

Then, the other guy landed a big right hook on Frankie's temple. I did my best not to cower and look away. I wanted to retreat to the back of the crowd so I could avoid watching the fight, but I didn't want Phoenix to think less of me.

Phoenix cupped his hand around his mouth and yelled at Frankie, "Keep those hands up!"

"Is Frankie going to lose?" I asked, trying my best not to sound smug.

"Why do you say that?" Phoenix replied, surprised I asked such a question.

"I don't know. Maybe because the other guy is twice the size of him. Frankie kind of looks like a twig."

Phoenix chuckled. "My money is on Frankie. Just because the other guy looks bigger doesn't mean anything. Frankie's got a longer reach, and he's got a chin on him. It's still early in the fight."

I was bummed to hear Phoenix say that. Maybe I could manage to get through watching the fight if I kept thinking Frankie deserved to get beat up.

Phoenix continued, "And as long as he doesn't keep letting Will get on the inside, he'll win."

The crowd began going crazy as Frankie shoved his foot into Will's stomach. Will hunched over, his wind taken from him. Frankie took advantage and started wailing on his opponent. Blood began to trickle from Will's brow, and I felt my stomach do some unsatisfying flips.

"Yeah!" the crowd yelled in unison, some throwing their fists in the air.

Involuntarily, my hand shot over my mouth, and the acid from my stomach traveled up my throat.

"You okay?" Phoenix asked, worried.

I closed my eyes. I didn't want to hurl all over Chad's parking lot. Luckily, I managed to gulp it back down and not embarrass myself further.

I nodded my head and hoped when I opened my eyes, everything would be over, and the bloodied man would be out of my sight.

Thankfully, he was, but I didn't expect there to be another fight after.

"You want to get out of here?" Phoenix asked gently.

"Yeah…" I whispered, and he wrapped his arm around my shoulders to guide me out of the ring of people.

Once we weren't surrounded, I took a deep breath, relieved I didn't have to watch another bloodbath.

"Where do you want to go?" he asked.

I wanted to go anywhere with Phoenix, any place that wouldn't trigger vomiting, but then I remembered I had brought company. "Oh, I almost forgot that Ben came with me," I mentioned.

"Right," Phoenix replied.

"I should probably go get him and head home."

"How'd you get here?" Phoenix wondered.

"We walked."

"All the way here?" he asked, concerned.

"It's not too far," I told him and patted my bag, "plus, I have protection."

"Oh, is that so?" Phoenix said and continued to stare at me, unfazed by what could be in my bag. I guess I was thankful for that.

"Okay…" I said, feeling a bit uncomfortable by the staring contest he initiated. "I'm going to go now."

I turned to walk away and find Ben, but then Phoenix grabbed my hand again. "Wait," he said, pulling me gently back toward him.

I was shocked that he stopped me and didn't feel the bag on my shoulder slide down my arm. It fell onto the ground, revealing the contents.

One of the guys in the back of the circle turned to see what had happened and laughed when he saw the contents of my bag scattered on the ground. "What's all that?" he mocked.

"Mind your own business," Phoenix snapped, and without another word, the guy turned his gaze back to the fight.

I bent down, frantically gathering my belongings. "I'm so embarrassed," I said under my breath.

Phoenix knelt beside me and helped me pick up the last of my stuff. "Don't be."

I wanted to sprint home and bury my head in my pillow, possibly until I stopped breathing, so I would never remember that moment again.

As we stood after picking up my belongings, Phoenix's eyes were still fixated on me. "Thank you," I said.

"Of course, but if I'm being honest, I'm a little offended you didn't think I would be enough protection," he smirked. "I told you I wouldn't let anything happen to you."

"I know, but Ben and I walked here, and I— I mean, we can't be too safe these days."

"Right…" Phoenix trailed off like he couldn't relate. "Uh, anyway. Maybe I should walk you home. Then I will know you got home safely."

I didn't think Ben would like that. "It's all right. We'll be fine." I patted my bag again. "I've got protection, remember?"

"Please," Phoenix insisted. "I wouldn't want something to happen along the way, and you said it yourself, *can't be too safe these days.* I would feel a lot better knowing you got home okay."

"I did say that, didn't I?" I admitted.

"You sure did," Phoenix chuckled to himself, and just as I was about to find Ben, he'd already found us.

"That was intense," Ben said with a grin.

"Glad you enjoyed yourself," Phoenix said.

I was surprised Ben had a better time than I did, and I was also a bit envious that he could watch the fights without throwing up.

"Phoenix is going to walk with us," I told Ben.

Ben's grin instantly vanished. "What? No."

"Why not?" I scoffed.

Ben leaned closer to me and whispered into my ear while eyeing Phoenix. "Because we don't know this guy, and you want to show him where we live? How do you know we can trust him?"

"He hasn't given us any reason not to, and he saved us from Frankie, remember? Would you rather get torn apart by vampires on the way home? Chad said it himself—these people are deterrents."

Ben thought for a moment as he pictured us getting mauled by vampires. "You're right. It might be a good idea to have someone else join us. Better to have another person in case we get ambushed."

"All right, I'm ready whenever you guys are," Phoenix said, and Ben began to lead the way.

Ever since we left the parking lot, Ben walked ahead of us, and it was obviously on purpose. I was unsure if it was because he was in a hurry to get home or because he didn't want to join our conversation. Probably both.

"So, how far is your place exactly?" Phoenix asked.

Normally, the scent of trees would've filled the air, but all I could smell was the leather jacket Phoenix was wearing as we walked. "Just another minute or two," I answered.

"Dang," Phoenix said as if he was disappointed.

"What's wrong?" I asked, wondering what was on his mind.

"Just hoped for a little more time with you," he explained.

"I'm sure you don't have much free time anyway," I shrugged. "Seems like you have quite a big group of friends to keep you busy."

"We're required to get along," Phoenix said. "I'd rather choose who I spend my time with."

"You mean someone like me?" I asked, confused.

"Yeah," he chuckled lightly. "Someone like you."

"Oh…" I trailed off. I was sure my cheeks were bright red.

"I've barely gotten a chance to get to know you," Phoenix continued.

I decided to stop staring at the ground while we walked and looked up at Phoenix. But maybe I shouldn't have. The moonlight shined down on him like it was placed in the sky specifically for that moment—to entice me and make me feel foreign emotions. His blonde hair and mystifying eyes almost glowed in the night. It was lit just enough to see his chiseled jawline and perfect grin.

The distraction caused me to pause on the side of the road—forgetting my destination. I didn't know why I couldn't turn away from Phoenix. In fact, I felt drawn to him, so I took a step closer. The autumn wind picked up, and my hair gathered in my face. Phoenix gently raised his hand to tame a strand covering my eyes, and he took his sweet time tucking it behind my ear.

It seemed like forever before one of us finally spoke, and that was okay. "Iron sharpens iron…" Phoenix whispered.

"*And one man sharpens another*," I finished.

Phoenix smirked. "You're different, Delilah," he said, almost in a whisper. "I knew it from the moment I saw you."

"I am?" I asked, worried it was a bad thing. I tried to come up with an explanation as to why I wasn't like him or the others he was with. "I mean, I, uh—"

"Hey!" Ben yelled in an angry whisper that surprisingly traveled far enough to reach me. Ben had gotten quite a bit ahead of us. "What are you guys doing? Hurry up!"

Phoenix and I began walking toward the house again, but I realized my home was in sight, and I, too, felt disappointed our night had to end.

"Well, this is me," I told Phoenix, and he took that as a hint that he'd joined us far enough. "Maybe we'll run into each other at Chad's again. During the daytime, that is."

I began to walk backward toward the house, not wanting to say goodnight—not wanting Phoenix to disappear from my sight, and I couldn't wipe the grin off my face the entire time.

I enjoyed hanging out with Phoenix, even if I had to watch someone get bloodied up. I had so many more questions I wanted to ask him. I wanted to learn more about the world he lived in, the world that allowed him and his friends to linger under the moonlight for as long as they liked. And more importantly, what was he hiding behind those mysterious eyes of his?

"I hope so," Phoenix said.

"I had a good time," I replied, walking slower. "Thank you for inviting me."

"Come on!" Ben yelled again before crawling inside through the window.

After stalling a moment longer, I waved goodbye to Phoenix and followed Ben inside. When I turned back around to shut the window, I expected Phoenix to still be standing there, but he wasn't. I didn't even see him walking away.

He simply disappeared into the darkness…

# Chapter Eight

## Good Morning Sunshine

I was startled awake by shouting coming from the living room. I think I heard Grandpa yell something about Nick, but I wasn't fully coherent yet, not after staying out so late last night.

I rubbed my tired eyes and squinted at the clock on the nightstand, trying to read the time. My eyes had a hard time focusing at first, but then I realized I'd slept later than I usually did.

As soon as the sun went down, people slept, and as soon as the sun began to peer over the horizon, they started their day. Waking bright and early made the day seem longer and less tempting to get into trouble after nightfall—less of a chance of going crazy sitting inside, locked away.

Since it took me more than a minute to get out of bed, Grandpa was soon knocking at my door and wondering if his shouting did the job. "It's past noon! Are you feeling ill? Should I tell Nick to come back another time?"

I flung the covers off in a hurry, remembering I had made plans to hang out with Nick that morning. "No, I'm fine. Just give me a few minutes," I replied. I didn't want Nick to leave.

I stared at my reflection in the mirror, which showed a girl with frizzy bed hair and eyes that looked like she needed another hour of sleep.

"Okay," Grandpa grumbled, annoyed I needed a wakeup call. "I guess I'll talk to the boy and keep him entertained while you get dressed."

"Thanks, Grandpa," I yelled and quickly changed out of my pajamas.

I walked into the living room to see Grandpa awkwardly explaining to Nick how his record player worked and was about to go through his record collection. Ben sat with Nick and Grandpa, but he was distracted by his Game Boy. Nick tried his best to seem interested in what Grandpa was saying, but only out of politeness.

"Hi," I said.

Nick abruptly stood, eager to escape my grandpa's attempt to entertain him. "Hey there, Delilah."

"Good morning, sunshine," Grandpa added. "What happened? You're usually up before the rooster crows. Sure you're feeling all right?"

"Uh, I…" My brain wasn't firing on all pistons, still groggy. There was no way I could tell Grandpa the truth without it blowing up in my face.

Ben chimed in, "It's probably that time of the month. She always sleeps in when she's got the cramps."

"Ben!" I snapped, embarrassed he would say such a thing in front of Nick.

Ben shrugged as if he did me a favor, covering up for our escapade to Chad's.

"Oh…" Grandpa said sympathetically. "Do you need the heating pad?"

I shrugged Grandpa off and gave Ben a death stare that I hoped would send him to Satan's doorstep so I wouldn't have to ever deal with him humiliating me again! "No, I'm fine!" I said under a hot breath. "Come on, Nick, let's get out of here."

"Where are you kiddos going to go?" Grandpa asked while staring at us over the frame of his glasses.

The annoyance I was feeling at that moment didn't disperse as quickly as I hoped it would. "Anywhere but here!" I yelled, stomping toward the door. Nick began to follow hesitantly, which wasn't fast enough to my satisfaction.

Nick glanced over his shoulder at my grandpa. "I'll take good care of her, Mr. Summers."

"I'm sure you will," Grandpa said with a grin. "But call me Bill."

Nick went to grab the brim of his hat to give a nod toward my grandpa, but mid-nod, I grabbed Nick's arm in hopes he would move a bit faster.

On our way out the door, I heard Ben tell Grandpa, "See, told you. Her hormones are going crazy."

I sat by the old oak tree to let out some steam, hoping Nick didn't hear that last line Ben spat out. As much as I prayed Nick might've missed what Ben said, I knew he heard every embarrassing comment my brother had made. But Nick was kind, so he sat beside me without hesitation.

"I have some pain meds in my truck if you need them," Nick said gently.

"My stomach is fine," I replied.

"Ah, you aren't on your—"

Before Nick could say it aloud, I cut him off, "No, I'm not."

"Ah," he chuckled. "Brothers."

"Yeah…"

"I know firsthand that the more a sibling picks on you, the more he loves you."

"I highly doubt that," I countered.

Nick nodded to himself a few times and pursed his lips as if he didn't want to make the conversation more awkward than it already was. I wondered if he regretted coming over. He probably wished he hadn't put effort into becoming my friend, and I couldn't blame him.

I picked up a leaf that had fallen, pinched the stem with my thumb and finger, and twirled the leaf back and forth. I set my chin on my knees that were bent in front of me and stared at the colors spinning above my fingertips.

"Sorry, I overslept," I apologized.

"No big deal," Nick said, adjusting his cowboy hat by the brim. "I enjoyed listening to your grandpa. Were you just extra tired today?"

"I had a longer night than usual," I explained.

"Doing what?"

I didn't want to tell Nick where I went. I didn't need that kind of judgment placed on me. Nick didn't know me too well, and I was sure he would make assumptions about my character if he knew what I was up to last night.

"Have you heard of a group of people who keep vampires away?" I wondered.

"No… why have you?" Nick asked as confusion caused his eyebrows to furrow.

"Yeah, I think so, well, maybe not. I'm not sure, actually."

"Uh… Okay?"

"Never mind," I recoiled when I realized he had a bundle of something tied in a white cloth beside him. "What did you bring with you?"

"Apple season is almost over, so I picked some for us in case we get hungry," Nick explained.

"Thanks, that's very thoughtful of you."

"It was no problem."

"So, what do you want to do today?" I asked.

"Nothing in particular. Just glad I was able to take some time off from work."

"That's good. I'm glad you're able to relax, too. I bet your parents are thankful they have you to help, though."

"Yeah, they're grateful, but they work hard. I almost feel guilty for taking a day off," Nick admitted.

"Why would you feel that way?" I wondered. "It's one day."

"Well, for as long as I can remember, my parents have worked every day from dawn until dusk. They taught me by example that being sick, tired, or injured, are never valid excuses to lie around all day, especially when running a farm. The livestock and fields won't provide unless they are tended to, and providing for the family was and will always be the number one priority."

"I guess that's where you get your work ethic from?" I grinned, trying to compliment him.

"They're good parents. I don't know what I would do without—" Nick added and then realized what he was saying. "Oh… I'm sorry. I-I didn't mean to—"

I guess Nick could assume where my parents were. It didn't take a rocket scientist to figure out why my brother and I lived with our grandpa.

I quickly changed the subject, "There's a creek that leads to a small lake not too far from here. Would you want to take a short hike?"

"That sounds perfect," Nick said, already standing before I had finished talking.

"Cool," I replied and tossed the leaf to the ground.

I learned a lot about Nick while we hiked along the creek, but he was also fairly predictable. He was the responsible type, never a rule breaker. He enjoyed the simple things in life, like tending to the animals and the fields. He talked about one of the horses becoming pregnant and how he'd soon be able to help with a live birth for the first time. He was a sweet guy, a guy who would never stab a friend in the back or even someone who had done him wrong, the type of person to bend over backward for a stranger.

"So, what do you like to do besides sit under trees and meander by the water?" Nick asked as we reached the lake.

I picked up a flat stone and chucked it across the still water. "Sometimes I like to write," I told Nick.

"That's neat. What kind of writing?" he wondered.

"Mostly poems," I explained. "Nothing all that great."

"Sounds fun. I wouldn't know where to begin with that sort of thing. What do you like to write about?"

I shrugged. "Whatever comes to mind, whatever I'm feeling at the moment."

"You'll have to share some of those poems with me," Nick urged.

"I've never read them to anyone. I like to keep them private," I said, hoping he still thought I was friend material even though I didn't want to share my hobbies with him.

Nick joined me in skipping rocks. His throw was much better than mine. All that farmwork must've given him strong arms. "I can respect that," he replied, and I was glad he understood where I was coming from.

After we got tired of chucking stones across the water, we sat on large rocks that lined the lake, surrounded by patches of tall grass. Nick untied the bundle of apples, and my mouth began to water. When I took my first bite, a loud crunch escaped. The apple was the crispiest, juiciest apple I ever had, and I couldn't help but let out a long sigh of pleasure.

For hours, we lingered by the lake, enjoying each other's company. It was easy creating a friendship with Nick—one that seemed would last a lifetime. I couldn't recall a time when I laughed as hard as when Nick told me a story about him falling into a cow patty when he was tending to the herd. Learning how much work it took to maintain a farm was intriguing. I could also tell Nick enjoyed hearing about how my family and I got by. I told him about some of our outings, and he seemed nervous about the dangers while on the road.

To each of us, our own life didn't seem exciting because it was the only life we had known since we were born, but the other life we learned about that afternoon by the lake seemed enticing. I wondered what it would be like to live on a farm and be around the animals. The luxury of having fresh food at my fingertips seemed like a wonderful life. Nick thought it would be amazing to be able to protect people like we did and learn a new trade. And although we both wouldn't have minded a taste of something different, something out of the ordinary, we agreed we were thankful for what we had.

Nick left before dinner, so he'd get home before dark, but not before making plans to meet again the following week. I liked him. I felt comfortable around him, and we had plenty to say to each other, never leaving a dull moment in the conversation. But he was also the kind of person I could spend time with and not necessarily feel pressured to fill the silence. I didn't have to pretend to be someone I wasn't with Nick. His heart was filled with compassion for others and all living things, and I knew he would make a good companion.

# Chapter Nine

## Make the Climb

"Come on," I yelled, looking down the ladder at Nick as we climbed the water tower. "Don't be afraid. It's not that high."

Apparently, he wasn't used to climbing higher than a two-story ladder. It seemed strange for a farm boy to be afraid of heights.

"I-I'm coming," Nick said shakily and eventually met me at the top where he sat beside me, somewhat relieved. "I think I prefer the walk along the creek better," he mentioned.

"But look at the view," I pointed out.

The sun had just fully finished rising above the horizon, and it was early enough that the sky was more red than blue. We were surrounded by miles of long blades of brown grass that had dried out from the lack of rain the previous season. There was a windmill in the distance by a rundown house, and I could hear the rusty blades rubbing as they turned, making an unpleasant squeaking sound.

"Wasn't it worth the climb?" I asked Nick.

"Mhmm," he mumbled, not all that convincingly. "Didn't take you for someone so wild and daring."

I laughed. "What? Me? Wild? *Hardly…*"

"Yeah, well, adventurous, at least."

I nodded, finally agreeing. "I guess you're right. For as long as I can remember, I've always wondered what else was out there. What else have I been missing all the past years?" I glanced over at Nick, "What about you? You ever wonder what it's like past Idaho?"

"Not really," he answered.

"Why is that?"

"Everything I love is here—my family," he explained. "I couldn't bring myself to think about leaving my little sis. Family is everything." Then Nick looked at me with wide eyes like he wanted to take back what he had said. "Sorry, I didn't mean to do that again. I should probably be more careful about what I…"

I shook my head and kicked my feet, which were dangling over the edge of the tower. "It's fine," I replied, but I knew my head hung a little lower, thinking about what I didn't have. "If my parents were here too, I know things would be different."

"I'm sorry," Nick apologized again.

I looked at him from the corner of my eye and smirked as I leaned toward him, giving him a gentle nudge with my shoulder so he would stop feeling sorry for me. "Don't be."

"So, where would you want to go if you could go anyplace in the world?" Nick asked, changing the subject.

"I'd love to find a little place by the ocean."

"I've never seen the ocean," Nick admitted.

"Me either," I added. "I bet it's more beautiful than the lake we went to or the grass fields or even the woods. The first thing I'll do when I get to the coast is run into the sea, even if it's ice-cold." I chuckled as I imagined squishing the sand between my toes and the waves rolling over me.

"Does sound pretty fantastic," Nick agreed.

"Yeah, it sure does."

"What about Ben?" Nick asked. "You going to take him with you too?"

"Don't know," I answered while biting my bottom lip since I felt guilty for the dreams I had that didn't necessarily include Ben. "I don't know what he wants. We aren't too close."

"I thought twins are supposed to have an inseparable type of bond," Nick mentioned.

"Not us," I scoffed but then sighed. "Maybe it has something to do with losing our parents. I'm not sure."

"Were, uh… Were you there when it happened?" Nick asked hesitantly, curiosity getting the best of him.

"My mother died giving birth to Ben and me. If she'd gone into labor while the sun was up, Dad would've driven her to the maternity ward, but right as dusk approached, she began having intense contractions. There was a midwife a few minutes away from our home who was willing to be on-call since we were close by, but the midwife couldn't stop the bleeding. If things were different, she might've lived, or maybe… she might not have," I shrugged, trying to keep my emotions intact. "So, I guess you could say Ben and I were both there. Our father is a different story though. He went out to help my grandpa with something and didn't come back."

"Wow, I can't imagine finding the strength to make it over another mountain after losing so much," Nick said, feeling even worse for me. "Your family's gone through a lot… a lot more than mine has."

"Yeah, I guess so…"

"Sorry, I didn't mean to compare our situations," Nick added, worried he'd said something to rub me the wrong way. "So, if you don't mind me asking, how have you coped with your losses?"

"I come here pretty often," I revealed. "It helps a lot, and of course, writing always makes things better, too."

"You mean… here? On top of the water tower?" Nick asked, shocked. "But why? It's so high."

I tilted my head to the sky which was filled with the fluffiest clouds. "To be close to them."

"Oh…" Nick trailed off, understanding completely.

I inhaled deeply, thinking about where my parents were, or rather, their souls. "My mom was cremated, and my dad… I just— it's a place where I can visit them, you know?" I explained.

"Thank you for taking me here and allowing me to share this spot with you," Nick replied.

"Of course. I have to admit, it's kind of nice to have company."

"Well, if you ever want to talk more about what happened to your parents, you know I'm here for you."

I smiled at Nick, thankful for his friendship. "I appreciate that. I don't like to talk about it too often."

"That's understandable. You are lucky to have your grandpa."

"Very…"

Nick didn't press the subject, but instead, we sat quietly on the water tower, gazing at the tangerine sky and the fields that seemed to go on forever. I knew one day I'd see my parents again, and that helped to put me at ease.

# Chapter Ten

## That One Time

I'd only seen a vampire one time face-to-face, and it was the time I almost died. The incident happened right before my dad passed away. It was midnight, and I was in bed when I awoke to a distressed animal outside my bedroom window. I threw back my covers and peeked outside to see a dog breathing heavily. It continuously switched from panting to licking a deep wound on its hind leg. He looked as if he could've been someone's pet at some point, but there was no saying for sure. His fur was matted, and mud was caked on all four of his paws. Every so often, he'd let out a painful whimper, and the longer I stared out the window at the poor animal, the sorrier I felt for him.

Ben and I were never allowed to have any pets. Dad said they made too much noise when danger was near, but more so, Dad never allowed us to have one because of the responsibilities that came with taking care of a living creature—not enough time and too costly. The reasons why we could never own a dog went on and on.

But that night, there was no way I'd pass up an opportunity to rescue a dog and possibly call it my own. If Dad saw that the dog needed someone to look after him, maybe he'd let me nurse the wounded animal back to health. At least I'd be able to keep him a little while, or maybe the stray would become part of the family, and he could stay forever.

It was a good plan, so I tiptoed to the front door in my nightgown in hopes of not waking Grandpa, who was asleep in the living room recliner. I descended the front steps of the porch to where the dog was huddled against the side of the house.

I crouched down and held out my hand while puckering my lips, coaxing the dog with kissing sounds. "Come here, Buddy," I said softly, slowly inching nearer.

The dog was frightened and curled his upper lip to display his teeth.

"It's okay. I won't hurt you," I continued.

But then the dog let out a warning bark, and I paused from trying to get closer.

"Shh!" I whispered loudly. "You'll wake up Grandpa and Dad, and then you won't have a home for sure."

I took another cautious step, determined to earn his trust, but it only scared him more, and he stood shakily on three legs while growling. I realized it would've been smarter to get some scraps from the fridge. He was thinner than I'd originally thought, and I noticed his ribs protruding like he hadn't eaten a decent meal in a long while.

"Here, boy," I encouraged, but with those words, he began to back away from me toward the darkness and outside of the UV perimeter. "No, don't," I said, worried he would go too far and out of my reach.

But as young and naive as I was, oblivious to the real dangers that thrived in the night, I followed the scared dog, even when he stepped past where I wasn't supposed to go. I walked a few feet into the darkness, but as soon as the night surrounded me, I heard rustling in the bushes nearby.

"Hello? Is-is someone there?" I asked. The dog directed his growls toward the bushes where the noise was coming from. "What's wrong, boy? What is it?"

His snarls grew more intense, and I became worried it might not just be a coyote or fox behind the bushes. That's when common sense finally came back, and I slowly began to walk backward toward the perimeter, never turning my back to the bushes. I noticed the dog was closer, his fur brushing against my leg as he followed me to safety. He was no longer frightened of me but rather something else that was truly a danger.

I prayed I would make it back under the perimeter before something happened. I was only a couple of steps away before a woman leaped on top of me like a wildcat pouncing on its prey, causing me to fall onto my back. Just as quickly, she retreated into the darkness to avoid being burned by the lights. I was worried for a second but felt relieved once I realized I had made it to safety. Vampires couldn't harm me as long as I had the light surrounding me.

But then, I felt something on my ankle, and when I looked to see what it could be, absolute horror overtook me. My feet were still outside of the perimeter, and my heart began to race. I could feel the rush of adrenaline pulsing through my veins. My body begged for me to fight back, so I kicked and screamed as hard and as loud as I could, but I was weak compared to my attacker, and I wasn't loud enough for Grandpa or Dad to hear me. The woman had ahold of my ankle and quickly dragged me back into the darkness. The dog cowered, whimpering, but stayed where the light was shining.

"Oh... you'd make the perfect addition," she smiled sinisterly at me as I lifted my head to get a better look at who was holding onto my leg.

I continued to try and scoot back into the light, but it was no use. She was unusually strong, and I couldn't budge. My elbows dug deeper into the dirt, but rather than moving me closer to where I wanted to go, it was as if I was digging myself a grave.

"P-please, please don't hurt me," I cried, giving up on screaming. Grandpa slept too deeply.

The woman crawled up my legs and then over my stomach until she hovered over me and met my gaze. Her eyes were black as if they were soulless and hollow. She let out a high-pitched screech into my face while presenting razor-sharp fangs. Her hair matched the darkness of her eyes perfectly, and her skin was whiter than the purest of clouds.

"Come with me," she cooed. "I have a nice place where you can stay."

The dog began barking uncontrollably, but the vampire ignored him as if he wasn't there. She was zoned in on me, and nothing else mattered.

"No— no, thank you," I said with a whimper.

My response seemed to amuse her, and she giggled to herself. "Don't think you have a choice, my dearie. But tell me, how old are you exactly?" Her eyes narrowed with curiosity, and her playful expression turned serious. "Will you be an asset to the hive or simply food? Now that I have you in my grasp, you seem a bit young. I love the taste of young blood, though."

"I, um, I…" I stammered, terrified and confused.

Then, it was as if she became distracted. I assumed she had noticed the cross that hung from my necklace, and it was confirmed when she slowly reached toward me. She took her time as she lifted the cross with the end of her long, pointed nail, knowing if it touched her flesh, it would burn. She hummed to herself as if she were inspecting my piece of jewelry.

I was thankful God spared me another moment from being dragged away into the night. I was certain that once she took me, I'd never be seen again. Although I didn't know what she meant about taking me somewhere. I didn't understand much of what she'd said since I was young and didn't know all the details about vampires yet.

Suddenly, a loud bang rang through the air, and the vampire on top of me recoiled. We were both shocked when we saw the wound on her shoulder. There was a gaping hole, but it began healing almost instantly.

"Get away from her!" I heard Grandpa yell.

I sat up and glanced over my shoulder to see Grandpa behind me, pointing a shotgun at my attacker.

"Get back here, Delilah!" my grandpa shouted, instructing me to get within the perimeter.

The vampire stood faster than I could blink, hunched over in a defensive stance, and hissed loudly at the human with the weapon.

The vampire was stunned for a few seconds, taken aback by the silver pellets that burned through her. The distraction allowed me to scoot back to safety, and Grandpa let off another round, hitting the vampire in her torso. The silver needed to touch her heart for her to die.

"The next one won't miss," Grandpa said confidently, but before we knew it, the vampire vanished into the night.

Grandpa let out a sigh of relief and lowered the shotgun to his side. "Are you okay?" he asked, worried as he hastily examined every inch of my neck. "She didn't bite you, did she?"

"She didn't bite me," I answered as Grandpa tucked his hand underneath my arm to help me up.

Once I was able to stand on my own, he looked at the gun in his hand and twisted it back and forth as if something was interesting about it.

"Would've killed that bloodsucker if I'd thought to grab my glasses," Grandpa murmured to himself, disappointed he'd missed his mark.

"What's going on?" my dad asked, peeking out the front door of the house.

Grandpa shook his head. "Delilah almost got herself killed."

My dad groggily stumbled down the steps, concerned. "What do you mean? What happened? Why are you out of bed?"

"Let's get inside," Grandpa suggested.

My dad wrapped his arm around my shoulder to urge me into the house, but I paused and looked down at the dog sitting by us. I bent down to see if he'd let me pet him and held out my hand again. I smiled when his wet tongue grazed my hand, forgetting about the horrific encounter I had moments ago.

"Not without, Buddy," I told my dad and grandpa.

"Huh?" my dad said in a daze, and after a few seconds, he understood what I was referring to. "You know the rules."

"But he saved me," I added.

"He did?" my dad asked, looking at Grandpa for confirmation.

Grandpa shrugged and nodded. "Yeah, I guess he did. If he hadn't barked, I wouldn't have woken up."

"I didn't hear anything," my dad added, his words tainted with guilt.

"I told you to stop taking those sleeping meds. They are still potent even though they're expired!" Grandpa scolded, but everyone knew it was easier said than done. It had been difficult for him since Mom died.

My dad held his hand to his head, pinching his temples. "I, uh, yeah. I guess you're right," he admitted. "I'll stop taking them."

"So, can we keep him?" I begged, forgetting how shaken up I was just moments ago.

"Bring the dog inside, and we can figure out what to do with him tomorrow morning," my dad instructed.

Dad ended up letting me keep the dog, but since we couldn't afford to take Buddy to the vet, he ended up dying shortly after the incident. The infection got to him, and my dad and Grandpa were already ticked that they had to dip into their stash of silver bullets because of my incompetence. They didn't come cheap and kept getting more expensive.

Money seemed to always be an issue since the war, but to a kid, it didn't mean anything. I didn't understand much when I was younger, like finances and safety and how they correlated to our survival. But I *did* know that I missed Buddy. I cried for a week straight, depressed that I couldn't save him. Grandpa said it must've been a bobcat or a coyote that got to Buddy since vampires didn't attack animals unless the animal made the first move. Grandpa said the vampire must've scared off the predator that attacked him. Grandpa was probably right, but all I could think about was how Buddy saved my life, and I couldn't save his…

# Chapter Eleven

## Come With Me

Nightfall came, and I should've been asleep like everyone else, but something kept me awake. I suppose it was because I knew the group was gathering in Chad's parking lot like they did every Friday night.

Hanging out with Nick helped get my mind off Phoenix and his friends, but only for a short amount of time. It was inevitable that the unanswered questions would eventually begin scratching at my door again.

I grabbed my notebook from the nightstand drawer. If there was anything that could help keep my mind from yearning for answers, it was writing. Writing was a way to escape reality—one that didn't involve monsters lurking in the shadows, a place that allowed me to lie in the fields at night and stare at the stars above, somewhere that didn't imprison me when darkness fell. Writing transported me anywhere I wanted to go.

But just as my pen hit the paper, I was distracted by loud screeching coming from outside. It was a horrid noise that wouldn't cease. The screeching could've been mistaken for a dying animal, but I knew better. There was no use in trying to jot down my thoughts, not with all that ruckus. So, I closed my notebook and put the pen aside. I peered outside the window to see if I could spot a pair of glowing eyes perched on a nearby tree.

"Ah, there you are," I said quietly to myself as I spotted the owl circling above the field behind the oak tree.

I sat on my bed with my elbows on the windowsill and watched enviously as the owl hunted under the moonlight. Anything with wings had the advantage in a world filled with bloodsuckers, and apparently, vampires weren't the only predators of the night.

Eventually, the owl swooped down into the field to catch his meal. I was finally ready to peel myself away from the excitement going on outside and give writing another go, but out of nowhere, a figure appeared in front of the window. It must've been crouching beneath the frame, so I wouldn't see it until the precise moment—only when it wanted me to.

I gasped in terror while falling off of the bed, clumsily rolling into a backward summersault as I hit the floor. "Ow," I cried softly, rubbing the back of my neck, and then remembered there was someone or *something* outside my window.

I stayed low, thinking if it didn't notice me, it would simply go away. It reminded me of the time when I had a nightmare as a child. As soon as I awoke from the horrid dream, I began to think the monster I dreamt of was real, and he was waiting to lunge at me from the blackness in the room unless I did something quickly like hide underneath the covers. I was convinced nothing could harm me as long as I stayed hidden.

"Hey!" the person outside my window said in a loud whisper.

"Huh?" I breathed softly. My heart still pounded wildly, and I was unsure if I should make myself known.

There was no possible way it could've been a vampire outside my window, not with the perimeter lights. So, I gathered what courage I could and crept closer to my bed. Although I was still hesitant to peek out the window.

"You in there, Delilah?" the person outside continued. His voice sounded familiar the second time he spoke, and he knew my name which made me feel more at ease.

I slowly stood to see who was there and sighed with relief when I saw Phoenix. But what was he doing outside my house? Shouldn't he have been at the fight with the others?

I crawled onto my bed and unlocked my window.

"Phoenix?" I asked in disbelief. "What are you doing here?"

"I came to say hi," he said with a grin.

I shook my head, unable to fathom why he would do such a thing.

"Oh," I replied, becoming embarrassed when I realized I was in my nightgown. I quickly pulled the covers over myself to hide what I was wearing, and Phoenix chuckled, but not in a rude way. "Hi," I said awkwardly.

Phoenix's grin still lingered. "Hi," he replied quietly. "So, are you busy?"

I looked around my room like there might've been something I needed to tend to. "Uh…" I trailed off and shrugged.

Phoenix ran his hand through his hair, brushing the front locks back into place. "Well, if you aren't busy, maybe I can take you somewhere."

"*Somewhere*?" I asked, wondering what he had in mind.

"It's a surprise."

Phoenix enjoyed keeping things a mystery, but I hated being out of the loop. I remembered Grandpa saying, "Curiosity kills the cat," and I suppose, if I was a cat, I would have used up my nine lives a long time ago.

"I have my motorcycle parked down the street," Phoenix explained. "I didn't want to wake everyone."

"Oh, uh, you do?" I stuttered.

I had never ridden a motorcycle before. Grandpa told me about how Mom made Dad sell his motorcycle as an ultimatum when he asked her to marry him. She didn't want to be a widow just as soon as she was a newlywed.

"Yeah, the place I want to take you is a little far on foot. I brought an extra helmet," he said, encouraging me to tag along.

"I, um, I don't know…" I mumbled, knowing I should've said no.

"Come on. It'll be fun," he promised.

"I mean, it's past nightfall, and I don't think it's safe. I probably shouldn't have even gone out that last time. I don't know what I was thinking."

"You were thinking you can't stay cooped up here every night for the rest of your life."

I chuckled lightly, "Yeah… I guess."

"So, come on. Let's have some fun. I told you a hundred times already that you don't have to worry about vampires. I'll protect you."

Phoenix was so confident he could protect me that it seemed borderline cocky.

"Like with your awesome fighting skills?" I said, almost too mockingly.

"You could say that," Phoenix said flatly without emotion.

He was difficult to read. He seemed fierce but gentle. Maybe outgoing but cautious? Sort of sweet, like I wouldn't mind growing up next door to him, but also like something had ruined his innocence. It was as if Phoenix had two sides to him, or maybe I didn't know enough about him to make such judgments.

I sighed, still not convinced I should sneak out again. "I hardly know you," I countered.

"Isn't that the whole point of hanging out? To get to know one another better?" Phoenix chuckled as if my excuses were silly.

He was right though, and I felt like every time I tried to come up with a reason to say no, he easily had a better reason for me to go with him.

"What if I said I would answer any five questions you have?" Phoenix volunteered. "I know you must have a lot of them."

"Huh?" I asked, confused. "What do you mean five questions?"

"Well, I know I gave you vague answers when we were at the gas station the other night. What if I told you I'd give you upfront answers this time? Any five questions you have."

"Really?" I asked, squinting at Phoenix, wondering if I should believe what he said.

"Yeah, I give you my word, and I never break my promises. Never."

And with that, I gave in. Forget about curiosity killing the cat. I would die from the unknown, spending the rest of my life locked away during the night. "All right. Give me a minute," I said and pulled the curtains to cover the window for privacy.

I quickly changed into suitable clothes but didn't grab my "go-to bag." I couldn't quite put my finger on it, but something about Phoenix convinced me I could trust him. I believed he would keep me safe.

# Chapter Twelve

## Tell Me Secrets

"Hop on," Phoenix instructed as he mounted the bike and handed me the spare helmet.

"Um," I stammered. "How do I get on… exactly?"

He chuckled and pointed to the foot peg on the side I was standing on. "One foot on there and then swing your leg over. There's nothing to it."

I took a couple of steps closer to the bike, and my heart began to beat hard. Where was I supposed to put my hands?

"You can use me for support," Phoenix added while patiently waiting for me.

"Oh, o-okay," I replied while setting one foot on the peg.

I slowly placed a hand on Phoenix's shoulder and did my best to swing my leg over but not without almost falling off the other side.

"Woah, woah," Phoenix said holding his arm behind him to catch me. He helped push me back onto the seat with ease.

"Sorry," I apologized, my cheeks becoming warm.

"No worries," he laughed. "Just make sure you hold on tight during the ride, okay?"

"What do you mean?" I asked, confused.

"You don't want to fall off the back while we're riding," he explained. I didn't have to see his face to tell he was smirking.

"Oh, right, yeah…" I said like I knew what he was talking about.

Phoenix could tell I had no clue what I was doing on the back of his motorcycle. It seemed pointless to put on a façade, but I would continue to do so because Phoenix was as wild as a tornado sweeping the fields of Idaho. He was as intriguing as the Fairy Shrimp that thrived in Tadpole Lake. Phoenix didn't let the type of world we were in weigh him down. He embraced the night and wouldn't dare allow the monsters to keep him from living. In a sense, I wanted to be more like him, and I was dumbfounded as to why someone such as him would give me the time of day.

With his feet still planted on both sides, Phoenix held his hands out behind his back. "Give me your hands," he told me.

If my heart wasn't beating fast enough before, it sure was then, and I hoped my palms weren't sweaty when I placed them in Phoenix's. He pulled my arms around his waist, giving me no choice but to lean against him.

"Hold here," he explained. "Lean forward and not back, all right?"

"Okay," I answered.

"Don't be afraid to get closer," he said, but I didn't see how that was possible. I could smell his leather jacket with my face pressed against his back.

"Um, okay…" I murmured awkwardly.

"All right, here we go! You ready?" Phoenix exclaimed, but before I could answer, he slammed his foot down, kick-starting the bike to life. It was louder than I expected, so I was thankful he didn't pull up to the house. "Hang on!" he yelled before taking off.

A scream escaped my lungs as we began our ride into the night. I was startled by how fast the bike was and gripped the front of Phoenix's jacket even tighter. Also, I guess he was right… I was able to scoot closer.

But after a few minutes, I realized it was just us and the road. Phoenix maneuvered the bike with ease, and since my arms were around him, I could feel how relaxed he was. I noticed the night air was crisper as we flew by on the motorcycle. The sky was brighter than I could've hoped for. It was as if there were billions of stars above. The balls of fire lit the dirt back road we were cruising on, and it was everything and more than I imagined it to be after nightfall.

After what seemed like too short of a drive, we arrived in the middle of nowhere. Phoenix turned off the motorcycle and when I dismounted, a castle that was falling apart came into view. Stones were missing and moss bred freely upon the structure, but it wasn't in complete ruin.

Around the perimeter of the castle were tall posts with lights similar to what Grandpa installed. Although I could tell they weren't UV bulbs. They were simply meant for seeing what was surrounding the castle. As I looked closer, I noticed lights coming from inside.

"Does someone live here?" I wondered. "Are we meeting people here?"

"We aren't meeting anyone here," Phoenix answered.

"But then who's inside?"

"Mostly just some of the training officers that are on duty. Everyone else won't be back until the sun rises."

"What do you mean? Who— wait, just to be clear, these don't count as my questions, right? I mean, I should know where you've taken me."

Phoenix smirked. "Yup, that's only fair. You still have five."

"Okay. Good," I said in all seriousness. "So, why are we here?"

"This is where I live or have been… or will be for the time being."

"You— you live here?" I asked and began to think about how I heard vampires like to dwell in castles.

"Yeah," Phoenix said, as if it was normal to live in a rundown castle.

"I didn't even know there was a castle nearby," I mentioned. "Don't vampires like to gather in them?"

"Yeah, they do, but the funny thing about castles is that although they are massive, many are hidden within nature. "Don't worry though, no vampires live in this one, at least not anymore."

"Oh, okay, that's good," I replied, nerves hanging heavily on my words.

I wasn't only nervous because I hardly knew Phoenix, and I let him take me to a place where no one knew where I was, but also because I just found out he lived in a castle, a place where vampires congregated. The closer I thought I was to finding out more about him, the more questions arose and the more unsure I became about my safety. I knew Phoenix gave me his word, but how much did his word really mean?

"I figured since I know where you live, you ought to know where I live, too," Phoenix said nonchalantly.

That helped put my nerves a little bit more at ease. Since Phoenix knew where I lived, he could've murdered my family and me in my sleep if he wanted to.

"That's fair," I replied.

"So, once we step inside, you'll have five questions," he explained.

I nodded more eagerly than I should've. Grandpa and Ben would've killed me if they knew what I was doing.

When I stepped into the castle, the inside didn't match the outside. It looked more like a military base. Crates were stacked on each other, and I assumed they were full of supplies and weapons. A woman stood by the door in black pants and a long-sleeved shirt. Her hair was pulled back into a tight bun, not a loose hair present. Above her shirt, she wore a tactical vest, and a pistol was attached to the side of her thigh. But what stood out to me the most was her eyes, which seemed to have a dark purple ring around the iris. At least, that's what they looked like from what I could see. Maybe I was wrong. I didn't want to stare too long.

"Welcome back," the lady greeted Phoenix. "Heard you pull up."

"Ma'am," Phoenix nodded to her before heading into another room that was being used as a kitchen.

The castle was old, but they had the newest and finest appliances set out on makeshift counters. There were many wooden tables with ample seating. Phoenix walked over to the fridge which was three times as big as the one we had at our house, and I wondered how they kept things running. It must've cost someone an arm and a leg to purchase the gas to run the generators.

"Oh, I'm not hungry," I told Phoenix.

"Me either," he added, which didn't make sense because he was rummaging through the freezer.

"So, then why are you—" I paused, remembering my questions had started.

He turned with a carton of ice cream in each of his hands. "What about dessert?"

"Oh, my gosh," I squealed with wide eyes. "Yes, please." I quickly sat at one of the tables, my mouth beginning to salivate.

Phoenix grabbed some bowls and spoons. "Chocolate or vanilla?" he asked.

"Both?" I said anxiously.

"Was that a question?" Phoenix joked.

"No!" I spoke too loudly, but not because it would be a strike against my question limit. It had been forever since I had ice cream, and it was difficult to contain my excitement. "I've only had ice cream one other time."

"When was that?" he wondered.

"It was for my fifth birthday. My dad did someone a big favor and brought me home ice cream." My excitement seemed to quickly disperse as soon as I began to speak about my dad and reminisce. "It was the best thing I've ever had. My dad even made sure it was packed in ice for the trip home. I've never tasted something so amazing before."

"What flavor did your dad bring you?" he asked.

"It was mixed with vanilla and chocolate and had some caramel."

Phoenix paused and went to the mobile pantry. He grabbed a bottle and held it up proudly. "How about that? Got some caramel right here."

Phoenix scooped me a generous bowl, smothered it in caramel, and took a seat beside me. The amount of ice cream he gave me was twice the amount he served himself, but I didn't question why. "Bottoms up," he said, holding his spoon up for a toast.

But instead of digging in like I thought I would, I sat and stared at the bowl. I didn't clink my spoon against Phoenix's for a toast because I was reminded of a special moment I had with my dad so long ago. I couldn't suppress the emotions rushing within me like an avalanche. I remembered my dad and I laughing as we ate the entire carton together in one sitting. He let me have most of it, and I wasn't forced to give a single bite to Ben. I didn't feel an ounce of guilt for not sharing since Dad brought Ben his favorite king-sized candy bar. I remember my dad rubbing my upset tummy as I lay in bed. I remember him kissing me goodnight and telling me he loved me.

"What's wrong? Want more caramel?" Phoenix asked before lowering the spoon, confused.

I shook my head, doing my best to tuck the memory of my fifth birthday back into the vault. "No, it's perfect," I said solemnly. "Looks delicious. Thank you."

Phoenix could tell something important was on my mind. "If you keep waiting, it's going to melt, you know?" he said, trying to make me smile.

I picked up my spoon. "I can't believe you guys have ice cream here," I mentioned, doing my best not to linger in my memory.

"It's one of the perks of our job."

"I see…" I trailed off, staring at the bowl of ice cream as I slowly swirled the caramel around with the spoon.

"You sure you're okay?" Phoenix asked, leaning closer as he tried catching my gaze with his.

"Yeah… yeah, I'm fine. Sorry. I-I just haven't had the most… *ideal* life," I explained and did my best to produce a half-hearted smile. He barely knew me, but he sincerely cared.

"Me either," Phoenix added. "But you know what helps me when I'm feeling down?"

"What?" I wondered.

"Eating ice cream," he grinned, "a crap load of ice cream."

"All right," I chuckled and began enjoying the dessert. "I'll give it a shot."

I don't know if it was the ice cream that helped ease the pain I was feeling, or rather that I was able to spend time with someone who could relate. Phoenix didn't pretend his life was perfect. He didn't deny that he felt down more often than not. I didn't have to pretend to be whole when I was around him.

"So, you want to start asking some questions or what?" Phoenix reminded me.

"Yeah, I almost forgot about that!"

"Told you, ice cream helps. It helps you forget," Phoenix added.

"You're right…" I agreed.

"So, go ahead, shoot," Phoenix urged. "Unless you plan on staying here all night with me."

"Uh… O-okay," I stammered, uncomfortable by the last part I hoped was a joke. "What is your job exactly?" I asked.

"I… I mean *we*," he corrected himself. "Everyone you saw at the gas station… we hunt down vampires."

My jaw dropped, "Wh-what?"

"Is that your second question?" Phoenix asked as if vampire hunter meant nothing.

"No. No!" I said urgently, afraid he would take another one of my questions away. "Questions relating to the same topic don't count! I just… I don't understand."

"*I*—hunt—vampires," Phoenix repeated slowly, almost demeaning as if I didn't understand the English language.

I shook my head and rolled my eyes in disbelief. "I didn't know there was such a thing. I didn't think something like that existed."

Phoenix shrugged. "Been around for about a decade now. We're the New Military. Was the President's idea. Well, the President who was in office twenty years ago. Took a while for the politicians to get things in order. I joined six years ago when I was sixteen."

"But why? Why would you want to hunt vampires?"

"Second question?" Phoenix grinned.

"Um," I thought for a moment, debating if it was something worth finding out. "Yes," I confirmed.

"Father was a drunk. Mom died when I was ten. Guess Dad was a drunk because Mom died when I was ten. Father liked to beat on me to let out his frustration that he lost his wife. Seemed like the best option when the New Military knocked on my door."

"I'm sorry," I said softly.

"Don't be. You know what it's like, too."

I nodded. "Yeah," I whispered. "I do."

We let silence have the room for a few minutes while we finished our ice cream and let the reality of losing loved ones wash over us and then move on. And for a brief moment, I wondered if people saw pain when they looked into my eyes—the same hurt I saw in Phoenix's.

Phoenix gathered our bowls and placed them in a tub filled with soapy water. "Want to go to the roof for a little?"

"Yeah," I replied. "That sounds nice."

When we reached the top of the castle, I noticed two other people on the rooftop standing on opposite sides of each other, keeping a lookout. The two were dressed similarly to the lady at the entrance, but they were both holding a rifle in their hands. They didn't greet us like the previous soldier at the entrance, and I assumed the rooftop guards' responsibilities were to keep their eyes on the perimeter at all times.

Phoenix directed me over to a bench that had been brought to the roof. It was toward the middle, between the two soldiers, who acted like we weren't there.

"Are you cold?" he asked.

"Not as cold as I was on the ride here," I mentioned.

"Sorry, should've told you to dress warmer. It's always chilly on the bike."

"It's fine. I didn't mind. I kind of enjoyed the ride."

"You did?" Phoenix asked, surprised.

"Mhmm. It's different being out at night."

"Yeah, it sure is," Phoenix replied.

I tilted my head back to gaze at the sky. The moon was so full that night.

"And God made the two great lights, and the lesser light to rule the night," Phoenix quoted.

"And the stars, too," I finished.

We both looked at each other simultaneously and smiled. At that moment, I was convinced Phoenix was good. His soul was damaged but filled with pure intentions. He wasn't just beautiful on the outside, his love for God shined from within him.

"I've never seen the moon or the night sky like this before," I admitted.

"What about the other night when you were with me?"

"I wasn't looking at the sky," I chuckled, thinking of how I was so fascinated by the group of people gathering, unafraid and free, and more so… *him*.

"If the night sky didn't catch your attention, then what did?" Phoenix smirked as if he knew what was on my mind.

I bit my lip, thinking I shouldn't have said what I did. "Nothing…" I brushed him off and changed the subject. "Thank you for taking me here."

"Of course," Phoenix said softly.

"It's like there's nothing else that compares to the night sky," I breathed in awe.

"I couldn't agree more," Phoenix said even more quietly, but his eyes hadn't returned to the sky above like mine had.

I could sense his gaze pressing down on me. I tucked my hands between my legs and pinched them tightly, becoming uncomfortable again. It wasn't because I thought Phoenix was creepy, though. Surely, he meant his intent stare to be a compliment, but I didn't know how to take it as something flattering. I didn't think I was ever worth a second glance, so his gaze felt foreign.

"So…" I continued in hopes of steering away from flirting. I didn't know how to do that and didn't want to make a fool out of myself. "Third question."

"Okay, sure, let's hear it," Phoenix replied.

"Why were you given orders to set up here in Hope?"

"Oh," Phoenix breathed out slowly. "That's a question that requires a long answer."

"I think we've got some time until I need to be back," I reminded him.

Then Phoenix sat up straighter and his voice became serious—military-like, and he spoke in a deeper tone, "Well, before the New Military was formed, we learned a lot about vampires, each year bringing in new information. Once the government felt that we knew enough to protect ourselves from the abominations, units were ordered to kill. In the process, we found out how vampires change people, and more importantly, that they have a system."

"System?" I asked. "What do you mean?"

"The best way I can explain it is they're like bees. You know how there are hives everywhere around the world?"

"Yes," I answered.

"You know how each one of those hives has a queen?"

I nodded, eager to find out more.

"Well, vampires thrive together in hives, and they rely on a queen to keep things in order. That's mainly why they haven't been so easy to get rid of. They aren't just mindless creatures. Each hive has vampires who lure or force humans back to the hive to eventually be changed by the only one who can turn a human—the queen. The vampires people encounter are workers, the only ones who leave the hive. The workers are disposable, unlike the queen who is faster, stronger, smarter… more sinister."

"How come I haven't heard of this before?" I wondered.

"It's not known to the public."

"But why?" I asked, becoming heated that the media and politicians would keep such important news from us.

"What does it matter anyway? The public can't do anything, and it wouldn't do any good if they knew. It would only scare them more knowing there are stronger vampires hidden away within hives," Phoenix explained.

"But it's still wrong to keep it from the rest of the world," I mentioned.

"Yeah, well, I don't make the rules. I just have to follow them," Phoenix added defensively.

"I know. Sorry, I didn't mean to seem like I was attacking you."

"Trust me, a lot of us feel the same way you do, but to answer your question, they think there is a hive nearby that has one of the eldest queens."

"A hive? H-here in Hope?" I asked, concerned.

"Well, okay… maybe not *nearby*, could be hundreds of miles away. Not like castles are abundant in Idaho," Phoenix laughed as if he was cracking a joke.

"Oh, um, all right…" I didn't think what we were talking about was a topic to be put lightly.

Phoenix continued, "Vampires can cover long distances in a short time as long as the moon is high. Anyway, if we can figure out where the hive is, it might give us a hint of where the Vampire King is. We thought, maybe, we'd find the queen we were looking for in this castle when we got here, but the queen who resided at this place couldn't have been older than a couple of decades or so. I'm not disappointed, though. I know we'll find what we're searching for eventually."

"So, you're here to what? Go in and exterminate them?" I asked, shocked.

"Yeah, something like that."

I began to ramble out of confusion, "How can you tell how old a queen is, and how can you tell which one is the leader of the hive? And what about a *king*?"

"That's a bunch of questions," Phoenix laughed, but I'm feeling generous tonight, so I'll count it as one.

My eyes squinted as he placed his hands behind his head and leaned back. "Thanks?" I said sarcastically.

I was starting to sense Phoenix was kind of arrogant, or maybe I was mistaking his confidence as something negative. I guess it didn't hurt to be confident, and doing what he did, confidence was probably a good thing for him to have. Confidence kept a person alive, not passiveness or second-guessing.

"You can tell the age of a vampire by its fangs. The longer they are, the longer the vampire has lived. It's easy to spot a queen. She's always dressed flamboyantly. The last one had some sort of gold outfit with jewels sewn on. I swear, it's like the Vampire King must've come from some tomb in Egypt or something because all the queens seem to resemble Egyptian queens. It's like the king had implanted demons from thousands of years ago into women's bodies, making them fulfill his wishes of conquering the world. Seems like he'll never stop spreading his disease. Well, that is… until we find him and kill him."

My adrenaline began to pump as I pictured Phoenix and the others attacking a hive full of blood-sucking demons. I tried to fathom vampires who were stronger than the ones we knew of. The world we lived in became dimmer, and being able to stare at the night sky in safety whenever we pleased seemed to be getting farther out of reach. I would've never guessed Phoenix would be telling me something so insane.

"Do you really think you guys can end the war?" I wondered.

"Last question?" Phoenix confirmed.

"Yes," I answered without hesitation.

He nodded. "I'd like to think we can complete our mission and rescue nightfall," he said while placing his hands behind his head to look up at the moon.

"Aren't you worried you're going to get killed?" I asked, which was maybe too blunt of a question.

Phoenix smirked. "You're at your limit."

"What?" I scoffed. "No!"

"Maybe I'll answer more of your questions another night," he added.

*Another night?* I wondered to myself. *Why would someone like Phoenix want to keep hanging out with a nobody like me?*

"Let's just enjoy the night and not talk about vampires for a little while," he suggested, and then I felt one of his arms relax from behind his head, finding a more comfortable spot around my shoulders.

I sighed, giving up on finding out more, and decided it was okay that Phoenix placed his arm around me. I joined him in admiring what was above us. I wanted to give the night sky the attention it deserved while I had the chance.

# Chapter Thirteen

## Big Brother Scolding

"Knock, knock!" Ben yelled from the outside of my bedroom door.

I sat up in bed, startled. The sun was shining through the crack in the curtains that covered the window. "I'm for sure moving my bed now," I muttered groggily, annoyed by the ray of light beaming in.

I held my hand to my brow in hopes of blocking out the brightness and blinked about a hundred times a minute so my eyes could drown out the blurriness. It took a long moment before my sight was clear again, but I guess that was what long nights did—made mornings difficult.

"It's past noon, Delilah. You missed breakfast."

"Go away," I grumbled.

"I will count to ten, and then I'm going to come into your room. So, make sure you're decent." Then Ben began to count, "One, two—"

"Just shut up and come in!" I yelled, annoyed.

Ben slowly cracked open the door, still unsure if he'd given me enough time.

"I'm dressed, you idiot!"

"Okay, okay," Ben said, entering. "Gramps wanted me to check on you and make sure you're feeling all right."

"I'm fine," I answered, glaring at Ben. "Just tired."

Ben leaned against the wall and folded his arms across his chest. "I can see that," he replied and pursed his lips for a moment. "You went out again last night, didn't you?"

I threw my hands in the air and let them flop down beside me with dramatic flair. "Yeah, so what?" I rolled my eyes. "*Now* are you going to tattle on me? I know things haven't changed much since we were kids."

Ben shook his head like I shouldn't have assumed that he was going to snitch. "No, I'm a good brother, even though you don't think so. I wouldn't intentionally try and get you in trouble. Although there might come a time when I need a favor…"

"Oh, geez, Ben…"

"I'm only joking," he countered.

"Yeah, uh-huh, sure you are. Keep in mind that *you* came with me just the other night," I reminded him.

"Right… So, what'd you do last night?" Ben asked too enthusiastically, as if he wanted to live vicariously through me. I knew firsthand it was hard being locked up every night.

"None of your business," I snapped.

"Gramps," Ben yelled, "Delilah has something she wants to tell you!"

"Ben!" I shouted hotly.

"Huh? What is it?" Grandpa said from the kitchen.

"Don't!" I snapped at Ben. "You'd risk Grandpa finding out you had a little outing, too?"

"I'll do what I have to," Ben said unwaveringly.

"Seriously?" I scoffed.

"Tell me what you did," my brat of a brother ordered.

The squeaking from Grandpa's knee brace was getting louder as he approached my room. I couldn't believe Ben was going to rat me out!

"Fine!" I gritted through my teeth.

"What does she need to tell me?" Grandpa wondered, peeking his head in.

I held my breath in anticipation. My eyes widened, and my spine sat straight as I angrily balled the comforter into my clenched fists. *You better keep your mouth shut, Ben!*

"Oh, nothing," Ben explained. "Just that she is feeling a little under the weather."

Once I knew Ben wasn't going to blab, I was able to relax.

Grandpa asked, unfazed, "Is it a cold? Flu? That time of the—"

I quickly fake coughed and sniffled a couple of times before Grandpa made his last assumption. "I think it's allergies," I lied while Ben tried to hide his laughter.

"Oh, okay. Well, you know where the medication is. It's expired, but it should still help," Grandpa said. Then he turned to Ben, "What's so funny?"

"Nothing," Ben replied, continuing to fail at hiding his grin.

"You're sure acting strange," Grandpa told Ben.

"Uh, you know, Gramps, I was just thinking that Delilah's room is weirdly decorated. There are posters of the beach everywhere," Ben tried to explain to suppress Grandpa's questioning eyes. "We live in Idaho, not California."

Grandpa's eyes went back and forth from Ben and me, giving us the same skeptical glare over the frame of his glasses.

I shrugged. "I think beaches are relaxing to look at," I added, hoping Grandpa didn't suspect anything.

"Uh-huh," Grandpa replied. Then he turned to walk out of the room while muttering to himself, "Must be the hormones. It has to be… What other explanation is there?"

Ben hunched over in the most dramatic way possible, finally able to let out his laughter.

"It's not funny," I scoffed.

"You totally sold it with the whole *coughing gig,"* Ben mocked.

"Just get out," I growled.

"But you're supposed to tell me where you went last night."

I sighed loudly, frustrated Ben always had to poke around in my business, but I knew I didn't have another choice. Grandpa was all for us being independent and being prepared for the future, but he would never condone reckless outings or bad decisions that might sacrifice our safety. Plus, Grandpa didn't know Phoenix. If word got out, he would scold me on how Phoenix was dangerous and bad company.

It was a strange feeling of being eighteen but treated like a child. As far back as I could remember, Grandpa consistently said, "My roof, my rules." I knew Grandpa's goal was to keep us safe, so I understood why he had boundaries, but since I had a taste of what the night had to offer, I didn't think I could resist going out again. I could picture Grandpa installing bars on my windows and a deadbolt on the outside of my bedroom door if he ever found out.

"Shut the door behind you," I told Ben.

He did and eagerly sat on my bed beside me.

"So, what'd you do?" he asked excitedly.

"I saw Phoenix again," I revealed flatly.

"I thought so," Ben replied. "Where'd you go? Chad's?"

"No. He took me to a castle."

"What? How far was that— wait… there's a castle around here?"

"I know, that's what I was thinking too. It wasn't all that far. Less than a twenty-minute drive."

Then Ben was really confused. "But why a castle?"

"It's his base," I explained, and I went on to tell Ben almost every detail about my night, from the lady with the weird purple rings around her eyes to everything Phoenix told me about the vampires.

"Holy shit!" Ben replied as if his eyes had been opened for the first time.

"I know, seriously…" I replied, understanding how Ben felt from the information overload.

"What are you going to do?" Ben asked.

"What do you mean?"

"I mean, you aren't going to hang out with him again, are you?"

I thought about how much I enjoyed myself last night. Phoenix showed me things I thought I would never see in my lifetime. He made me feel like there was hope for the world, and I admired that he was so open to sharing what he'd been through.

"Maybe," I shrugged. "I don't know."

"He sounds dangerous, Delilah," Ben scolded.

"You sound like Grandpa," I countered defensively.

"I'm just trying to give you some advice. Tell you what's best for you. Keep you safe."

"And how would you know what's best for me?" I asked, becoming heated. I was thoroughly offended that Ben thought he knew what was good for me, and I hated when Ben acted like he needed to dictate how I lived my life. Who was he to tell me what decisions I should and shouldn't make? "You aren't Dad! You— So… so, stop trying to act like him!"

Ben retracted from my outburst by holding his hands up in defense. "I'm not trying to act like—"

"Yes, you are!" I yelled. "Get out of my room!"

"I didn't mean to make you mad," Ben said as he stood. "I'll make sure I stay out of your business from now on. If you get into trouble, don't come crawling to me for help."

"I'm not going to get into trouble," I spat through my teeth. "And if I did, I wouldn't expect help from you!"

"Good!" Ben shouted, his words as hot as mine.

"Good!" I countered, making sure to get in the last word.

Ben stormed out, slamming the door behind him. Without another thought, I retrieved my notebook to transfer my anger toward Ben onto paper. Even after everything I told him, all he could think about was how Phoenix was a potential danger. All Ben focused on was the choice I made regarding who I kept as company. Ben never cared about companionship. His video games kept him distracted from typical human desires and needs.

It was sad that my brother wasn't able to see what I saw in Phoenix—someone caring and brave, someone willing to sacrifice his life to save others and end the war for good.

# Chapter Fourteen

## Sunflower Fields Forever

Joseline invited us over for brunch. Also, one of the bulbs needed to be replaced because Nick's dad accidentally broke it with a rake. Grandpa was nice enough to bring them a few spares. It was the least we could do since they offered to feed us a nice meal. I suppose my friendship with Nick might've had something to do with the invite to stay and eat, or maybe Nick and his parents were just those types of people—too caring and too generous. Whatever the reason, it was clear that it made Grandpa happy that we had become friends with the Bryers.

After we ate, Nick gave me a guided tour around the farm. It was larger than I had assumed. The fields seemed to go on for miles, and I understood better how much work went into tending to the animals and land. I enjoyed every aspect of the tour, but Nick saved the best part for last when he introduced me to baby Mable, the foal that was born only days ago. Mable's coat and mane were as white as milk. She stood close to her mother, soothed by her presence.

"She's beautiful," I told Nick.

"She sure is. Do you want to feed the mama?"

I looked at Nick excitedly. "Uh, yeah!"

"All right. Let me grab a bag of feed, and we can go into the corral."

As Nick poured the grain into the feeding bins, the older horses eagerly walked over.

We watched as Mable suckled from underneath her mother, and then she wandered over to me.

Nick began to refill the water trough when I asked if I could pet her.

"Of course. She's friendly too. Not scared at all," Nick explained with a grin. "At least not of you."

I stroked my hand across her mane. "This is amazing," I mentioned.

"Yeah, it's pretty awesome," Nick agreed.

"Now I see why leaving home never crosses your mind."

"The farm life isn't for everyone, but it is for me," Nick added and wiped his hands on his blue jeans. "Come on. I want to show you one other thing before you have to get going."

"Okay," I replied, even though I didn't want to leave Mable's side.

"You can always come back another day, and we can take a couple of the horses on the trails nearby."

I finally pulled myself away from Mable and turned my attention to Nick. "I'd really like that."

I followed Nick as he took us on a short walk to his neighbor's.

"There it is," he said, but I didn't know what he was referring to until he pointed it out.

It was the largest field of sunflowers I'd ever seen.

"Mr. Terry doesn't mind if we go through the field," Nick explained. "He's one of the friendliest folks I've ever met. Plus, we make sure he's well fed."

We spent a good amount of time walking through the field of sunset orange, and as we strolled through the sea of flowers that were as tall as us, I felt at peace. There wasn't a worry that concerned me. I wasn't thinking about when it would be dark like I usually did. I didn't think about what the future would hold or the wonders of Phoenix. I simply enjoyed the time I had with Nick and our casual talks.

Before heading back to the farm, Nick pulled out a pocketknife and cut the stem of a sunflower. "For you," he said, handing me the flower.

"Thank you," I replied with a smile.

"In a couple of weeks, the seeds will form in Mr. Terry's field, and I can bring you some."

As we walked back, I began to feel guilty about my friendship with Nick. Maybe it was because I knew Grandpa wanted me to reap the rewards of having Nick in my life. Maybe it was because I felt like he had more to offer than I did. I couldn't quite put my finger on the reason, but I knew that being around Nick made me happy.

"Nick," I said softly as we left his neighbor's.

"Yeah?"

"I just want to tell you that I value our friendship, and not because of all the food on your farm. I enjoy talking and spending time with you. Before we came to your house a couple of months ago, I didn't know what I was missing out on. Being homeschooled and all, I didn't have an opportunity to create friendships. I'm truly thankful for your company."

"You didn't have to tell me that," Nick chuckled to himself. I wasn't certain, but I thought I saw him blush. "I know you're not the kind of person to take advantage of someone."

"How do you know?"

"I just know…" Nick said confidently as his pace slowed, and eventually, he came to a full stop.

The farm was just a few yards away. "What's wrong?" I wondered.

"Nothing's wrong," Nick said and placed his hands in his pockets. His gaze was tilted downward, and the brim of his cowboy hat covered almost his entire face. He began to rock back and forth, digging the heels of his boots into the soft earth. "I just— I just wanted to…"

I bent down to look under Nick's hat and make eye contact. "What's wrong?" I asked again, letting out an awkward chuckle. "Why are you acting so weird?"

Then suddenly, Nick straightened up, finally meeting my gaze, and began to say, "Delilah, you make it seem like you don't have much to offer, but you do. The way you talk about helping people and keeping them safe setting up perimeters shows that you genuinely care about others. The losses you had to overcome in your life prove that you are resilient. You're smart and adventurous and—"

"Wait," I interrupted. "Are you still talking about me?" I joked.

"And you're funny."

"Depends on who you ask," I countered.

"Modest, too."

"Maybe you bring out the best in me," I pointed out.

Nick continued, "And while I'm also grateful for the friendship we've formed, I can't help but feel like it's turning into something more."

"Oh…" I trailed off, finally understanding where the conversation was going. It was all so unexpected.

"I don't want to ruin what we have," Nick added, "but I also don't want to ignore my feelings for you. If our friendship can bloom into something more, why not find out and take the risk?"

I nodded, not sure how to respond. I liked Nick. I loved being with him. He was a good-looking guy, very handsome. He was kind, generous, and a hard worker. All of those were a given, but more importantly, he wasn't the slightest bit dangerous. He was safe…

"Uh," Nick stammered and removed his hat to scratch his head, breaking the silence. "So, what do you think?"

"I've never been on a date before," I answered.

Nick laughed for a good minute. "That's all right. All you have to be willing to do is let me pick you up and take you somewhere."

"Okay, I think… I can do that," I replied, wide-eyed in shock.

"All right. Sounds good," Nick smirked. "Better get you back. I'm sure your grandpa is probably ready to leave."

"Uh-huh," I managed to say but didn't move.

Nick slowly swung his hand, directing me which way to go.

"Oh, yeah, right," I shook off my awkwardness and began walking toward Nick's house again.

As we drove back to our place, Grandpa stared at the sunflower I had set between us on top of the center console. He couldn't help but stick his nose in the honey pot. "So, you and Nick?"

I pushed my foot down on the gas, wanting to get home sooner. The sooner we got home, the sooner the questions would stop since I could hide in my room until dinner.

"I saw the goodbye exchange," Grandpa pointed out, referring to the long hug Nick gave me and the weird reaction when I wrapped my arms around him five seconds longer than I should've.

I shrugged, not wanting to answer.

"At least he's not bringing you to castles in the middle of nowhere," Ben murmured from the back seat.

I glared at Ben from the rearview mirror. I would've normally said something nasty in return, but I was ignoring him for trying to tell me what to do. I knew holding grudges was bad for the soul, but I couldn't help it. Even knowing it was wrong to do so, I couldn't let it go while the anger still lingered.

"What did you say?" Grandpa asked Ben.

My heart started to beat hard, and I gritted my teeth as I kept my eyes on Ben, praying he wouldn't open his big mouth.

"Nothing, Gramps," Ben responded.

"So, Joseline and Kirk made it seem like you were really growing on Nick," Grandpa continued.

I knew there was no way of escaping the inevitable. "He asked me on a date, okay! That's it. No big deal."

"I had a feeling there was something more," Grandpa smiled.

"It's just one date," I explained. "It might not amount to anything."

"Maybe now is the time," Grandpa mentioned.

"What are you talking about?" I asked, confused.

"You always wanted to wear your mother's dresses," Grandpa added. "Ever since you were a little girl. I think they'll fit you now."

"I— I don't know. I don't think I should," I said, thinking about how the dresses belonged to my mom. They would always be hers. It felt wrong to wear her clothes. When I was younger, her belongings didn't have the same meaning.

"Why not?" Grandpa wondered. "Better they get worn than letting moths feast on them until they become rags."

"You should, Delilah," Ben agreed.

I looked in the mirror at Ben again. I didn't continue to glare at him but wondered if he was secretly rooting for Nick, hoping Phoenix would disappear from my life.

Yeah, that was probably what Ben was hoping for…

# Chapter Fifteen

## How to Date

It had to have been at least a decade since I stepped foot into my mom and dad's room. I couldn't quite remember how it looked since it had been so long. It was *theirs*, and every time I thought about taking a peek inside, I felt like I was intruding. I would've continued to avoid my parents' room, treating it as a forbidden space for the rest of my life, but Grandpa was right, I shouldn't let my mom's belongings wither away. She'd want me to have them. She'd want me to think of her and remember her the way she was.

I hesitantly turned the knob on the bedroom door and breathed deeply before entering as my heart thudded violently. The bed was still made and waiting to be slept in. The curtains seemed darker from the layers of dust that coated them, and the vanity beside the nightstand had gone untouched.

I slowly walked toward the vanity mirror and stared at my reflection. It was the same mirror my mom looked at herself in for all the years before I was born, *all the years before she lost her life.* My eyes became watery as I thought about the mother I never knew. Then I noticed a bottle of perfume sitting on top of the vanity, and without thinking, I spritzed it into the air. I closed my eyes and inhaled, picturing what it would be like to hug my mom and take in her scent. She would've smelled of honey, jasmine blossoms, and hints of musk that I imagined one would find in the deepest woods of Idaho. I couldn't contain the tears, and they angrily trickled down my cheeks.

As my chest became heavier with heartache, I sat on the bench in front of the vanity. I slid open the drawers that held her makeup. I didn't know what she did with all the sticks and brushes, but when I found the lipstick, it reminded me of the pictures of her. I pulled the top off and twisted the tube, revealing a bright shade of blush pink, which was painted on my mom's lips in every photo. She was so beautiful and always smiling. I wiped away the moisture on my face. I wasn't sure how to apply the lipstick, but I did my best as I slid the color along my lips. Then I took a long, hard look at myself in the mirror again and tried to smile. I tried to smile like my mom did in all the pictures scattered around the walls of the house. It was hard though… to smile while missing her.

And I believe I felt a tinge of anger wash over me, thinking about how a mother was supposed to teach her daughter certain things. I was supposed to be able to ask her questions such as, "Is it normal to want to be desirable to men?" And then she was supposed to give me advice and say, "It doesn't matter what you look like on the outside. It only matters what's inside of you, and it's okay to want to drop the tomboy act you were forced into. It's all right to be a lady as long as you don't forget what's important."

I held back more tears as I abandoned the vanity and opened the closet that held my mom's beautiful dresses, some I never knew she had. The long ivory dress with red-orange flowers and deep green leaves caught my eye. It seemed like something she would wear during autumn. I pulled the dress off the hanger and held it to my chest with my chin pinched tightly against it.

"I miss you," I whispered, realizing I missed her just as much as I did my dad.

It didn't matter if I didn't know my mom because I wanted to. I desperately wanted to know her, to talk to her, to hug her tightly. Maybe I had been lying to myself all along that it didn't hurt as bad to lose her. I deceived myself into believing it was easier not to know her, and suddenly, I felt deprived, like something was ripped from my arms that was meant for me and only me…

Grandpa was sitting in his recliner in the living room, listening to the radio, and Ben was also doing what he usually did—playing on his Game Boy. But as soon as I descended the stairs, Ben dropped his video game onto his lap as if it involuntarily fell from his hands, and his jaw drooped while Grandpa stood from his chair in awe.

"You look lovely, Delilah," Grandpa said while folding his hands across his belly. "Doesn't she look nice, Ben?" Grandpa asked, and I hoped my eyes were less red than they were a minute ago from crying.

Ben smirked and decided to be the typical Ben we both knew he was. He shrugged, "Eh, now you can tell she's a girl."

"Why do you have to be so rude?" I asked.

"All right, you two," Grandpa said. "Let's not get into it."

Luckily, Nick was on time, and I didn't have to deal with Ben any longer.

"Oh, wow," Nick said, handing me a bouquet of wildflowers he must've picked near his farm.

"Thank you," I replied.

"You look… different," Nick continued.

I could feel my cheeks becoming warm. "Really?" I asked. "A good different or bad different?"

"Definitely a good different," Nick nodded.

"All right. I'm out," Ben said, removing himself from the couch. "It's getting too lovey-dovey in here." But before he left the room, Ben patted Nick on his shoulder. "Have a good time, kids."

Nick looked at me, confused. "*Kids*?"

"Just ignore him," I told Nick.

"Oh, okay," he replied with an awkward chuckle as we headed out the door.

"Bye, Grandpa," I waved while glancing back to see that he seemed pleased.

Nick opened the truck's passenger door to let me inside. Then he quickly ran around the front to the driver's side and hopped in.

"You ready?" he asked as he cranked the ignition.

I met his smile. "Yeah, I've been waiting all morning. Where are we going?"

"You'll see," he said, tilting his hat toward me. "It's one of my favorite places to spend my days off. And as you know, days off are rare, so I haven't been able to go in a while."

The sun shined down on us as we drove, and it was the perfect autumn day. I couldn't help the urge to roll down the window and stick my hand out to feel the breeze. Along the road, the leaves on the trees had changed, and many were falling from their branches. I unbuckled myself so I could lean farther out the window with my head and arms outside. I wanted to feel the wind against my face.

"What are you doing?" Nick asked with worry tingeing his voice.

"It's fine!" I yelled as the breeze caught my hair and swirled it wildly.

"You're nuts!" Nick chuckled nervously.

"It's like I'm a bird flying down the back road. I feel free, and it's amazing!" I shouted with a grin.

Nick gently tugged at the side of my dress, pulling me back inside the truck. "I don't think it would be a good idea to let you fall out of my truck on our first date. Or if we get in an accident and you're not buckled up, it could be dangerous. There might not be a second date if I bring you home all black and blue."

"I was fine," I said, grinning from the adrenaline, and brushed my hair out of my face. "Plus, I'm sure you're a safe driver."

"You're so sure?"

"Yeah, I can just tell," I said half-jokingly.

"Please, buckle up," Nick told me more firmly, and I did as he asked since I knew he didn't want anything to happen to me. "I know you want to be free and fly away like a bird, but gosh damn, don't scare me, okay?"

"Sorry, it won't happen again," I smirked.

Nick took me to a meadow somewhere between his farm and my house. He laid down a blanket and unpacked a lunch for us. All around us were wildflowers that stood as tall as we sat. Honeysuckles and lilies danced around us, swaying ever so slightly.

"Thank you for coming here with me, Delilah," Nick said, leaning his shoulder toward me.

I nodded. "How could I say no?" I said as the sleeve on my dress slid down my arm.

Nick and I glanced down simultaneously, but before I could adjust my sleeve, he quickly raised his hand to my arm. He was such a gentleman.

I looked up at him and smiled as he slowly placed the sleeve back onto my shoulder. The touch of his fingertips sent chills along my arm.

"Where did you find such a beautiful dress?" Nick wondered.

"It-it was my mom's," I explained, a bit hesitantly.

"Sorry, I didn't know. I— I didn't mean to bring that up…"

"It's fine," I exhaled.

"I can tell you really miss her."

"Yeah, I do," I admitted. "A lot. More than I thought I did."

Instead of allowing me to put a damper on our date, Nick decided to throw out some positivity which I appreciated. "She'd be proud to have a daughter like you. Such a hard worker, and more importantly, someone who helps others the way you do."

"Thank you, that's nice of you to say," I replied, doing my best to produce a halfhearted smile.

"Don't worry, you'll see her one day," Nick assured me.

"I know, but it seems like forever…"

As sweet of a guy as Nick was, he couldn't permanently wash away my hurt.

"Why is that?" he wondered.

I shrugged. "I don't know. I guess because I think if we could live how we used to before everything happened, it'd give us more opportunity to enjoy life how God intended. Not to sound ungrateful, but sometimes I feel like this life drags."

"So, you're saying you want more out of life?"

"I know I shouldn't. I know I should be thankful for what I have— I mean, I am… most of the time, but some days are harder than others."

"I understand," Nick replied and slid his hand over to mine, attempting to comfort me. "I had a hard time when my grandma passed away."

I sat up a bit straighter. "Your grandma? Did the vampires get to her? If I remember correctly, I thought your mom said your family hasn't had many encounters with bloodsuckers."

"No, it wasn't vampires. It was old age. She lived a long, healthy life until the age of ninety-three."

"That is a long life," I added.

"Yeah, but it still wasn't long enough. I wanted her to stick around ninety more years," Nick chuckled, trying to lighten the mood.

I nodded. "So, did she pass recently?"

"Three Christmases ago," Nick replied as if time had already done some healing.

"Were you close?"

"Sure were. We used to make Christmas cookies together every year. She taught me how to bake."

"Hold on," I interrupted. "*You* know how to bake?"

Nick shrugged as if it wasn't a big deal. "Yeah, what about it?"

"Nothing, I just didn't picture you as the 'baking' type."

"What's that supposed to mean?"

"I mean… you work the farm. It's hard labor. Baking is kind of the opposite. It's difficult to imagine you wearing an apron and pulling goodies out of the oven."

Nick smirked proudly. "I got a soft side to me, too."

"Who would've known?" I laughed. "So, tell me more about her."

Nick continued, "I always looked forward to spending the holidays with her. She was my best friend. I could confide in her about anything, and she was funny as hell. You would've loved her. She would've been able to kick your worries away with just a couple of knee slappers."

"She sounded like a wonderful person. I'm sorry for your loss."

Nick hid his eyes under the brim of his hat for a few seconds before responding, "I just do my best to look in the right places, you know, to fill the void. If you constantly keep your eyes on the good things in your life, it can help ease the past."

"Maybe," I agreed, although I wasn't so certain.

But I did know that it felt good to hold Nick's hand. It felt right looking into his eyes as we talked about anything and everything or nothing at all. It was nice being around someone like Nick—every ounce of him was pure and loving in the most positive of ways. He was so innocent and a beautiful human, one who brought joy to a world that desperately needed it.

But that day in the meadow, I realized happiness came easier for Nick than it did for me. Maybe I needed to view life differently, somewhat like Nick did. Maybe he was right about moving forward and hoping for a brighter future. Maybe I could do that with him by my side.

# Chapter Sixteen

## You Can't Resist

Just as Ben had hoped, Nick began replacing my thoughts of Phoenix. For a while, keeping Phoenix out of my head didn't seem possible, but it must've helped that many of my questions were answered that night on the rooftop of the castle. What might've helped even more was that I could see a future with Nick. It was easy to envision myself with him. He was such an easy person to fall for.

Although there was a detail about Nick's and my relationship that always made me a bit uneasy, *one minuscule* detail that shouldn't have been an issue. Unlike me, he was content with where he was, never questioning if the grass was greener elsewhere. I could never stop wondering what more the world had to offer. That was something Nick never thought about, so I didn't have much faith that Nick would be able to tame the curiosity inside of me. The question of wanting to know what else was out there would forever burn red-hot, and there was no way of calming the fire unless I left Hope.

I cared deeply for Nick. He meant a lot to me. I knew he was more than a friend, and that's how I wanted it to stay, but just as soon as I was beginning to see Nick in a different light, another night rolled around when Phoenix came knocking.

I couldn't resist another ride on the bike and the view of the night sky. I couldn't say no to following Phoenix whenever he called. Even more insane, I came accustomed to never asking where he was taking me. I simply went, knowing he would take me on another adventure I wouldn't be able to experience without him.

"Just a little farther," Phoenix urged as we walked along the forest.

Ahead, I could see trees bent in odd ways, creating a tunnel.

"What's over there?" I asked.

"A tunnel made of branches," Phoenix answered.

"I've never seen anything like it before," I said in awe, and as we began making our way through the archway, I admired the thin beams of moonlight that snuck through the cracks of the branches to light the path. "Is this manmade?"

"Nope, Mother Nature gets all the credit for this one."

"But how? Did they bend toward the moonlight like plants do during the day to get more sunlight?"

"Who knows? It's Nature's wonders."

"It's so strange, but not as strange as you knowing more interesting places in Idaho than me."

Phoenix shrugged. "It's my job. I need to know what's—"

"Oh, no," I breathed in a panic as I frantically felt my bare chest.

"What's wrong?" Phoenix asked while I bent down on my knees to feel around on the ground.

"I-I… my necklace. It must've fallen off," I explained, worried it was gone forever. There was nothing but earth and dead leaves on the forest floor.

"You mean the silver one with the cross you always wear?" Phoenix wondered.

"Yes!" I said, practically yelling.

"I'm sure it's around here somewhere," he said calmly, bending down beside me. "It'll be fine," he chuckled as if I was overreacting.

"This isn't really a laughing matter," I reminded him.

"It's just a necklace. I can always buy you another one when I go into town."

"No, you can't!" I continued heatedly, my jeans quickly becoming filthy from crawling on the ground.

"Uh… I can't?" Phoenix asked, confused. "Why not?"

I exhaled sharply and paused from my frantic search with watery eyes to stare down Phoenix. "Be-because… it belonged to my mom, okay?"

"I see…" Phoenix replied, finally understanding the importance of the necklace.

We spent a long while in silence, searching for something that seemed lost for eternity. More than once, I glanced over at Phoenix, who made me believe he would stay there all night until he found it. Not once did he suggest coming back when there was more light, not once did he suggest giving up on the search, and I appreciated that more than he knew. We didn't speak too much about the pains of our past, but we were both aware of each other's wounds that would never fully heal. We were the same, and I didn't have to go into detail for Phoenix to know what that necklace meant to me.

After what seemed like an hour, Phoenix stood with something in his hand. "I found it!" he shouted excitedly.

I ran over to Phoenix, who had found my necklace. "Thank you," I sighed in relief. "Thank you…"

Without another word, he draped the necklace over my chest and clasped it behind my neck. Phoenix smirked, pleased I was okay.

"Come on, let's go," he urged, and I followed.

Soon, I could hear water in the distance.

"Is there a stream nearby?" I wondered.

"The Pack River isn't too far."

I felt embarrassed like I should've known that. "Oh," I laughed, shaking off my nerves. "I guess I haven't explored much. Didn't know there was access through these woods."

"It's hard with everything going on. I'm sure your grandpa would worry if you explored on your own, and I bet you stay busy helping with the lights."

"You know about the lights?" I asked, wondering how Phoenix knew what my family did. "I don't think I mentioned…"

"Uh, Frankie told me you had some fancy UV light your brother shined on him. Looked homemade," Phoenix explained. "Plus, I've seen the perimeter around your house, and at the gas station, so I asked Chad about them."

I must've been paranoid from Ben's warnings. Even though I'd like to think I didn't care what Ben had to say, I still took my brother's opinion to heart.

"Sorry, I didn't mean to sound like a creep," Phoenix laughed and then paused underneath the branches just before the tunnel ended, his blue eyes piercing mine. "I'll admit that I still have secrets, things you don't know, but you can trust me. I will never hurt you and will always protect you. You know that, right?"

I couldn't help but believe every word he said. Maybe I was entranced by how beautiful he was, or was it his dangerous spirit that was like a siren calling? I couldn't read Phoenix like a book, so could it have been that I enjoyed a mystery?

"Do you trust me?" he asked almost in a whisper.

"Mhmm," I murmured. "I trust you."

He took me to the edge of the river where there was a military boat tied down to the side of the forest floor.

"We use the river to scout areas and for an escape plan."

"Why are you telling me all this?" I wondered.

"I trust you," Phoenix said and guided me into the boat. "Have you ever been on the river before?"

"No," I answered as a coyote howled nearby, and Phoenix untied the boat from the shore.

"Your home is something else," Phoenix added.

"Where are you from?" I asked.

"Grew up in the desert," Phoenix explained. "Arizona. Nothing but crackled earth, dust storms, and cacti."

"I've heard there are also breathtaking sunsets and rolling mountains everywhere," I added.

Phoenix smirked and started the boat's motor, "Yeah, those too."

"Doesn't sound so bad," I mentioned as Phoenix stepped into the boat.

"Can't compare to seeing the rest of the world, though," he replied.

"I'm sure."

"So, Delilah, is it my turn?"

"What do you mean?" I wondered, confused.

"To ask you questions. You got five. Do I get five, too?" Phoenix asked, holding his hand out to help me into the boat.

"Oh, uh. I-I guess it's only fair," I replied hesitantly as I placed my hand in his. "What do you want to know?"

It would've been a stress-free night with the wild animals hidden along the tree line and the restlessness of the river crashing onto the rocks. It seemed like a perfect night to admire the stars and speak of how full the moon was, but instead, Phoenix wanted to know more about me, and I wasn't so sure how much of myself I wanted to reveal.

"For starters," Phoenix began, "tell me more about the family business."

Phoenix sat at the back end of the boat, steering as I sat at the front. "Um, there's not much to tell," I admitted.

"Sure there is," he urged. "Tell me how things started, where the business has taken your family."

"Okay, well," I said slowly. "My grandpa was in the military for a little while and learned some engineering skills. Eventually, when vampires started emerging, and the military fell, he took what he learned to keep fighting back. He's taught my brother and me some stuff. Ben is handier building the lights and knowing what pieces we need and whatnot. I'm pretty good helping set up the perimeters, or rather, Ben prefers not to do too much heavy lifting," I joked.

Phoenix chuckled, "Right, I can see that."

"Yeah, the business is what helped us get by. It's what's keeping us alive."

"It's tough times," Phoenix mentioned.

"I know. We're doing ok, though."

"Soon, humans won't just have to *get by*. Hopefully, we can change things."

I nodded, agreeing, but Phoenix always seemed so optimistic when he spoke of changing the times and turning back tides. Although I wasn't sure the New Military would be enough to take back the night.

"What do you want most out of life?" was his next question.

It was a question I had an answer to, but one I hadn't revealed or admitted to anyone. "That— that's kind of a deep question," I said, stalling to answer.

"I'm good at asking intimate questions," Phoenix grinned.

"Uh, all right," I stammered. "I guess I want to be… *free*."

"Interesting. How so?" Phoenix asked, confused by my unclear answer.

"Free to leave the house when I want to, even when the sun goes down. Free to stargaze without worrying about dying. Free to take a night drive."

"I like that answer."

"Of course you do. Isn't that what your 'cause' is all about?"

"Mhmm," Phoenix hummed as he gazed over the water. "Third question. What do you enjoy most out of life?"

"That one's easy. Writing poetry. Spending what time I can with my grandpa." I left Nick out of the conversation.

"I could've guessed that," Phoenix said, his eyes narrowing like he already knew everything about me.

"I'm that easy to read, huh?" I laughed.

"Actually, the opposite," he answered, which didn't make sense to me.

"Oh, um, okay," I said, becoming self-conscious by the way he was staring at me.

His grin tilted to the side, and he didn't say a word for the next few minutes as we glided down the river. The moonlight shined generously on his face, and I could see he wasn't interested in the night scenery. The way Phoenix looked at me made me feel like I was the only thing that mattered, like he wouldn't have noticed if the boat hit a rock and we began to sink to the bottom of the river.

"So, what else?" I asked, wondering if he planned to continue questioning me or stare me down for the rest of the boat ride.

"Are you seeing anyone?" he asked bluntly, catching me more off guard than when he suggested that he be the interviewer this time.

I scoffed, "Wh-what?"

"Is there someone special in your life?" he clarified.

"That's kind of private," I snapped under my breath.

"I'll take that as a yes," Phoenix replied.

I angrily folded my arms across my chest and scrunched my lips. I couldn't believe I agreed to this extent of an interrogation. I didn't know my personal life was up for questioning.

"That's fine. I understand. I mean, you are special," he said. "I wouldn't expect less."

"Huh?" I asked, confused.

"Do you like me, Delilah?" Phoenix asked nonchalantly, his last question making my heart race.

"I think I'm done with the questions tonight," I gritted.

"It's a simple question," Phoenix smirked. "Yes or no?"

I opted to ignore him, focusing on the ripples the boat was creating on the river.

But then Phoenix idled the motor and leaned across, his body stretching along the entire boat as he kissed my cheek.

I instantly felt guilty as my thoughts went to the time I spent with Nick in the meadow just days ago.

"Uh," I stammered, my eyes wide as an owl. I sat a bit straighter, surprised by what Phoenix had done. "I— is this a date?" I asked, demanding clarification.

"Do *you* want this to be a date?" Phoenix asked.

"No," I said flatly, feeling like I betrayed Nick one way or another.

"Then, no, it's not," Phoenix smirked.

"I should get back home," I suggested.

"Of course," Phoenix said smugly and turned the boat around.

But the entire ride home, I couldn't stop replaying the conversation I had with Phoenix in my head. No one had ever told me I was special. No one made me feel the way he did.

# Chapter Seventeen

## Anything but Ordinary

"*Happy birthday to you, happy birthday to you…*" Ben and I sang as we entered the living room.

When I spotted Grandpa on his recliner, I noticed he was on the verge of falling asleep, and his eyes were beginning to droop. But once Ben rushed over to Grandpa and placed the cone-shaped birthday hat onto his head, Grandpa's eyes popped open wide, and he sat up with a smile.

I held the poorly frosted cake that had three lit candles as I walked slowly across the living room toward Grandpa.

"Where are the rest of the candles? Looks like I need eighty-eight more," Grandpa joked.

"We didn't want to burn down the house," Ben added.

"Ben!" I yelled, frustrated by his bluntness.

Once I was close enough, Grandpa leaned forward to blow out the flames, and he chuckled, unfazed by Ben's comment. He had a good sense of humor.

"Not like they'd all fit on the cake anyway," Grandpa chuckled. "So, what flavor is it?"

"Your favorite," I began.

"Carrot," Ben chimed.

"Nick gave us the carrots," I mentioned.

"Oh," Grandpa sighed contently. "You will have to tell him thank you when you see him next time."

"I sure will," I replied, and then unexpectedly, a big yawn escaped from within me. "Gosh, excuse me! I don't know where that came from."

"Why so tired?" Ben asked, squinting hard at me.

I glared at him without words and turned to Grandpa, "Should I go ahead and cut you a slice of cake?"

"Sounds delightful," he said, settling back into his chair again as I returned to the kitchen.

I grabbed the plates from the cabinet and began to cut the cake while listening to the conversation going on between Grandpa and Ben. "I couldn't have asked for better grandchildren. You two are truly special and such a blessing," Grandpa said.

*Special.* Grandpa mentioning I was special made me think of Phoenix and made me realize that guilt would continue growing inside of me, even though I prayed it died the same night Phoenix kissed my cheek. It thrived within me because I allowed it to, and if I was being honest with myself, I would never fight it. The enormous guilt I was housing would never change my actions. No matter how well I suppressed the guilt, I knew it would linger forever…

As more months passed and winter quickly approached, I continued to spend days with Nick and nights with Phoenix. It was as if I was living two different lives with two people who were just as different from one another as the moon was from the sun.

One had his roots planted deep into the Idaho soil and loved his family more than himself. He was a simple guy who found happiness working the land and reaping the benefits. He loved talking about the animals he tended to and the fields that surrounded him. Nick was someone who wanted to settle down, someone who didn't require much to live a fulfilled life. He was grateful for what God gave him, never asking for more.

The other was a wanderer, someone who didn't mind a change of scenery. He had a family but not like one would expect. He often spoke of the dangers he'd been in, what the world could be, and how he would be a part of the change. Phoenix was wild and unpredictable. Some would say he was dangerous. I couldn't deny that he was intriguing in all the wrong ways because he made everything feel so right.

The issue was, I wanted both in my life. And even though I knew it was wrong to keep each hidden from one another, I couldn't bring myself to tell either of them there was someone else. I felt selfish but fulfilled. I was wrong but denied what I was doing. I knew I should've been punished for keeping such secrets, but I didn't want to let Nick or Phoenix go.

Even worse, I couldn't say that either of them was just a friend. Friends didn't look at each other the way Phoenix did when he looked at me, and friends didn't want to hold hands like Nick always did.

# Chapter Eighteen

## Fall for You

"Knock, knock," Phoenix whispered through my window which was already open and waiting for him.

I was dressed and ready to go for a bike ride. I was all set to wander off into a field somewhere and stare at the night sky with Phoenix, but when I realized I might've been underdressed, I paused from climbing out the window.

Phoenix stroked his hair that was stiffly held in place. Then he adjusted the bowtie that accompanied his black tuxedo, and I noticed that one of his hands was tucked behind his back.

"I know, weird without the leather jacket, right?" he chuckled uncomfortably.

"No, you clean up nicely," I told him. "But what's the occasion?"

Phoenix coughed into a loose fist before revealing a single red rose that he was keeping hidden behind his back. "Delilah," he whispered while smirking. "Will you go to the Holiday Ball with me?"

"Uh, thank you…" I replied, caught off guard. I slowly reached through the window and took the rose from Phoenix's hand. I pushed the petals against my nose, inhaling deeply. "It's beautiful. Smells amazing."

Roses were meant for the wealthy. I wasn't certain I'd ever held a rose in my hand before, let alone knew what they smelled like until that night. It wasn't like roses grew abundantly where I lived, not like wildflowers.

"So, you will be my date tonight?" Phoenix said in a joking manner as if he knew I would never say no to him.

"What's a Holiday Ball?" I wondered.

Surprisingly, Phoenix took a moment to chuckle to himself as if he was nervous. It seemed odd because he was never anything but confident. "It's like a party," he explained.

I had never been to a party, so I was eager to say yes, but then I remembered what I was wearing, and I was overcome by disappointment. "I-I don't have anything to wear," I stammered.

Phoenix pointed his finger in the air like he had an idea, but instead of speaking, he bent down to pick up something beside his feet. When he stood, he handed me a white box with a black bow.

"Try this on," he suggested, passing me the box through the window.

I opened the box, wondering what he could have brought me.

I held up the dress that was smooth as silk and as dark as night. I admired the long sleeves that were made of lace. I never saw anything so extravagant, not even in my mom's closet, not even through a window in a single shop.

"Do you like it?" Phoenix asked. "I don't think I've ever seen you in a dress."

"I love it. It— it's…" I stumbled over my words, speechless and on top of the world. Never in a million years would I have imagined I would be able to wear something girls only dreamed about. "It's perfect."

I closed my curtains to slip into something more appropriate for the Holiday Ball. Once I had the dress on, I couldn't believe how soft it felt and how elegantly it hugged my body. It was as if I was wearing a foreign object, something made for a different time, and then I realized something important or possibly embarrassing…

"Is everything ok in there?" Phoenix wondered since I was taking a while. "Did I get the wrong size?"

"It fits," I replied.

"Okay, so then…" Phoenix pressed.

"I, um, I only have sneakers," I admitted.

"Oh, well, won't the dress cover them?" he suggested.

I slid on my only pair of shoes and was thankful Phoenix was right. "Yeah, they do," I sighed in relief.

"Then we're good to go. Come on."

With that, I clumsily climbed out the window as if it wasn't hard enough to do so in jeans and a jacket.

Once I made it out, Phoenix stood frozen, staring at me like he often did. It was as if there was nothing else that mattered to him besides me, like nothing could pull his gaze away.

"What?" I asked, becoming self-conscious. "I look weird, don't I?"

Phoenix shook his head. "Since the day I saw you, you've always been the most beautiful girl I've ever seen, but tonight, there's no question, you have to be the most gorgeous person that has ever walked this Earth."

Warmth brushed over my cheeks, and then I wondered how I was supposed to ride on the back of Phoenix's bike with a dress. "Do you have any tips for riding a bike with what I'm wearing?"

"Don't worry. I brought one of the work trucks," he reassured me.

"Oh, phew!" I sighed with relief. "I was worried the dress would catch the wind like a parachute, and I would go flying off."

"I would never let that happen. I wouldn't dare risk losing you," Phoenix said smoothly.

"Right…" I chuckled uncomfortably as my cheeks heated up again.

*****

When we arrived at the castle, I heard loud music coming from inside.

"Don't worry, some of the officers are protecting the perimeter," Phoenix explained as he helped me out of the truck.

"How come the training officers are always the ones working?" I asked.

"We get at least one night off a week," Phoenix answered.

"Oh," I replied, "Like your Friday nights?"

"Yeah."

"I guess I could've figured that out on my own."

"I'm sure you could've," Phoenix grinned and held out his elbow. "You are just as smart as you are stunning."

I placed my hand on Phoenix's arm, and he escorted me in. Again, there was someone at the entrance dressed in tactical gear. As we passed the guard, I tried to get a better view of his eyes. I could see the violet ring around both of his irises, and it was confirmed… the training officers were *different.*

I wanted to know more about them, but my attention was averted as soon as Phoenix opened the door that led to the Ball. I was in awe. Long satin cloths of dark gray were draped from the ceiling, trailing along the stone walls. Everyone was dressed in formal wear, and I was consumed by a sea of black and white. The table that held the food seemed endless, stretching from one end to the other end of the room. When I looked up, there was a disco ball spinning freely, casting spots of silver light all around. Frankie was on a makeshift platform, playing music between two large speakers. And as Phoenix pulled me deeper into the crowded room, I noticed the floor I was walking on felt strange. I peered down at my feet and saw thousands of red rose petals covering the stone floor.

"We go all out during holidays," Phoenix mentioned.

"I see that," I replied, wondering how they accumulated so many roses.

"Would you like to dance?" Phoenix asked, and by then, I realized we were in the center of the room. Everyone around us was dancing to a fast-paced song.

"Oh, I, um," I stammered uncomfortably. "I didn't know this was going to require dancing. I sort of have two left feet."

I didn't know how to dance, and I never went to school functions seeing as I was homeschooled. To be honest, I was kind of thankful for the lack of social events I missed out on. I never had to put myself in an awkward situation in that sense.

"Sorry, I should've told you," Phoenix apologized, his gaze fixated on me.

Then the song ended, and everyone started clapping. Phoenix stared at me and clapped along with them. I felt like I should've been doing the same, so that's what I did.

Next, a slow song began to play, and Phoenix held out his hand, asking me to dance again. I felt like I didn't have a choice, so I placed one of my hands in his and the other on his shoulder. I remembered seeing my mom and dad dance on a video from their wedding, but I knew it was much easier to watch someone dance and envision going through the steps rather than doing it.

I moved my feet back and forth, shifting my weight, and began to feel even more self-conscious. My eyes began to wander to other couples dancing beside us, curious if they were laughing at me.

"You're doing great, Delilah," Phoenix encouraged. "Best dancer in the room."

I let out a sarcastic laugh, but Phoenix's humor brought me back to him, and I looked up to see his gaze locked on me. His eyes were piercing. His side smirk—always mysterious, and his protective embrace—always comforting.

"I-I don't know what I'm doing," I continued.

"Just keep looking at me. It's only me and you in here," he told me.

As long as I kept my eyes on him, maybe I could pretend no one was watching me make a fool of myself.

"What are you thinking about?" Phoenix asked as we continued to sway to the music.

I smiled, not wanting to reveal my thoughts, which I preferred to keep private.

"Come on, tell me," he urged.

Phoenix had a way of persuading people, making them bend to his every wish.

"I was thinking that you're kind of— I don't know… angelic."

Phoenix chuckled loudly. "Angelic? I always thought I was tougher than *angelic*."

"I mean, you're beautiful," I tried explaining.

"Oh," Phoenix replied, his laughter dying a bit. "Well, thank you."

"You're welcome," I said awkwardly and proceeded to ask the question that had been stuck in the back of my mind. "How come the training officers' eyes are different?"

I could feel Phoenix's chest fill with a deep breath. He held it inside and slowly released it, telling me he either didn't want to talk about it or it wasn't a simple answer.

"They're, uh… different," he said.

"And how are they different?" I pressed.

Phoenix pursed his lips tightly together.

"You thought I wouldn't notice?" I wondered.

"I knew the question would arise eventually."

"Okay, so tell me," I demanded. "You've told me everything else. What's the big deal?"

"All right. Fine," he nodded. "They're stronger and faster than a typical human by a lot. Their skin is thicker too, harder for vampire fangs to pierce through," Phoenix explained quickly as if he wanted the conversation to move on.

"How?"

"From drugs," he answered.

"What kind of drug can do that?" I questioned, shocked.

"One that the government made, derived from vampire DNA."

"What?" I gasped in disbelief.

"It's not known to the public because it could cause—"

"Mass chaos!" I finished Phoenix's sentence. I could feel both our bodies become a bit more tense as we tried our best to continue dancing. "Seems like you guys keep a lot from everyone."

"Not my choice," he reminded me.

"I know," I said more calmly, realizing I might've been ruining our night. "But I don't understand. Why would the government do such a thing and tamper with vampire DNA? Isn't that dangerous?"

"Yeah, but that's what has given us a fighting chance," Phoenix countered.

"Then why don't they give it to more people?"

"You have to earn it. Put in the time and prove you're worthy. Plus, not everyone wants it."

"Why not? If it enhances a human's abilities then…"

"The drug does amazing things, but it also takes away some of the humanity a person has."

"You become more like a vampire?"

"They describe it like always having to contain rage within oneself, always angry, always wanting to destroy anything and everything."

"That sounds terrible. So, I bet you don't want anything to do with the drug if it has those side effects?" I assumed.

"I think in the next year or so, I'll be considered for the injection," Phoenix said with a stern expression. "If it gives us a better chance to take back the night, I'm in."

I shook my head, wondering how Phoenix could agree to something that would dehumanize him. "B-but that's crazy!" I unknowingly stopped dancing due to the shock I was enduring from Phoenix telling me something so bizarre, something I never would've imagined he'd say, not in a million years.

"I didn't want to talk about this tonight," Phoenix said and reached for my hand.

"Well, if not tonight, then when?" I asked hotly.

"Any other night," he said. "I'm sorry I've kept you wondering. I would've told you sooner, but I thought I'd revealed a lot already. Didn't want to overwhelm you, you know?"

I nodded, understanding, and realized I was being selfish because I was putting a damper on our night. I knew he wasn't trying to hide anything from me. He was always honest when I asked him about anything.

Phoenix didn't like the few seconds of silence. "Delilah," he begged, "please forgive me."

"No, don't apologize. I should be the one saying sorry," I told him. "I didn't mean to get so upset. You're right, we can always talk about it another night. I didn't mean to get so worked up. I realize a lot is going on in the world that I don't know. You and everyone else here are just trying to do what's best."

Phoenix shrugged. "It's all right. I'm glad to know you care so much about me."

"I do," I admitted. "I just want you to be safe."

"Aw," Phoenix cooed. "Do you worry about me, Delilah?"

I let out an awkward laugh. Funny how easily Phoenix could turn a sour situation into a good one. I admired his forgiveness and willingness to move on. So, I wrapped my arms around his neck to finish the dance, and Phoenix's hands found their way back to my waist, but instead of pulling me close, he kept some distance between us to look at me as he spoke.

"You're amazing," he told me.

It wasn't hard to take him seriously, to believe every word he said. He seemed so confident when he spoke. There was no ounce of doubt in his voice. The way he let compliments roll off his tongue sounded more like facts than opinions.

"Thank you," I said.

"How was I lucky enough to come across someone like you?" he wondered. "Someone good with her hands."

Phoenix was too much.

"Someone who loves the night just as much as I do," Phoenix continued. "Someone who craves adventure as much as I do. Someone so..."

"Stop," I urged, worried my palms would start sweating from Phoenix's flattering words.

"You want me to stop?" Phoenix asked, inching closer.

"Yeah," I breathed, becoming nervous, anticipating what he planned on doing next.

The bluest of eyes was all I could see, and my heart began to pound as Phoenix closed the gap between us. So close, I could feel his breath on my lips.

"Okay, I'll stop," he said softly, and before I could say another word, he pressed his lips to mine.

And when he kissed me for the first time, it was as if the world stopped spinning. The music went silent, and the only sound I could hear was the pounding of my heart about to burst out of my chest. I truly believed no one was in the room, just us. Everything went pitch black, but in the best way, and I became lost in another universe with Phoenix—somewhere only we could go, a place made only for us.

The longer we kissed, the hotter I became. It felt like flames were engulfing my body, fire igniting from my lips. I could feel Phoenix's strong embrace continuously pulling me to him, but even though our bodies were against one another, it was as if Phoenix thought we could never be close enough.

"Excuse me, Phoenix," a training officer interrupted, bringing me back to reality. "I know it's your night off, but the Upper wants to have a word with you."

"Right now?" Phoenix said, annoyed.

"Sorry. She wants an update," the officer explained.

Phoenix sighed loudly. "Fine, tell her I'll be there in a minute," he said, and the officer excused himself.

"Sorry," Phoenix apologized, "bad timing. It'll only be a few minutes."

I nodded as Phoenix turned to deal with his business, leaving me alone in a crowd of strangers.

I wandered over to the table overflowing with several types of food that someone like me would never be able to afford or come by. There was a tall glass sitting on a skinny stem. It was filled with some kind of light pink bubbly drink. It looked like the soda pop my dad brought me from one of his outings when I was little.

I eagerly picked up the glass and took a sip, thinking I would enjoy the sugary goodness, but it wasn't what I had expected. The drink didn't taste anything like I remembered. It burned the back of my throat when I swallowed, and I coughed it back up, spraying one of the guys next to me.

Through my continuous coughing, I tried to apologize, "I— I'm so… I— I didn't—"

"Gross," the guy said, reaching for a napkin and retreated across the room to get as far away from me as possible.

I wiped my mouth on the sleeve of my dress and prayed no one else saw what had happened.

"What's gross," I grumbled to myself while setting the glass back on the table, "is that drink."

"Ew," I heard someone say next to me.

"Great," I breathed heavily, realizing it was Veronica.

Although she wasn't by herself. Veronica had a posse with her, who happened to glare at me the same way she did.

"Did I see you take a drink from that glass and put it back?" Veronica scoffed.

"It tasted weird," I explained. "I didn't know where to put it."

Veronica flung her hair behind her back and crossed her arms along her chest while popping her hip to one side. She leaned forward so her narrowed eyes were inches away from mine and said slowly, "You—are—disgusting."

I don't know if it was the nice dress I was wearing that gave me confidence or maybe I finally had enough, but I knew I was done with Veronica being so rude to me.

"What's your problem?" I snapped.

Veronica retracted, her hand moving to her chest as she gasped, shocked I spoke back.

"Oh, hell no," one of the girls whispered behind her.

"Excuse me?" Veronica sneered.

"I don't understand. You don't even know me and every time you see me, it seems like I've done something to upset you, but really, I haven't done anything at all," I explained.

"You think so?" she said, her eyes squinting harder at me.

I threw my hands down. "Is this about Phoenix? He told me you guys aren't together anymore."

Veronica's tongue clicked inside her mouth, grazing the edge of her teeth. "Did he now?" she said.

"Yeah," I replied.

Then her eyes became fierce and sad at the same time before leaning closer to me to whisper into my ear. "Did he also tell you that you're *special?* That there's no one else like you? That he was so lucky to find you?"

"Wait, what?" I breathed in disbelief. How did she know?

"Oh, you poor girl," she laughed. "He's using you."

Veronica must've been trying to scare me away. I was a threat. She wanted Phoenix and knew I was standing in her way.

"You're just jealous," I told her.

But then she laughed even harder, like I'd made a funny joke. "Of *you*?"

I felt my insides becoming hot with anger and embarrassment all at once.

"How do you think the New Military is made?" Veronica asked me.

"Wh-what do you mean?" I asked.

"Phoenix is recruiting you," Veronica said with eyes that pitied me.

"You're lying," I countered.

But surprisingly, the expression on her face changed. She seemed sincere and almost sorry she was saying what she had to. "I wish I could say I was," Veronica admitted. "I was you not too long ago."

"No…" I trailed off, processing everything.

"It's true," one of her friends chimed in. "I think he only needs to recruit one more before he's considered into the Vamp program. Word has been going around that you have a family business that would be beneficial to our cause, too."

"He doesn't care for you," Veronica added. "It's all part of the recruitment process. I'll be punished for telling you this, but I thought you should hear it sooner rather than later. I thought it was only fair to you. I wish someone would've told me."

"No…" I repeated, trying to convince myself what Veronica was saying wasn't true.

But what she was telling me made sense. If Veronica wanted to scare me off, there were other ways. She wouldn't have made something like that up.

Lies. So many lies! Phoenix wasn't someone I could trust, and he was only using me. He manipulated me into believing he cared for me. How could I have been so dumb? My brother was right. I should've forgotten about Phoenix!

As I stood in front of Veronica and her friends, I didn't know what else to say. My eyes began to water, unable to hold back tears.

Another of Veronica's friends giggled, "I think you made her cry."

I took off running and made my way out of the castle, out of sight from judgmental eyes. My heart felt like a thousand pounds, and I couldn't bear the load. I fell to the ground, dirt covering my dress. I didn't care if it got ruined because my insides felt like they had been torn to pieces. I sat there, alone and sobbing, unable to pick myself up.

"There you are," Phoenix said from behind me. "What are you doing out here? It's freezing. Why are you sitting on the—"

I quickly stood and wiped my tears, attempting to be brave. "Stay away from me," I said.

"What?" he chuckled like I was joking and took a few steps closer.

I retreated farther away from him. "You heard me. Stay away."

"What's wrong?" he asked, realizing I'd been crying.

"I know what you're doing."

"What do you mean?"

"Veronica told me everything!" I yelled.

"What did she tell you?"

"Stop pretending!" I continued to shout.

"I don't know what's going on. Please just tell me what Veronica said."

"That— that… you— you're just using me. That I don't mean anything to you!"

"Oh…" Phoenix trailed off. "Veronica doesn't know what she's talking about."

"Stop, just stop! Stop lying!"

Phoenix exhaled loudly as if he didn't know what to say or how to make things right.

"How could you do such a thing?" I said, wounded.

"I was going to tell you. I was, really. You weren't supposed to find out like that."

"When? After you told me how amazing I am a hundred more times? Or— or after kissing me again?"

"Delilah, please, let me explain," Phoenix pleaded. "It's complicated, but I'll admit, at first, I wanted to spend time with you because I thought you would be a good asset. Then I got to know you and—"

"*Then you got to know me* and realized I would have even more to offer because of my family's business," I pointed out. I didn't want to hear his excuses.

"No, that's not it at all. I have feelings for you," Phoenix said softly. "I'm sorry I didn't tell you sooner. I wanted to. I did. I— the Upper doesn't allow it until the person becomes a recruit and signs the contract."

"So, you're saying that you trick people?" I scoffed. "How can I trust you? Why— why did I ever trust you?" My face contorted in ways I didn't want it to, but I couldn't help it while trying unsuccessfully to hold back more tears.

"You *can* trust me," he countered and held his hand out.

I don't know what he expected me to do. Did he want me to simply forgive him? I couldn't do such a thing. Not after all the lies.

I glared at him with stern eyes and spoke, "I will *never* be able to trust you!"

"Delilah…" Phoenix said as his hand dropped down to his side, knowing I wasn't going to place mine in his.

"Stay away from me," I said through a clenched jaw and turned to run away.

"Where are you going?" Phoenix asked. "There's a storm that's supposed to pass by."

"Home!" I yelled angrily.

"It's too far!" Phoenix shouted. "And too dangerous!"

But I didn't care. I didn't care if I ran into a dozen vampires, and they dragged me back to their hive. I didn't care if I lived or died. I only cared about getting far away from Phoenix and running away from the betrayal.

I would never be able to deny the feelings I had for Phoenix were real, even if he didn't want me like I wanted him. I couldn't tell myself it didn't hurt finding out the truth because I felt used, like Phoenix thought my feelings didn't exist. I was something to be found, seduced, and kept for "the cause."

# Chapter Nineteen

## Wandering Through Town

A few minutes after running away from the castle, I felt confident Phoenix wasn't going to chase after me. Although, what was I thinking that he might actually come looking for me in the first place? After all, he didn't care about me. Phoenix's goal was to climb the ranks in the New Military and take back nightfall… or whatever it was he wanted to do.

I slowed my pace as my adrenaline began to die down. My heart and head calmed, which made me realize how tired I was, not just physically but mentally as well. All the emotions that erupted when I found out the truth about Phoenix's deception had completely drained me. I knew I would have to dig deep to make it home before sunrise, and Grandpa noticed I was gone.

The hours I spent walking felt like days, my limbs turning into popsicles, and although I covered more miles than I could count on one hand, I was also aware I still had a long way to go. I decided to stick to the road because it was less likely that vampires would attack somewhere lit rather than in the darkness of the woods. Thankfully, I was wearing the right shoes for a long walk, but my feet still ached, and my legs were beginning to feel numb due to the harsh chill in the air. No cars came or went because everyone knew better than to be out during such a time, but I still prayed anyway that someone—anyone would drive by and offer me a ride.

My dress began to fray along the hem as it dragged on the road. To get my mind off the cold and how badly my feet hurt, I fantasized about curling up in my bed and sleeping well after the sun came up. I even thought about how lying in the middle of the road didn't seem all too bad of an idea. Camping out under the stars would've been fine if Grandpa didn't notice I was gone, and of course, the fact that monsters were real.

Then I felt a drop of water hit the top of my head, and I looked at the night sky. "Great, just my luck," I murmured as rain began to fall.

At first, it wasn't so bad. The raindrops came down slowly, but soon it became a heavy downpour. The dress I was wearing became drenched, and I felt like I was wearing a thousand-pound sack.

I wanted to find someplace to hide from the weather. Anywhere would do. I looked around, hoping to find shelter, but it was hard to see anything in the distance. The houses in Hope were spread out, and nothing was close to the edge of the road, but then I noticed one of the street signs at a crossroad. I squinted hard through the rain and realized I knew exactly where I was. I was getting closer to home, probably only another two or three miles. I felt a sense of relief and urged myself to push through.

But just as I was about to pick up the pace, eager to get home, I heard a branch snap loudly, and my head shot over to the forest lining the road. I stood alert as a frosty tingle trailed along my spine. Maybe the storm caused a tree branch to break off?

Suddenly, my soles weren't so achy, and my legs didn't care if they had been abused or frozen. I tried to stay positive—that Phoenix was wrong, and I'd be fine. Maybe the storm would ease up soon.

Then I heard someone speak, and it came from somewhere in the trees. "Well, well, look who we have here." The voice was deep, and strangely, it easily cut through the sound of the rain.

I frantically searched all around me, attempting to locate the person or… vampire, but I couldn't see past the road where the streetlamps shone.

I wasn't sure if I should try and make a run for it since I didn't think I could move very fast. If it was a vampire, there was no chance of outrunning him. Even if it wasn't raining and my dress wasn't weighing me down, vampires were *always* faster than humans.

I spun around in a circle, wiping my wet hair away from my eyes, desperate to figure out if there was a real threat. "Wh-who's there?" I said, my voice shaking.

I expected a response, but instead, I jumped when I heard glass shattering and the fizzle of a lightbulb. I felt small shards of the streetlamp's cover and lightbulb shower down on me as they fell to the ground. The street was darker, and then suddenly, a second light went out, and then another. Someone was throwing rocks, intentionally breaking the lights.

Laughter rang through the wet air, and I could feel a second round of adrenaline kicking in again, so I ran. With a false sense of hope, I ran as fast as I could, believing I could outrun whoever was taunting me. Maybe if I ran far enough, I could find help.

But just as I was starting to build up confidence that I was going to get away, my foot caught on the bottom of my dress, and I took a tumble. In an attempt to break my fall so I didn't hit my head, I braced myself with my arms and shredded the sleeves of my dress on the ground. I cringed, knowing I thoroughly scraped both my forearms.

When I sat up, I was caught off guard. Not one but three men were standing around me, and two of them were still laughing.

There was one with a thick chain wrapped around his waist who spoke to the others, "Told you she wasn't going to get very far."

"Oh," another cooed and bent down beside me. "She's prettier than I thought."

His breath smelled like rusty old pipes from drinking blood. I noticed his eyes were black, and he wasn't a man at all.

The last of the three looked quite a bit older than the other two, and he seemed more serious. He didn't laugh along with the rest of them, and he didn't smile. He quickly suggested they take me back to the hive and not waste more time.

"No, no," I pleaded. "Please…"

They ignored me and continued to chat amongst themselves. "We're allowed to feed and have a little fun, you know," the one with the chain belt added.

The vampire who was beside me stood. "I agree. We found her."

Maybe if I had my bag, I would've tried to fight back. Maybe if there was only one vampire, I would've tried to make another run for it. Maybe if I wasn't in shock, I could've done something to try and get away—anything at all to get help, anything but sit there like I'd already given up.

The older-looking one sighed, disappointed he was outvoted. "Fine, but make it quick, and don't kill her. Our queen will be furious if we don't bring someone back to change. You know how she's been since she got word of the military gathering nearby."

I hoped it would be quick. I hoped they would accidentally kill me so they wouldn't be able to drag me to their hive to be changed. I didn't want to become a vampire, something so monstrous. I would rather die than be made into something that murders people.

"Me first!" the one with the chain said as he knelt beside me.

The others allowed it and stood by, waiting patiently.

"Hello, there," he said to me, his fangs already in place for a meal.

Water trickled rapidly from my eyes.

"Aw, don't cry," the vampire said as if it would make it less pleasant for him to feed off of me. I was surprised he could tell I was crying since the water from the sky also ran down my face. My distorted expression, which showed panic, and my chest rapidly rising and falling, must've given it away. "It'll only hurt for a moment until the venom paralyzes you and takes away all the pain," he assured me.

I shook my head and pushed my shoulders higher to shorten my neck, hoping it would prolong the inevitable.

Then, with a blink of an eye, his fangs plunged into my neck like two daggers, and I screamed aloud until I couldn't scream any longer—until the venom took its toll and my body became a limp noodle. I lay lifeless in the vampire's grasp as he fed. Although, oddly enough, tears were still able to flow freely, streaming down my cheeks.

Once the vampire was satiated, he handed me over to the next. I assumed he would do the same as the other, but instead, he laid me back on the ground.

"You know, I think I'll have a different kind of fun with this one," he laughed sinisterly.

My body was stiff and unable to move, but I could see what he was doing. His hands were busy unbuttoning his jeans. His long fingernails seemed to make it more difficult, but he was able to get it done. The way his body shook from excitement made him move more slowly, prolonging the inevitable.

"You are utterly disgusting," the serious one said and turned to walk away. "I'll be waiting in the forest for you to finish." After taking a few steps toward the trees, he paused and glanced over his shoulder. "Make it snappy. I can feel the queen calling to us to get back to the hive."

I was helpless. I felt weak, like a vulnerable roly-poly bug on its back being prodded by a toddler—waiting for the torture to end. I begged for God to let me die. I couldn't begin to imagine the horror I would have to endure next.

The vampire's pants fell to his ankles, and I told myself to think of something else, anything that would get my mind off what was happening. I repeated bible verses that comforted me as the venom slowly began to wear off.

It sounded gargled and almost inaudible as my lips quivered, unable to fully move.

"The Lord is my light and my salvation; whom shall I fear? The Lord is the stronghold of my life; of whom shall I be afraid?" I said, doing my best to ignore the pain caused by the puncture wounds on my neck.

"What?" the vampire with the chain asked. "What's she saying?"

"Who cares," the other replied.

The two vampires laughed even harder, and then the one whose turn it was, began to remove his underwear, but before he could, he was interrupted by the sound of a loud motor approaching. The vampires' gazes shot up in surprise as a motorcycle stopped a couple of yards away.

I attempted to tilt my head to get a better view of who was approaching. It was a dark figure on a bike, but I couldn't make out who it was.

My lips began to move a little more. My insides felt like they were slowly coming back to life, and I screamed as loud as I could, "Even though I walk through the valley of the shadow of death…"

"I will fear no evil," the man said as he dismounted the motorcycle.

"Look at this guy," the vampire with the chain mocked, referring to how he was dressed.

"Do you think that's one of the military people our queen was so worried about and told us to stay away from?" the other mentioned lightly.

As the dark figure approached us, he reached for something on the side of his thigh. He lifted his arm in front of him as he began to run, and silver bullets flew across me as I lay on my back helplessly. Both vampires moved in blurs, dodging the bullets. The monsters made it seem effortless to avoid contact. It was as if they barely moved from their spots, their upper bodies contorting in odd ways, allowing the bullets to continue past them.

Still running, the man quickly placed the gun back into its holster and reached behind his back, retrieving a weapon in each hand. The weapons looked like axes, but the blades were large and circular. Once he was close enough, I realized it was Phoenix.

"What the—" the half-naked vampire breathed, scrambling to pull up his pants. But before he could finish, Phoenix slid across the wet pavement on one knee, precisely swinging his weapons in front of him. The blades cut clean through the vampire, slicing the bloodsucker in half at the waist.

The vampire's body twitched, lying in the street in pieces. A couple of seconds longer, and the bottom part of the body vanished to ash. Phoenix calmly stood and walked over to the upper half of the vampire's body. Phoenix thrust down the weapon in his right hand, causing a silver stake to appear at the bottom of the handle.

"Do something!" the sliced-up vampire screamed to the other.

The vampire who sunk his fangs into my neck moments ago quickly removed the chain from his waist with one pull. Phoenix heard the chain rattle and turned to face his next opponent. The vampire wrapped the end of the chain around his fist as a smirk formed on his face.

I was finally able to sit up, the vampire venom continuing to dissipate. I assumed I would watch Phoenix put an end to the next vampire, too, but out of nowhere, the vampire who was lingering in the trees ran over to me in a blur and grabbed me by my hair. Before I could do anything, I realized I was being dragged through the forest like a gazelle being carried away by a lion. I desperately clawed at the hand that held me by my hair as if it would help me escape, but it was useless.

The roots of the trees that protruded from the forest floor, ripped the rest of my dress to shreds. The rain falling made the earth soft, covering every inch of me with mud. The pebbles that were scattered everywhere were sharp, each taking their turn to bruise and cut my body.

"Delilah!" Phoenix's voice rang through the branches, but I knew he was preoccupied, and I was already too deep in the woods for him to track me down.

"Almost there," the vampire said, still running at full speed. It was as if he was speaking to himself. He didn't want to disappoint his queen.

A couple of minutes ago, I thought I was saved. I thought my prayers had been answered. How was I supposed to get out of this one? I didn't think there was any chance of survival. My fate was sealed, and there was nothing I could do. I was a rabbit caught in a vampire's snare.

But just as I was about to give up hope, I was released, and my body dropped to the ground. The vampire who was dragging me wailed in pain, and I quickly gathered myself and scooted to where I could lean my back against a tree. I was a wounded animal. All I could do was try and catch my breath.

I couldn't see much in the darkness but noticed the vampire's hand had been severed from his body. His dismembered appendage was inches from my feet, which was disgusting to look at. I used all my strength to kick it farther away while holding back vomit that was crawling up my throat. His hand turned to dust as it rolled farther away. The vampire's wails of agony continued to ring throughout the woods, but I couldn't pinpoint where he was.

I squinted, searching farther in the distance. Eventually, I spotted two silhouettes fighting under the moonlight. One of them had a sword and seemed to have the upper hand. My body tensed again, wondering who was out there. The person slid the sword up the other's hip and through to his shoulder, similar to what I witnessed Phoenix do to the other vampire.

I was finally able to relax as I watched ash float through the air, knowing I was safe. But who was my savior? If he killed a vampire, he had to have been a good person, someone I could trust.

I was surprised when a woman came closer and knelt beside me. My body was beaten from being dragged through the forest, so I couldn't do much besides sit there. She leaned closer to look me in the eyes, and all I saw were two violet circles as if they were glowing in the night.

"Are you okay?" she asked, concerned.

I nodded and was about to speak, but the ache from the vampire's fangs reemerged. I held my hand against the wound, but I quickly retracted while wincing from the pain and decided it was best not to touch it. I glanced down at my hand, but it only made me woozy since it was covered in blood. I waited for the rain to cleanse the red that stained my skin, but as I looked up, I realized the water ceased and white powder was falling. I felt lightheaded, and my vision became blurry.

"Hey, stay with me," the woman said as she placed her hand on my cheek to keep my head steady.

But it was no use. As I stared at the snow falling from the clouds, my eyes rolled back, and I went unconscious.

# Chapter Twenty

## Rise and Shine

I dreamt of the vampires dragging me back to the hive. I pictured myself under their queen's grasp as she sunk her teeth into me. I imagined myself becoming one of them, but even worse, I dreamt of Phoenix wrapped in a chain, unable to fight. I saw him being drained of blood and his life slipping away.

But someone's voice pulled me from the nightmare, the voice speaking something familiar…

*Born From Ashes*

*Wildly free like the wind,*
*And untamable like storms.*
*Unbreakably fierce like a beast,*
*And fearless like God.*

*Oddly mysterious like the Heavens,*
*And perplexing like Hell.*
*Undeniably alluring like the moon,*
*And dazzling like the stars.*
*Ultimate temptation like the fruit,*
*And enticement like none.*

My eyes shot open, my heart beating faster than a racehorse, and I sat up in my bed, hyperventilating.

"Shh. You're safe," Phoenix said as he sat beside me.

He placed his hand on mine, reassuring me I wasn't in danger.

I sighed, relieved I was home safe in my bed and Phoenix was alive, but I quickly noticed he was holding something in his other hand. "Hey!" I shouted and yanked my notebook from his grasp. "That's private!"

"Oh, sorry," he apologized. "It was sitting on your nightstand. I didn't think it was—"

"Well, it is!" I shouted, hoping he didn't read more than I heard. "Ow," I winced and moved my hand to my neck. There was a bandage covering my wound, but it still hurt, and getting worked up didn't help the pain.

"Careful," Phoenix told me. "It's going to be tender for a while and will take a few weeks to heal."

I remembered everything from last night. What I was most surprised about was that Phoenix came after me. Maybe he meant what he said all along, and I did mean something to him.

"You— you came— I didn't think you would come after me," I said, my words still a bit icy.

Phoenix's sapphire eyes stared back at mine. "Of course. I told you everything I said was true. I care for you." He raised a hand to stroke my cheek, and surprisingly, I allowed him to touch me. "You mean more to me than you realize," Phoenix continued. "I'm sorry I didn't tell you sooner. I shouldn't have cared about the rules. I should've done what was right. I'm sorry you had to find out everything from someone else. I'm sorry I hurt you. I'm sorry I didn't get there sooner…" he trailed off while staring at my neck, disappointment present in his eyes. Then he turned his head away from me completely, ashamed of what he had done.

The coldness I held in my chest began to disappear. Phoenix saving me had chiseled away at the ice that surrounded my heart, and his apology melted the rest away. How could I hold a grudge? What kind of person would I be if I wasn't able to forgive him?

"Thank you for saving me," I whispered. "I was worried you weren't going to make it through the fight."

He nodded solemnly as if he couldn't forgive himself. It was strange because Phoenix was always so confident, borderline cocky. Humility didn't fit him well.

"The vampires I fought were young. Their fangs were short."

"They seemed long to me," I pointed out, referring to the punctures on my neck.

"That's understandable," he whispered with disappointment.

"But what matters is I'm safe," I reminded him.

Phoenix sat in silence, continuing to punish himself for the lies and late appearance.

"So…" I urged, doing my best to pull Phoenix out of his head. "Can you tell me more about what goes on in a vampire hive?"

"You really want to know after everything you went through?" Phoenix scoffed, surprised by my curiosity.

"Yeah, now more than ever, if anything."

Phoenix couldn't hide the somber grin forming on his face. "You're a strange one, Delilah," he added. "Maybe braver than you should be, too."

"Some would agree. Others might say I don't have any common sense," I joked.

"Right… Well, in a vampire hive, the vampires tend to their queen and protect her. It's where they take humans back so the hive can feed and where the queen changes humans into vampires. I'm sure there's a lot more that goes on that we haven't learned about, but I can tell you, anything that goes on in one of those hives is evil."

"*Really* glad you showed up when you did," I mentioned again.

"I can't take all the credit," Phoenix admitted.

Then I remembered the training officer who intercepted me in the woods. "Oh, yeah. I should probably thank her. I— who…"

"That was Sasha who found you. She must've heard your screams. Not sure I would've been able to take on the older one by myself, the one who was supervising the other two. I shouldn't have put you in that situation. I shouldn't have let things get so out of hand," Phoenix said angrily, still beating himself up.

"It all worked out," I assured him. "I didn't get dragged back to the hive."

"Yeah..." Phoenix replied. "I know, but you still got hurt, and it was all my fault. If I hadn't lied to you, you would've never run off."

"They know you guys are coming."

"Huh?" he asked, his eyes widening as he put his emotions on the back burner.

"The older vampire said something about how their queen was adamant they bring people back to be changed because you guys were in town."

"Like they want to grow their ranks," Phoenix stated as if he were talking to himself. "You know, I better get back. The Upper will be wondering where I am, and I'll need to be debriefed."

I was disappointed to hear he had to leave. If I had the strength, I might've tried to stop him, but I also knew I couldn't keep him here forever.

Before leaving my room, he peered over his shoulder at me. "Please forgive me, Delilah. I never meant to hurt you."

I wasn't used to the whole forgiveness thing. I was better at holding grudges. But something inside me told me I should let this one go. Something told me Phoenix was telling the truth, and he cared about me.

As soon as Phoenix left the room, Ben entered.

"Told you," he snickered.

I shot a fiery glance his way, wondering if he had been standing outside the bedroom door and listening in on the conversation I was having with Phoenix.

"I warned you, didn't I?" he sneered.

I tossed my notebook aside onto the nightstand and pretended Ben wasn't in the room, but even though I did my best to act like Ben was invisible, he still had the nerve to take a seat beside me. I would've shoved him off my bed if I hadn't noticed the smugness on his face was quickly vanishing. Ben twiddled his thumbs for a moment in hopes I would stop ignoring him.

"I'm glad you're okay," he said quietly.

I could see the worry I caused him, so I finally responded, "Me too."

"I mean, it was raining, and then it started to snow," Ben began to ramble. "You know, I have a hard time going to sleep when you're gone. It's like I have twin telepathy or something."

Then, my gaze wandered to the window, curious about how much snow collected from last night. "Oh, no!" I yelled, realizing Phoenix was outside talking to Nick.

"Something wrong?" Ben wondered.

"No, no, no," I chanted, throwing back my covers, which smacked Ben in the face.

"Ouch!" Ben exaggerated.

I ignored him and hastily slipped my shoes on. For a second, I wondered how I got into clean pajamas and out of my dress. More so, I was concerned about *who* changed my clothes, but only for a brief moment. The imminent issue was that Phoenix and Nick ran into each other for the first time, and I wasn't ready for Phoenix to meet Nick or for Nick to find out about Phoenix.

I sprinted out of the room, ignoring the painful black and blue lumps that formed over various parts of my body and were causing me constant discomfort. With each stride I took, my muscles protested, aching in ways I didn't know they could. I was determined to get to Nick and Phoenix, and I wouldn't let any amount of pain stop me.

I hurried to the living room, ready to leap out the door, but before I could make my move, Grandpa interrupted. "Sit," he said firmly. Grandpa was reclined in his chair, and by the look of how comfortable Grandpa was—his body sinking into the cushions, he must've been waiting a while for me.

With all the commotion, I had forgotten about Grandpa. What did he know? What did Phoenix tell him? At that moment, I knew I would be chained to the house as long as Grandpa was alive.

"B-but I— I need to—" I stammered, worried about what was happening outside.

"Sit!" Grandpa yelled, sitting up straighter. "Now!"

Since Grandpa was serious, I thought it would be best to take a seat. So, I sat on the couch beside him with my hands folded on my lap.

"Wh-what did you hear?" I asked.

"Oh, Phoenix told me everything," Grandpa said, heated. "I got to know him pretty well, actually. The lady with the weird eyes, who helped drop you off, took a minute to chat, too."

"Every— everything?" I asked, hoping Grandpa didn't know *everything*.

"Yup, told me about the New Military, recruiting you without your knowledge, taking you around town and sometimes farther without me knowing, putting you in danger, the works!"

"So, you're going to tell me to stay away from him, right?" I assumed.

Grandpa leaned back into his recliner and sighed. "I think that would be the right thing to say, but that boy did bring you back in one piece… kind of, and he refused to leave until he knew you were okay. He stayed the entire night. Don't think he slept a wink, not that I did either."

"Wh-what? Really?" I replied, surprised by Grandpa's response.

Maybe Grandpa had a soft spot for people in the military since he put in his time when he was younger. Maybe Phoenix and Sasha took the blame.

"But it doesn't mean you'll be going out at night anymore! And more importantly, the sneaking around behind my back is going to stop."

"I'm sorry, Grandpa," I said, lowering my head in shame. "I shouldn't have lied to you."

"Well, you aren't a little girl anymore," he sighed, disappointed. "You were bound to do what you want sooner or later."

I felt like a hypocrite lying to Grandpa, even if he was more understanding than he should've been. I was so angry that Phoenix lied to me when I was doing the same thing all along.

Grandpa continued, "You're free to do as you please, but I want to know when and where you are going. It's for your own safety."

"I will let you know," I responded submissively.

"And if I'm being honest, that boy reminds me of when I was younger," Grandpa admitted. "So determined to make a difference, and the military isn't a bad way to do so. Little rough around the edges and a tad too adventurous, but he seems like a good kid. His heart is in the right place."

"It almost sounds like you think I should join…"

"Well, I'm not saying it would be a bad idea if you decided to work for them," Grandpa mentioned. "They would train you, and then you wouldn't be a sitting duck. You'd be able to protect yourself."

"I'd also be putting myself in more danger," I pointed out.

"It would be for a good cause, but from what the woman with the weird eyes and the boy were saying, it sounded like you'd be behind the scenes most of the time."

"What do you mean?"

"They seemed like they were interested in you making weapons for them."

"They did tell you *everything*, didn't they?" I said, annoyed. I shook my head in disbelief. I couldn't believe what Grandpa was suggesting, but then I remembered what my purpose was—Phoenix and Nick. "May I be excused now?" I asked urgently.

Grandpa nodded and shooed me away with his hand. I ran out of the house and bumped into Nick. I looked around for Phoenix, but he was driving away on his bike.

"Woah, are you okay?" Nick asked, catching me in his arms.

"Yeah, sorry," I apologized.

"Phoenix warned me you were hurt," Nick said, worried.

"What else did he say?"

"Not much," Nick explained. "Said it was up to you what you wanted to tell me. Who is he anyway?"

"Oh, um, that guy? He's nobody," I quickly replied. "J-just someone from the military."

"Really?" Nick asked, confused, "because he seemed to know you pretty well. He seemed really concerned about you and—"

"Maybe we should sit down?" I suggested while letting out a nervous sigh. I didn't have a choice but to reveal the secrets I'd been hiding.

Nick agreed and helped me over to the oak tree where we sat. The ground was still covered with a thin layer of snow, and I wondered how upset Nick would be when I told him the truth—that there was another guy I had spent nights with. I figured Nick would never want to talk to me again, and I would deserve whatever distance he decided to put between us.

"So, what's going on? What happened to you?" Nick asked, concern tainting his voice.

"I was attacked by a group of vampires," I explained, calmer than I should've.

Nick sat straighter like a chill had crept up his spine. "Vampires?" he asked, shocked. "But how? Did they attack you here? I mean, you have lights, and the main roads aren't for miles. I don't understand how you—"

"It wasn't here," I answered. "I, uh, I was walking home."

"At night?" Nick continued, becoming more confused.

I nodded.

"Why?" Nick's tone became harsher as if he were scolding me. "Why were you out at night?"

I turned toward Nick, barely able to look directly into those chestnut eyes of his because his eyes told me he couldn't tell a lie, especially to someone he cared for. He was genuine and honest, something I couldn't say about myself. I didn't want to hurt him.

"I've been spending time with Phoenix," I said slowly.

"Oh…" Nick breathed in disbelief. He rested his back against the tree trunk, and his gaze wandered to the branches as he tilted his head to the sky.

"I'm sorry," I told Nick.

He shrugged with pursed lips and brushed off whatever emotions he was going through like it wasn't a big deal. "It's not like we were anything."

"What?" I scoffed, offended he would say such a thing. "What do you mean?"

Obviously, we cared about each other. We had been more than just friends for months.

"Well, it's not like you're my girlfriend," he explained.

Nick was right. We weren't exclusive, but something told me Nick had been hoping for more than just casual dating for a while.

"Uh, yeah, I guess," I stammered. "But we were— *are* more than just friends."

Nick's gaze stopped fluttering from the sky to the ground, and then he looked at me with fierce eyes. "Do you love him?" he asked.

"Wh-what?" I scoffed, surprised by Nick's bluntness.

"Do you love him?" he asked again.

"No!" I laughed like it was an absurd question.

"Okay…" Nick trailed off.

"No, I don't love Phoenix," I tried to say as convincingly as possible.

"Have you *kissed* him?"

I wanted to continue to be honest with Nick, but he was making it so hard. The things he was asking me… I didn't want to answer.

But I did what was right. "Yes…"

Nick nodded over and over again in silence. It was almost like he was having a private conversation with himself inside of his head.

"I'm sorry, Nick," I apologized and realized I was beginning to sound a lot like Phoenix—trying to right my wrongs.

"You have nothing to apologize for," Nick said. "I should be the one apologizing for not realizing I needed to fight for you."

"Huh?" I asked, taken aback.

Nick turned toward me, riled up about something. Maybe it had to do with what he was thinking about?

"Shame on me for only holding your hand and not expressing how I truly feel about you. Shame on me for not asking you to be my girlfriend months ago. Shame on me for thinking you were already mine!"

"I didn't know you liked to write poetry, too," I smiled, trying to joke. I was just glad Nick wasn't upset at me.

Nick lowered his chin to his chest and chuckled softly to himself while adjusting his cowboy hat. His square jaw tightened and released repeatedly. He did that when he was nervous or embarrassed.

It took him a minute to regain more confidence, but eventually, he looked up at me with swoony eyes. "I love you, Delilah," Nick whispered. "Some might call me selfish for wanting you all to myself, but others would say I was a fool if I gave up and let someone else have you."

Nick was everything I needed—everything I wanted. He was perfect and too good for me. I could live a hundred lifetimes and still never deserve his forgiveness… or him. Nick never grew tired of hearing my sorrows about my parents. He always listened with an open heart. He learned all there was to know about me. He knew how to love someone properly and could forever continue to make me a better person.

*I was a better person when I was with him.*

There were endless characteristics that I admired about Nick, and I would be crazy if I said I didn't want to be with him. It would be crazy for me not to say the same…

"And I'm not going to be labeled a fool," Nick finished. "My parents raised me to be respectful to women and not cross boundaries, but maybe I'd been taking things too slowly."

I couldn't stop staring at his beautiful brown eyes. I ran my fingertips across his chiseled jawline and then my thumb along his bottom lip.

"I love you too," I said softly.

"Yeah?" Nick smirked. "You do?"

"Mhmm," I smiled.

But the smile on my face instantly vanished once Nick pressed his lips against mine. All those months prior, I was content lying in farm fields next to Nick. I'd been fine with sweet words and flirtatious glances. I was happy with walks along the creek and holding hands, unaware of what I was missing out on.

Nick's kiss was gentle and kind. It was the type of kiss that made me feel comforted and loved, the kind of kiss that told me he meant to keep me forever. And I wanted to stay there, under the oak tree, with Nick for as long as I could. I wanted to feel the way he was making me feel for the rest of my life, like I was worth everything and more, like I could move forward with him, never tempted to look back.

# Chapter Twenty-one

## Breathe You In

I made promises to Nick that I sincerely intended to keep. One—I told him we would be exclusive. Two—I promised I would be truthful with him, and three—I would never see Phoenix again.

The first two promises would be easy. I deeply cared for Nick, and he deserved the truth. He had given me another chance, which I didn't deserve but was thankful for. The third promise would be more difficult to keep, but I was determined to make things work between me and Nick.

So, I finally rearranged the furniture in my bedroom, moving my bed to the wall farthest from the window. I wrote in clear words on a piece of paper, "I forgive you, but I can't see you anymore. Thank you for saving me. I will never forget that you put your life on the line for me, but please don't come back."

I left that note for Phoenix taped outside of the window.

"Please, don't do this," he pleaded the night he read the letter. "Talk to me, Delilah. We can work this out."

Even though I didn't say a word or acknowledge his presence, Phoenix didn't take off immediately the first night. It wasn't until a long while before I finally heard him drive away on his motorcycle. Phoenix had to have spent hours sitting outside my window, hoping I would have a change of heart.

Week after week, Phoenix returned. Each time, it was harder for me to pull my covers over my head and continue to shut him out. I wanted so badly to let him in, but I had promises to keep, and I couldn't do that without a clean break between us.

As months passed, his visits became shorter and shorter until… he didn't come at all. It sounded selfish to say I was hurting just as much as Phoenix was, but it was the truth. I missed him, but I also hoped that time would help me forget how much Phoenix meant to me.

Thankfully, time did help ease the pain. The distance I put between Phoenix and me didn't hurt as much as when it was fresh. The feelings I used to feel for Phoenix eventually left my heart, and I was okay with that since I had other things to be thankful for and focus on in my life.

*****

"How have you been?" Nick asked me while we sat on the water tower, watching the sun as it finished rising past the horizon.

Nick seemed somewhat comfortable with heights after climbing the tower over a dozen times. It meant a lot to me that he overcame his fear. He knew how important the place was to me.

The air was beginning to warm as spring began to take over. The rains revived the fields, and there were endless patches of lavender among the grass where wild lilies thrived.

"I've been good," I replied. "What about you?"

"Same, but I'm glad I could finally spend some time with you. It's been a long work week," Nick mentioned.

"Me too," I said, gently nudging his shoulder. "I've missed you."

Nick slid his hand over to mine. "So, have you been writing lately?" he asked.

I nodded, hopeful Nick wouldn't try to persuade me to let him read my notebook like he often did.

"So, when will I get to read your poetry?" Nick continued. "I know you like to keep it private, but…"

"My writing isn't all that great," I reminded him.

"I know you're just being modest like always."

"No, I'm not."

"Come on," Nick urged. "We've known each other for practically a year now, and you know I've been dying to read your poetry. How much longer do I have to beg for?"

Those sweet chestnut eyes of his that were slightly hidden underneath the brim of his hat were all too convincing. How could I say no?

I sighed, giving in. "All right, if I share one with you, will you leave it alone for at least a little while?"

"Heck yeah!" he grinned.

"Okay… then I'll tell you one, but only *one*!"

"Huh? Right now?"

"Yeah."

"But you don't have your notebook," Nick said, stating the obvious.

I smirked while pointing to my head.

"Oh," Nick breathed excitedly. "Must be an important one if you know it by heart."

"Yeah, you could say that," I said under my breath, becoming nervous about reciting one of my poems. "Um, so it's titled *Breathe You In.*"

"Sounds amazing," Nick said too enthusiastically.

*"I breathe you in like the crisp spring air.*
*All I want is to start anew.*
*I breathe you in like life itself.*
*I desperately yearn to be more like you.*
*I breathe you in like it's my last breath.*
*Because I know you love me too."*

Nick sat in silence.

"Th-that's it," I announced, wondering if he might've thought I wasn't finished.

"That *was amazing*," Nick said in awe.

"You think so?" I said, assuming he was trying to be nice.

"Yeah! Truly amazing! It should be a song that plays on the radio."

I shook my head in disbelief. "I'm glad you think so."

Nick kissed me shortly after, so grateful I finally shared something with him that I intended to keep to myself. He could break down my walls so easily, and with each kiss, I fell deeper into him. I knew I had made the best decision by keeping my promises. Nick was who I was supposed to be with.

# Chapter Twenty-two

## About to Break

"So, Delilah," Grandpa began as we sat around the breakfast table. He had the morning paper in his hands. "Any late-night outings planned that I should know about?"

I shook my head as I poked at a piece of scrambled egg on my plate.

"I knew there were some brain cells in there somewhere," Ben said, violently jabbing the top of my head with his finger as he stood to put his plate in the sink.

I twisted around in my chair, hoping to give Ben a good smack, but unfortunately, Ben dodged his beating.

"That's enough, you two," Grandpa said with stern eyes as he looked up from the newspaper. He took a sip of his coffee before continuing his morning reading. "Looks like the New Military has finally made their official debut in Hope," he announced.

"Huh?" I asked, confused.

Grandpa laid the paper on the table and pointed to the front page. "Looks like the government decided to tell the public what's really going on."

I yanked the paper away from Grandpa to get a better look. I glanced at the black-and-white picture that was of a soldier being carried away on a gurney and quickly read the article. It explained that a hive was located in Wyoming which was one of the states that bordered ours. Phoenix's hunch was accurate; there was a hive hundreds of miles away, but it was still right on the edge of Idaho, and that felt too close for comfort.

The article also explained there was an incident near a small town in Idaho that led to where the hive was, and instantly I understood. The incident they referred to had to have been the one I was a part of. *I* was the clue to finding the hive. When the vampire dragged me toward the castle, it pointed the military in the right direction.

The article went on to say that the New Military wasn't successful in storming the castle, but they weren't going to give up after one attack. During the first raid, it was confirmed that the queen was one of the eldest the military had ever encountered. Therefore, they strongly believed the vampires' archives contained information that could help end the war.

Many lives were lost during the attack, and the New Military was in dire need of recruits. They listed endless incentives to try and get people to join the cause.

Once I finished reading the article, I inspected the picture more closely and realized the soldier lying on the stretcher wasn't just any soldier... *It was Phoenix.*

"Oh my gosh!" I gasped.

"What is it?" Grandpa asked, surprised by my reaction.

"I have to go!" I shouted, standing frantically.

"But you haven't finished your breakfast," Grandpa pointed out.

"I have to go now!" I continued, clumsily reaching for the keys that hung by the door.

"Okay, but where are you going?" Grandpa wondered.

"I'm going to make sure Phoenix isn't dead!" I yelled as I rushed out of the house.

As my heart flooded with mixed emotions, I could picture the disappointment on Grandpa's face, and I could imagine Ben making some smart-ass remark.

"Wait!" Grandpa yelled with authority, peeking his head out the door.

After Grandpa confirmed I wasn't going to take off right away, he disappeared inside. I anxiously stood by the van, wondering what my grandpa could be making me wait for.

Grandpa hurriedly stepped down the front porch steps, his knee brace squeaking, desperately in need of another lube. Once he made his way over to me, he tried to hand me something.

"Here, take this," he said.

It was a revolver. "Uh…" I stuttered.

"You remember how to use it, don't you?"

"Yes, but I don't need—"

"Just take it!" Grandpa demanded. "Good for both humans and vampires. Just in case. Better to be safe—"

"Than dead," I finished while hesitantly reaching for the weapon.

Ben came out with my bag. "And don't forget these," he said. "You never know."

I took the bag and placed the gun inside with the other weapons.

I gave them each a hug. "Don't worry. I'll be home hours before the sun starts to set. I'll make it back safely. I promise."

Grandpa patted my back, and Ben had begun to retreat inside before I finished talking. I knew they were concerned about my safety, and they had every right to be, but they were also learning they couldn't keep me locked away forever.

"Drive safe, Delilah," Grandpa told me before I got into the van and drove off.

During the drive, all I could think about was Phoenix dead on the cot. All I was focused on was getting to the castle to make sure he was alive. I wasn't too optimistic about a positive outcome, and I began beating myself up for shutting him out and ignoring him for so long. If he didn't make it, I knew regret would gnaw at my insides for as long as I lived. I had to make sure he was alive... *I had to.*

I reached the castle and had planned to pull into an open field to park, but instead, the area surrounding the castle was occupied. A barricade made of thick silver posts filed to points and barbed wire encircled the military base about a hundred yards out from all directions. So, I was forced to come to a stop, wondering how I was supposed to get in. The barricade reminded me of what Nick's dad put up around the farm to keep the animals safe. Although Nick's dad had a slimmer budget, so his wasn't nearly as extravagant as what the New Military had put up.

Before I got out of the van, I shoved my bag into the glovebox. I wouldn't need it anyway, not at the military base. I cautiously walked up to the barricade, wondering where the entrance could be. Maybe it was on the other side of the castle?

"Hey!" I heard someone yell from afar. "What are you doing?"

I had caught someone's attention who was inside the barricade.

"I, um, I'm looking for Phoenix," I yelled back as the soldier carrying a rifle approached.

"Hands up!" he commanded, and then he said something into the radio on his shoulder.

"Wh-what?"

"You heard me," he said with authority and pointed the rifle at me. "Hands above your head!"

I did as he ordered without another word.

"What's your name?" he asked, and once he got close enough to where I could see his eyes, I noticed he was a training officer.

"M-my name?" I stammered.

"Yeah! You heard me! Give me your name now!" he shouted angrily.

"Delilah," I answered quickly. The officer didn't have much patience if any at all.

Again, he jabbered something into his radio, but I couldn't make out what he was saying. Although I think I might've heard him mention my name.

A lady responded. She rambled some string of numbers and said, "But still confirm."

"Last name?" the officer asked.

"Um, S-summers," I answered.

"It's her," he said over the radio.

The soldier glanced over his shoulder at the castle. I followed his gaze and realized he was looking at the second story where there was a lady standing by a window, but she quickly disappeared within seconds.

"Bring her in," the lady said over the radio.

"Let's go. Follow me," the officer ordered.

I followed him outside of the barricade to a guarded entrance which was on the other side of the castle.

"Why is all this necessary?" I asked the officer guiding me as two other soldiers moved separate sections of the barricade to allow me inside.

It should've taken twice as many people to move something so heavy. Just as Phoenix mentioned, vampire DNA made humans a lot stronger.

"Our failed attempt," the officer explained. "Everyone's weary there will be another attack before we strike again."

"But it's daytime," I mentioned, still not convinced such an extensive barricade was needed.

"And then it will be nighttime," the officer countered.

I was led up a curved stairwell constructed entirely of stone to the room I saw the lady in. The officer stood a bit taller before he knocked on the door. Maybe Phoenix was in there too.

"Is Phoenix in here?" I asked, hopeful.

"The Upper wants a word with you," he explained, ignoring my question.

"Come in," the lady said.

The officer violently shoved me into the room before shutting the door behind me.

"Ow, you don't have to be so rough!" I said under a hot breath, as if the officer could hear me through the closed door.

A woman in a black button-up blouse with curly blonde hair sat at a desk in front of me. She briefly glanced up and held up a finger, telling me to wait a minute while she finished her conversation on the phone. I couldn't help but notice her eyes were the same as the training officers, and I remembered what Phoenix said about them.

The soldier who shoved me into the room was a perfect example of how they lost their humanity. They were rough around the edges, and all the gentle bones in their body disappeared.

"Yes, send the recruits as soon as possible. We can prepare them in a couple of weeks since we will be promoting the ones who survived. Uh-huh. All right. Thank you," the lady said before hanging up the phone.

She gathered loose papers in front of her and tapped them on the desk to straighten them into a neat pile. "Please, have a seat," she instructed without making eye contact.

I stared at her, still standing, and wondered what would happen next.

After a moment, she finally looked up from her desk. "Don't be afraid. I know my soldiers don't give the *warmest* welcome."

"Why do you want to talk to me?" I asked, guarded.

"Sit," she repeated more firmly, becoming annoyed.

I assumed she wasn't used to having to ask more than once, so I did as she said, and thankfully, she seemed less agitated.

"Thank you," she said and cleared her throat. "So, you are Delilah?"

"Yes, I came here to see Phoenix."

"I've heard," she replied, sitting back in her rolling chair while folding her hands in her lap.

"Um, so, then… Can I see him?" I asked hesitantly.

"But why?" she asked.

"I-I'm sorry, what? What do you mean why?"

"Well, it doesn't make sense as to why you want to see him all of a sudden. He reported to me that he lost contact with you months ago. Last I heard, you wanted nothing to do with him."

"I saw the article in the paper. I wanted to make sure he's still alive."

She nodded but didn't reveal whether he had survived or not. "You were the one he was recruiting most recently," she stated, disappointment tainting her words. "Not his best attempt, I might add."

"Yes, and yes," I answered and began to stand again in hopes I could go and see Phoenix. I wanted answers, and I didn't want to have to go through an hour-long interview before I got them. "If I can just find him—"

"Sit!" she gritted through clenched teeth while slamming her fist onto the desk, rattling the neat pile of papers she had recently created.

The Upper, as they called her, rolled her neck as if she were attempting to release the tension built up by me. Her eyes were closed as she took a minute to inhale deeply.

My spine straightened, and I eased back into the seat while holding my breath, speechless.

"I'm sorry," she exhaled heavily and opened her eyes. "My apologies."

"I, uh— it's okay," I murmured submissively and accepted I wouldn't be leaving until she allowed it. "I just want to know if he's still—"

"Oh, the price we pay for freedom," she chuckled, ignoring what concerned me. "Sometimes I wonder if it's even worth it." Then she started to nod her head rapidly as she organized the papers a second time. "Oh, it'll be worth it!" she growled passionately.

For a moment, it was as if she was having a private conversation with herself. I didn't want to interrupt and anger her further, so I didn't dare say another word.

Once her papers were in a neat pile again, she released another long breath and smiled at me. Calm seemed to wash over her each time she inhaled deeply, but her grin seemed forced. "I would like to ask you a couple of questions if you don't mind," she said. "Then I will give you the answers you came here for."

I nodded, agreeing. What other choice did I have?

"Have you considered helping the cause even though the recruitment process didn't go as smoothly as it should've?"

"No, ma'am," I replied, unsure why I was suddenly referring to her as ma'am. It seemed like the right thing to do. She had a sense of authority radiating from her.

She sighed, disappointed, her body becoming more tense. "Even with all the new incentives we put in the paper?"

I shook my head, hoping I wouldn't enrage her by my honesty. I could picture her reaching her boiling point, grabbing me by the neck, and tossing me out the window.

"You know, we could win this war," she stated confidently.

"That was what Phoenix always said."

"It's the truth," she continued. "We're this close to taking back what is rightfully ours." She held up her hand and pinched her fingers together. "This close!"

"That's good…" I trailed off, unsure of how to respond.

"Phoenix told me your family has been producing UV lights, perimeters, and whatnot?"

"Mhmm," I replied, wondering if there would ever be an end to the interrogation.

"I've seen them mounted at the gas station, the one the lower ranks like to hang out at. I feel like the lights would do sufficient damage in the right hands."

"I don't know. I— I guess they could. I've never used it on a vampire firsthand, but my grandpa says they fry them and make them turn to ash within seconds."

A satisfied smirk formed on the lady's face. "Hmm," she hummed. "Could be more useful than silver bullets."

"I-I guess… maybe," I mumbled.

The Upper leaned forward, resting her elbows on the desk. "What if I were to give you a different offer? What if I were to say the government would be willing to supply your family with food for the rest of the war and even after?"

What she was offering didn't seem real, but I didn't want anything to do with the New Military, so it didn't matter what she was trying to bribe me with.

"No, thank you," I said firmly but politely.

"Ah-ah. Hear me out," she went on. "What if I were to say if you helped us win the war, you'd be taken care of, your *entire family* would be taken care of. No worrying about your next meal, no more dangerous outings, and your grandpa… how old is he?"

"He just turned ninety-one."

"Wow, that's getting up there. Do you really want your ninety-one-year-old grandpa to live his last years slaving away, making lights?"

"He keeps people safe," I explained. "He's proud of what he does."

"As he should be, but don't you think it's time for you to take the reins and give him a break?"

"I-I, uh…" Talk about a guilt trip. "My brother and I help as much as we can."

"You'll have the finest foods. The best of the necessities," she continued. "You'd be set for life. Your grandpa wouldn't have to worry about you and your brother starving to death after he's gone. More importantly, if we win the war, which we most definitely can, your grandpa can rest easy knowing you will be safe from vampires. Don't you want to go out at night and not have to worry about infinite dangers? Phoenix told me how much you love stargazing."

I felt violated. Everyone knew so much about me without my consent. Fire ran through my veins as I thought about Phoenix manipulating me and toying with my feelings.

"No, thank you," I answered, frustrated.

She sighed again but even louder. I noticed her grinding her teeth, trying to keep her cool.

"Seems like there's no convincing you," she said. "I guess I'm to blame, too, for this. Well, just know, you could be the deciding factor in ridding this planet of the monsters that own the night."

"Are we done now?" I asked as politely as I could. "Can you please just tell me if Phoenix is alive or not?"

"He is," she said without emotion.

"Thank God," I breathed in relief. "Can I see him now?"

She nodded and allowed me to leave.

The officer waiting outside the Upper's office didn't say a word as I followed him down the stairs. The place he took me to was familiar. It was the same room they threw the holiday ball in, but instead of rows of tables filled with food, there were rows of cots filled with injured soldiers.

"Oh, dear God," I gasped.

"Right this way," my guide told me and led me through endless bandaged and bloodied bodies.

Then I spotted someone familiar a few cots away. Frankie slept with his arm in a sling, and he had quite a few scratches on his face too.

"Hey, man. It's time to get up," a guy said, walking toward Frankie while holding a cup of water in one hand and pills in the other.

It was Phoenix. He was alive! And without another thought, I ran up and wrapped my arms around him, causing the water in the cup to slosh back and forth and spill onto Frankie.

"What the hell?" Frankie said angrily while sitting up, alarmed. He wailed in pain as he clenched his ribs that must've been bruised or maybe broken.

"Delilah?" Phoenix whispered like he'd seen a ghost.

"You're alive," I told Phoenix.

"Yeah, I'm fine," he said, confused.

Phoenix's hands were still full. It felt weird he wasn't hugging me back.

"I saw you in the paper," I explained, letting him go.

Phoenix placed the pills in Frankie's hand—the one that wasn't bound to the sling. Frankie glared at me while taking his medication. Then he closed his eyes again and went back to his restful state. He must've felt terrible if he didn't have anything inappropriate to say to me.

"I didn't think I'd see you again," Phoenix said, and I could sense he was upset.

"Can we talk?" I asked.

"I guess we can… since you're here," he replied with coldness radiating from his voice.

Phoenix had every right to be mad at me, so I didn't blame him for his animosity toward me.

"Come on," he said, tilting his shoulder toward the door leading outside.

I followed him, relieved I didn't have to stay in the infirmary longer.

Once we stepped outside, Phoenix leaned his back against the stone wall of the castle and folded his arms across his chest. It seemed as if he was avoiding eye contact.

"So, what do you want to talk about?" he asked flatly.

"I just wanted to make sure you were okay," I explained.

"Yeah? Well, you did that. So, you can go back home now."

"Listen, Phoenix. I'm sorry I had to cut you out of my life."

"*Had to*?" he scoffed.

"You know what I mean."

"I know you made your decision," he said, biting the inside of his cheek.

"Just tell me what happened," I pleaded.

"Not much to tell. Got the shit kicked out of me and went unconscious for most of the fight. If it weren't for all the dead bodies that piled on top of me, I probably wouldn't be here talking to you right now."

"That sounds terrible…"

"Are we done here?" he asked with a clenched jaw.

"Okay, yeah," I replied, giving up. "I can see you don't want to talk, so I guess I'll go."

But just as I began to walk away, Phoenix grabbed my arm. "No, wait, I'm sorry," he sighed, turning me to face him. "I didn't mean to— it's been a rough couple of days."

"I can see that," I said hesitantly, taken aback by his sudden mood change.

"And it's been hard… It's been hard not seeing you," Phoenix said softly, his eyes finally making their way toward mine.

I fully intended to find out if Phoenix was alive and then leave. I made promises that I genuinely meant to keep. The last thing I wanted was to betray Nick, but if I was honest with him, maybe he wouldn't be upset. I would tell Nick right away why I went to see Phoenix and that my only purpose was to make sure Phoenix was alive. Nick would understand.

"The Upper made me another offer," I told Phoenix, steering away from where the conversation was going.

Luckily, Phoenix took the bait. "Oh, yeah?" he asked. "Was it a good one?"

"She said my family would have everything we needed… *forever*, but only if we help provide UV lights for the war."

"Let me guess, you told her no?"

I nodded. "You guessed right."

Phoenix let out a quiet chuckle. "There's no swaying, Delilah."

"I guess not," I added.

"Not even after seeing what you saw in the infirmary? You'd be saving a lot of lives, you know?" Phoenix pointed out.

"It's their choice."

"Yeah, it's their choice to sacrifice their lives because they believe in something better, something worth fighting for. If it weren't for them, it would be someone else. You should show a little gratitude."

"I— I do. I mean, I am grateful for their service. As you know, my grandpa served."

"Yeah, that's right," he said mockingly. "Just go on living in your little bubble and ignore what's going on in the world."

"Is this another recruitment tactic?" I sneered.

"Whatever, Delilah. Take my words however the hell you want," he said, frustrated. "I've got to get back to work. Don't worry about me. I'll be gone after we put this hive to rest, and you'll never have to see or think of me again."

I watched as Phoenix walked inside in disbelief, and I didn't try to stop him. I'm sure he'd be given the injection soon from the sound of it, and he'd become an entirely different person. He was better off without me on his mind and vice versa.

But if I thought we were better off avoiding each other, why was I crying as I walked back to the van? Why was my chest rising and falling so rapidly at the thought of never seeing him again? Why did it feel like I couldn't breathe after the fight I just had with Phoenix?

I pressed my back against the side of the van and slid down to sit on the grass. I didn't know what to expect. I hoped Phoenix was alive, and he was, but maybe I needed closure or resolution. Maybe I was wrong about my heart getting rid of the feelings I used to have for Phoenix. Maybe they were locked up for a time, a place where they went unnoticed. Maybe after seeing Phoenix again, those feelings escaped their cage—flooding my heart, reminding me how I truly felt about him.

# Chapter Twenty-three

## Those Three Hearts

Hearts can thrive with another.
Hearts can flourish from a single kiss.
Hearts can become more than expected.
Hearts can begin to transform into bliss.

I thought one heart was meant for one other.
I thought it wasn't possible to love two.
I thought loving was supposed to be simple.
I thought fate said I would be with you.

Hearts can shatter so easily.
Hearts can only bear so much.
Hearts can wither away like flowers.
Hearts can falter with a single touch.

I thought one heart was meant for one other.
I thought it wasn't possible to love two.
I thought loving was supposed to be simple.
I thought fate said I would be with you.

I didn't think it was wrong to love two people as long as I committed myself to one. I truly believed I could fully give myself to another if my will was strong enough. I could make the decision and ignore the conflict brewing within my heart.

# Chapter Twenty-four

## The Honest Me

The sun had begun to rise behind the endless hills that lined the horizon, painting the sky the same color as the peaches that grew on Nick's farm. The grass was tall and lush from the first spring rains, and Nick lay beside me with his hand entwined in mine while we watched the sunset sky transform into light sapphire.

"What's on your mind?" Nick asked as he glanced over at me. "You've been more quiet than usual."

My stomach felt heavy with guilt, and my heart was stained with worry. Nick had already given me too many chances, and I seemed to always take advantage of his grace. I didn't know if he'd forgive me again, but I knew what I had to do to rid myself of the shame.

"I-I… broke a promise," I admitted, my gaze fixated above. I couldn't bear to look Nick in the eyes.

Nick let go of my hand and grabbed his cowboy hat that was resting on his chest. He slowly sat up and placed it on his head. I could see the tension in his jawline building. "You saw Phoenix again," he gritted. Nick spoke as if it was a fact rather than a question.

I propped myself onto my elbow, nodded remorsefully, and picked a blade of grass from the earth. "Yeah," I replied, ripping the piece of grass into tiny pieces, making it my main focus to get through the rest of the conversation.

"Why?" Nick asked gently, hurt from my betrayal.

Nick made it harder than it should've been. He made the shame inside of me quadruple because he wasn't like a normal person. He was always slow to anger and never one to judge. He was always more kind than one would expect. If only he yelled more often, and let his temper fly once in a while, then maybe I wouldn't have felt so terrible for breaking my promise.

"I thought he was dead," I explained. "I saw an article in the newspaper."

"About the New Military?"

"They stormed the castle nearby…"

"Yeah, my dad and mom couldn't stop talking about it over breakfast when the news came out," Nick added. "I know what you're referring to."

"There was a picture in the paper, and Phoenix was— he was on a cot. I— I'm sorry I broke my promise to you."

"I— mmm! Delilah!" Nick lifted a tight fist and shook it. His lips were pursed like he wanted to curse my name to the Heavens. "Delilah! I just…" Then, his fist that was so tightly clenched relaxed into his lap, and he let out a deep sigh.

"I know I'm a terrible person. I-I was just worried, and I didn't think things through… I shouldn't be making excuses. I know what I did, and I didn't mean to hurt you again."

"You're not a terrible person," Nick said.

"I, um… I'm not?"

"No, I mean, I understand."

"You do?" I asked, surprised.

"I can't blame you for wanting to make sure someone was alive."

"You're too good for me, you know that, right?" I reminded Nick.

Nick's chin lowered as he took in my confession. I couldn't see anything but the top of his hat when all I wanted was to stare into his earthy eyes and apologize a hundred more times.

After what seemed like a lifetime, Nick eventually looked up. "So… is he alive?"

"Huh?" I asked, confused.

"Is Phoenix alive?" Nick clarified.

"Oh, uh, yeah, he's okay. He's alive."

Nick chuckled softly to himself.

"What's so funny?" I wondered, taken aback by Nick's laughter.

"Wish I could say I wasn't disappointed by that answer," he admitted.

"You don't mean that."

Nick shrugged. "If he didn't make it, then I wouldn't have to worry about losing you."

I scoffed, "You're not going to lose me."

"You sure you can say that so confidently?" he asked.

"Yes," I said sternly and placed my fingertips on Nick's cheek, turning his gaze to where it mattered most. "I choose you."

"Yeah?" he asked, a thin smirk appearing.

"Yeah," I breathed. "I choose *you*."

I kissed Nick fiercer than the tornados that swept the land. I kissed him like there was no one else that could compare to him, like my lips pressed against his was the only thing I would ever need to survive.

# Chapter Twenty-five

## Delivery Gone Wrong

"It was supposed to be slightly cloudy with a chance of drizzles," Grandpa said as we sat in the van.

Ben peered out the window, examining the heavy rain which was the culprit for us getting stuck on the dirt road back to our house.

"If I knew it was going to rain cats and dogs, I would've told you to go the longer way," Grandpa explained.

I pressed my foot on the gas again to try and get the van loose, but the tires spun in place, and it was no use.

"I told you, stop doing that!" Grandpa said frustratedly. "You're only making things worse. Just wait until Nick gets here with his truck."

I slammed my palms on the steering wheel, annoyed at how helpless we were.

"She thinks she knows best," Ben murmured.

Just as I was about to say something smart to counter Ben's remark, I was distracted by Nick pulling his truck around to the front of the van. I hopped out, instantly becoming drenched. Nick quickly retrieved the chain with the hook from his truck and attached it to the van.

"Thank you for coming," I told Nick as the sun began to descend in the sky.

"Of course. Let's hope this works," he said and ran back to the truck.

I returned to the driver's seat, hopeful we'd be unstuck within seconds, but as I watched Nick's truck through the front windshield, his truck tires spun, splattering mud, unable to gain enough traction.

Nick yelled for me to gas it, thinking if we worked together, we could get the van out. But it was still useless. Nick and I stood in the rain again, trying to figure out how to resolve the issue.

"I should've brought the tractor," Nick said. "I didn't think it was this bad. It's like a swamp out here."

"I don't think it's ever rained this hard," I replied.

Nick nodded. "Get back inside, and I'll get the tractor. It'll be a while, though, since it doesn't go as fast."

"Okay," I said and retreated to the van to get some cover.

"What's going on now?" Ben asked from the back seat.

"Nick is going to get the tractor, but it's going to be a while until he returns," I explained.

Grandpa glanced at the sky, worried by the cloud coverage and lack of sunlight. "Hopefully, it doesn't take him too long."

"I don't want to die," Ben said.

"Everything's going to be fine," I said confidently.

"Why didn't you call Chad to come and get us?" Ben wondered. "He's the one with the tow truck."

"Because I don't have Chad's number memorized," I snapped, "and Nick's place is closer to where we are at the moment."

"Tow trucks are faster than tractors," Ben continued to argue. "Go back to the house where you used the phone and tell Chad we're stuck."

"I already told you I don't know Chad's number. If you, by some miracle, have his number memorized, you're more than welcome to use your own two feet," I pointed out.

"Okay, kids, that's enough," Grandpa said. "I'm sure Nick will be back sooner than we think, and Chad is probably about to close up for the night anyway. There's nothing else we can do but be patient and wait."

"Go get the bag and light from the back of the van," Grandpa told Ben.

"Good idea," Ben replied, his voice shaking.

"We're going to be fine," I repeated, but less assured than before.

"Let's hope so," Grandpa added.

I nodded, but panic began to set in when I gazed out the window into the dark forest, reminding me of the woods I was dragged through, the place I thought would lead me to my grave.

Luckily, Grandpa knew how to get my mind off a stressful situation. "So, Delilah, you never told me how your trip to the base was. Was your friend all right?" he wondered, changing the subject.

"Huh?" I asked, peeling my eyes away from the trees.

"Your friend," Grandpa said again. "Is he well?"

"Oh, yeah… he's fine, but they are in desperate need of soldiers. Many didn't make it, and there are a lot that are wounded," I explained.

"Hmm," Grandpa hummed like he was reminded of his days in the military. "It's the price of war and fighting for what's right."

"You believe that?" I asked, skeptical.

"Believe what?" Ben asked, sliding the light into the back seat.

"Grandpa and *I* are having a conversation," I sneered at Ben.

"Sorry," he apologized in a snooty tone.

"Yes," Grandpa continued. "Freedom never comes without a price. Nothing worth fighting for is ever simply handed over."

"You sound a lot like Phoenix," I grumbled.

"It's a tough job, but someone has to do it," Grandpa said, stretching his stiff leg under the dash. "I have something to tell you both. It's important."

It seemed as if Grandpa was about to reveal a secret he'd been hiding. I wondered what he had to say, and why did he want to tell us now while we were stuck in the mud?

"I've been working on a project," Grandpa began.

"You have another customer?" Ben asked.

"Not exactly. It's a project I've been working on since you two were born."

"Like what kind of project?" Ben wondered.

"Something I strongly believe will help end the war," Grandpa continued. "I've invented a different kind of light that can be used as a weapon."

"But you've already built hundreds of perimeters," I pointed out.

"This one is more of an offensive weapon than a defensive one," Grandpa added.

"It sounds awesome, but you're not making any sense, Gramps," Ben said, intrigued. "What do you mean? Is it like—"

"Can you just shut up for a second and let Grandpa finish?" I scoffed.

Ben rolled his eyes and folded his arms across his chest, but he didn't say another word.

"The plans are in the basement, and they are locked away in the safe with the guns. The past couple of years,

I've only been able to make a dozen. Light bombs are what I like to call them. They took a while to perfect and are time-consuming to make, but they are very effective. Think of them like the sun," Grandpa explained, forming a small ball with his hands, no bigger than a tennis ball, "with the power and intensity of the sun."

"So, why are you telling us about these now?" I asked.

"Many reasons," Grandpa sighed. "That night Phoenix brought you home, he told me a bit about the hives. I suppose I can thank you for that information seeing as you brought him to my door. I've been staying up later than usual ever since I found out there is a hive nearby."

"I thought you were trying to avoid us," Ben jeered.

"Ben!" I yelled.

"What do you mean?" Grandpa wondered, confused.

"Oh, nothing. Ben just… we just know it's been hard after losing Dad and Mom. How you have a hard time— I know I look a lot like them," I finished, not wanting Ben to say something even more stupid.

"Delilah," Grandpa said softly while stroking the back of my head. "You do remind me of your dad in more ways than one, I'll admit, but I don't try to avoid either of you. My goal in life, ever since you two were born, was to keep you kids safe. That's why I don't sleep. That's why I spend every waking moment in the basement, to keep what matters most to me safe!"

Ben leaned forward from the back seat and placed a hand on Grandpa's shoulder. Grandpa patted Ben's hand and smiled at both of us. "You two are my world."

"We love you too," Ben said softly.

"Anyway!" Grandpa continued. "I wasn't sure how the light bombs could make a difference, seeing as the vampires need to be in one place at the same time. The bombs can wipe out endless numbers of monsters as long as they are confined to a certain area. Once I found out there were hives, I knew how the bombs should be used. You can help Phoenix and the—"

"I told him I wasn't going to help," I interrupted.

"But why?" Ben wondered.

I guess I didn't have a good explanation. "B-because."

"Because why?" Ben asked, annoyed.

"Because they lie to people," I answered hotly.

"So do you," Ben pointed out.

"I-I know, and I said sorry," I reminded him through gritted teeth. "But it's not the same. They manipulate people in worse ways."

"How so?" Grandpa chimed in.

I shook my head. "Never mind," I said. "You guys won't understand."

"They might've gone about things in the wrong manner, but their hearts are in the right place, Delilah," my grandpa mentioned.

"If you say so," I grumbled, and then I raised my voice in frustration, "and you know what? They tried bribing me again to help the cause. Can you believe that?"

"What'd they offer?" Grandpa asked.

"To give us supplies and food for as long as we need."

"And you refused?" Ben scoffed in disbelief.

"You know how many people are struggling to make ends meet, and the New Military has all the finest amenities? I think they could spare some without something in return," I added.

"No payment or food or supplies will ever be enough for the men and women who put their lives on the line," Grandpa said, upset.

"I'm sorry, Grandpa. I didn't mean to sound—"

"Until you walk in their boots, don't judge, Delilah," Grandpa reminded me.

I hung my head low. "You're right." Grandpa was right. Phoenix was right, and I had been so selfish.

"I wanted to tell you because I know my time is ticking," Grandpa explained. "And I need to know you guys will continue my work. Tomorrow, we can practice building a light bomb together." Grandpa placed a gentle hand on the side of my head again and smoothed my hair against my head. "I love you, kiddos. I know you guys will do wonderous things when I'm gone."

"Stop talking like that, Grandpa." I didn't want to think about Grandpa leaving us. "You know I hate when you do that."

"I can't deny the inevitable," Grandpa countered.

Just then, Nick returned, and the sun began to slip past the horizon.

"Look, it stopped raining," Ben mentioned, hopeful we'd be on our way home soon.

"Things are looking up," Grandpa added, and we all got out of the van since the rain had stopped.

Nick hooked up the chain again. "Ol' Faithful should get you out of here in no time," he said, referring to his family's tractor.

In less than a minute, Nick freed the van from the muddy hole I had dug it into.

Nick jumped out of the tractor. "Done and done," he smirked.

I hurried over and wrapped my arms around him. "You are the best. Our knight in shining armor," I said with a hint of sarcasm, but grateful as ever.

Nick patted the hood of the tractor. "Thanks to my trusty steed," he joked along.

Grandpa shook Nick's hand. "Thanks for the help. I'll have to pay you back for everything."

"No need, Mr. Summers. It was my pleasure," Nick said, tilting the brim of his hat.

"We all should get going," Grandpa announced.

Everyone looked at the horizon simultaneously and stared for a few seconds in horror as the moon began to rise.

"Yeah, you're right," Nick replied shakily.

"Hurry up, now, and get home safely," Grandpa told Nick before hobbling to the van.

I gave Nick a quick kiss before saying goodbye and turned to join Grandpa. "I'll call you when we get home," I told Nick.

He nodded and got back in his tractor, "Please do. I won't be able to sleep not knowing if you made it home okay."

"Bye, Nick," I waved, but before I knew it, he was far enough down the road to where I could barely make out his tractor.

When I turned back around to get into the van, I expected Ben to be sitting in the back seat. I expected him to be yelling at me to hurry up, but instead, he was unmoving like one of the spruces in the forest. He stood on the grass, past the muddy road, while staring off into the woods.

"Ben, what are you doing?" I asked, confused.

"Shh!" he snapped.

"What?" I said, meeting his hostility.

"Do you hear that?" he asked, whispering.

"I don't hear anything. Let's go," I urged.

"There's something out there," Ben said, his voice trembling.

"All the more reason to get going!" I told Ben.

Again, I thought about my near-death experience. It was déjà vu. I grabbed Ben's arm and attempted to yank him toward the van, but he didn't budge.

"Let's go!" I shouted again.

Ben shook his head, releasing himself from whatever had a hold over him. "Yea-yeah. Let's go," he said, looking at me with horror glazed over his eyes.

I nodded confidently. "We're going to make it home," I assured him, and we began walking toward the van with me leading the way.

But then Ben's scream rang through the damp air, "Delilah!" I never heard him scream like that before.

I quickly turned to see what had happened. It was like I was trapped in the same nightmare, and it was impossible to escape the horrors of the night.

A vampire with eyes as dark as the shadows in the forest had wrapped her arms around Ben from behind him. Ben was frozen again, and tears began to trickle down his cheeks.

"Delilah, h-help m-me," he stammered.

"Aw," the vampire cooed and ran one of her sharp fingernails that was as long as a petal on a sunflower along the side of Ben's cheek. "You're precious. My queen is going to love you," the vampire giggled like she was amused by Ben's vulnerability.

"Let him go!" I yelled, doing my best to hide the terror growing within me.

"Oh, hi, there," she smiled at me and sniffed the air in my direction. "This must be your brother."

"I said, let him go!" I gritted louder, balling my hands into fists. I could see her fangs, and they seemed short, which allowed me to conjure more courage. "You will not be taking him to your queen!"

As the vampire held Ben against his will, memories began flooding through me. I thought about all the hurtful jeers siblings say to one another. I remembered all the good times we had together growing up in a world we shared with monsters. Memories of leaning on one another when we lost Dad and all the talks about what we thought Mom was like flashed in my mind.

I thought about how much I would miss Ben if I lost him, how I couldn't bear seeing him dragged away to the hive to be changed into a soulless creature. He was my brother, the same flesh and blood. I loved him, and I'd do whatever it took to save him.

The vampire laughed so hard that her head tilted back to the moon above as if I said something funny.

"I said…" I began again.

"Let him go!" Grandpa shouted from behind me as he flipped the switch to the light he had retrieved from the van.

A beam of bluish-purple shot through the night sky toward the vampire. She wailed loudly, releasing Ben as she closed her eyes tightly. Her legs crippled, and her elbows, wrists, and fingers contorted in pain. Before she realized what the cause of her death was, she had turned to ash.

"Ben!" I screamed as I ran over to him. I fell beside him, joining him on the muddy road. I wrapped my arms around him tighter than I ever had before. "Are you okay?"

"Just dandy," he joked, poorly shaking off the shock.

"You kids are going to be the death of me," Grandpa said breathlessly, turning the light off.

"Come on," I told Ben, guiding his arm over my shoulders to help him up.

Grandpa continued to urge us into the van, "Let's get—"

I glanced up to see why Grandpa stopped mid-sentence, and my heart plummeted to my stomach when I saw a blur circle around him. Another vampire had made his way to us and was standing beside Grandpa with a smug expression.

This vampire was different, though. His fangs were long and hung over his bottom lip, and his hair flowed freely past his hips. The hem of his raven cloak dragged along the muddy ground, and the gold band around his skinny waist reflected the moonlight. All of us, including the vampire, seemed frozen in time as we stared at Grandpa.

Grandpa's eyes widened, and the flashlight he had in his hand seemed to slip out of his grasp, falling to the ground. Grandpa slowly lifted his hands to his neck as blood began to trickle down his chest, staining his jacket with bright red. My gaze shot from my grandpa to the vampire who ran his pointed fingernail along the tip of his tongue, which was grossly dangling from his mouth.

"Not as tasty as I was hoping, but what was I hoping for in such an elderly human?" the vampire murmured disappointedly to himself. "I shouldn't have such high expectations."

"Grandpa!" I wailed when I realized what had happened.

I ran over to him as he fell to his knees.

"There's not much you can do now," the vampire whispered as if he were chatting about the weather, still licking Grandpa's blood off his fingernail.

I couldn't think about the abomination standing next to me. All I could think about was saving Grandpa. I placed my hands over his in hopes of stopping the bleeding, but I could feel his grasp become weaker. Strength was absent as he collapsed into my arms.

"You're going to be fine," I told him through heavy sobs. "Ev-everything's going to be okay."

Grandpa tried to speak, but it was more of gurgling sounds than coherent speech.

"Shh, Grandpa," I urged. "Don't talk. You'll only make things worse."

But Grandpa didn't listen, and I knew what he was trying to tell me by the way his mouth moved. He was trying to tell me that he loved Ben and me. Grandpa removed one of his hands from his neck and held it to my cheek while doing his best to smile, pretending he wasn't in pain.

"Please, Grandpa," I cried softly. "Please. You're— everything is going to be— I— we love you too. I'm going to get you to someone who can help."

Then Grandpa's body went completely limp, his hand fell from my cheek, and his eyes closed.

"It's done," the vampire said nonchalantly. "Can't use the old ones. They aren't quite as spry once they hit a certain mark."

The only two things I could hear were Ben wailing loudly behind me and my heart violently pounding inside of my head. I continued to hold Grandpa in my arms and screamed into the unforgiving night sky. I never felt so much misery in all my years. I would've stayed there forever, holding the man who raised me. I could've let the agony infest me as I hung onto my grandpa's corpse. I didn't want to let him go. I needed him. *We* needed him, and no matter how many times Grandpa spoke about leaving us, nothing could prepare Ben and me to live our lives without him. I didn't want to believe he was gone. I couldn't believe such a thing…

But the panic in Ben's voice as he yelled my name again caused me to snap out of the continuous downward spiral Grandpa's death was sending me through. The vampire who killed Grandpa was holding Ben upside down by his ankle. Ben was a rabbit caught in a snare, and he was helpless.

I laid Grandpa's body gently on the ground and stood, fists and teeth clenched. I wouldn't dare lose Ben, too.

"Run, Delilah," Ben quivered.

"I'm not going to let him take you," I said as convincingly as possible.

The vampire smirked without moving. "Don't worry, darling," he cooed. "Another is right behind me to fetch you. You won't be left behind."

"Why are you searching for humans? I would've assumed older vampires didn't h-have t-to do such, um… *lowly* jobs. D-did you get demoted?" I said, hoping to stall and keep him there for a moment longer.

He moved Ben to the side, still holding him by the ankle. Ben's face was flushed due to the blood rushing to his head. The vampire let out a hiss, displaying his fangs in all their glory. He was offended by my remark.

"How dare you question my place in the vampire hierarchy!" he spat.

"You guys desperate or some-something?" I stuttered.

"You'd like to think that, wouldn't you?" he sneered.

Ben's eyes rolled to the back of his head as he fainted.

"Ben!" I screamed.

The vampire sighed like he didn't want to be out in the night just as much as me, and I knew he was going to run off with Ben before I could say another word. The moon was at its highest, and it didn't seem like the night could become any darker. I knew that was the last time I would ever see my brother.

But rather than witnessing a blur dragging Ben to the woods, three things happened simultaneously. One—the vampire holding Ben wailed so loudly, I had to cover my ears. His high-pitched scream drowned out the sound of the blade that cut through his wrist. Two—Ben fell, hitting his head hard, but luckily, the ground was still soft from the rain. And three—the vampire grasped his forearm that was spurting out blood.

"*You*," the vampire said to me as if he was accusing me of something.

"Me?" I wondered, confused.

Then someone brushed past me, and I wasn't certain the vampire was talking to me. He tilted his nose higher and sniffed the air around him.

"Familiar," he said, scanning the area. "Scents are familiar."

"Wh-what?" I asked softly.

"I remember your scent in the woods… I mean, two scents," he said, taking a defensive stance, still grasping his arm tightly. "That night… when our scouts didn't return, but they were so close to home. *You* must've been the one who led them to our hive!"

"I-I…" I stammered.

"*You* are one lucky kitten," he chuckled in pain. "But remember kitty cats only have so many lives. Tell me, how many have you used up? *You*… yes, I remember your…"

I didn't fully understand what the vampire was rambling about. Maybe he'd lost too much blood, or maybe he was in shock. I wasn't sure if vampires even reacted the same way humans did to a lost limb…

"Funny, because no one will remember you after tonight," a stranger growled through the chilled air. His voice sounded close, but he was nowhere in sight.

I couldn't believe someone was there to save us—to save me… again.

Soon, a figure seemed to emerge out of nowhere from the darkness of the night. He stood facing the vampire with his back toward me. The man wore the same gear and seemed the same height as Phoenix, but his voice sounded slightly off, and whoever it was, he stood differently. The man's body was thicker, and his demeanor was fiercer, so I was almost certain it couldn't have been Phoenix. What I was sure of, though, was that we were saved.

But then suddenly, another male vampire dressed in similar clothing, emerged from the trees and took his place by the injured vampire.

Even though I wasn't certain it was Phoenix, there was still a part of me that thought it could be. "Ph-Phoenix?" I whispered.

The man glanced over his shoulder at me, which seemed strange because why would he dare take his eyes off the threats in front of him? But when he looked at me, I noticed the violet rings emanating from his eyes.

"Get Ben into the van," he ordered, his voice still deep and unrecognizable.

I was scared to move him in case he was badly hurt. "B-but," I stammered.

"Do it now!" the man's voice boomed, and I crawled over to Ben, realizing if the vampires killed the soldier, Ben would be a sitting duck.

Ben was quite a bit taller than me but skinnier than a twig. He probably didn't weigh much more than me, but it was still difficult to move him. I struggled, falling into the mud over and over again while trying my best not to focus on the fight going on in front of me. Although I couldn't make out much of what was going on since they were moving so fast in the darkness.

I looked behind me to see how much farther I needed to go before reaching the van. I was almost there, just a few more feet.

I opened the door to the back seat of the van and tried to pick Ben up to set him on the seat, but it was no use. I didn't have an ounce of strength left. I fell to the ground, out of breath. My legs and arms felt like limp noodles.

"Come on," I said, giving myself a pep talk. "Ben wouldn't let anything happen to you. Do the same for him." But what brought back my strength was when I looked at Grandpa lying on the ground, lifeless. I wouldn't let what happened to Grandpa happen to Ben.

I stood again, adrenaline pumping, and placed my hands under Ben's arms. I lifted him into the van and hurriedly buckled myself into the driver's seat. I cranked over the engine and put the van into gear, but just as I was about to floor it to make our escape, I abruptly slammed on the brakes, my lungs filled to the brim, gasping deeply.

I couldn't believe what I was looking at, or rather *who* I was looking at. It was Phoenix standing in front of the van, the headlights creating a spotlight on him. He held a circular sword in each of his hands. Ash swirled behind him before the remains of the vampires' bodies were swept away with the wind. He calmly placed his weapons in their place on his back.

I put the van in park, but I didn't bother taking the time to turn off the ignition. I bounded out of the van and rushed over to Phoenix, wrapping my arms around him as rain began to pour again. I expected Phoenix to say something or at least embrace me. Or maybe that's what I *wanted* Phoenix to do, but then I remembered how upset he was the last time I saw him. He didn't want anything to do with me. He made it clear that if he didn't die from storming the nearby hive again, he would move on to his next mission. Ending the vampire species was his number one priority.

I wouldn't, in a million years, have expected him to show up again and save me. I would've bet everything that he would've never broken down the wall we built between us. Why did Phoenix always come back for me?

As I embraced Phoenix, I assumed his breathing would be heavier after defeating the vampires. I expected his body to be riddled with injuries, and for him to be exhausted, but he stood strong and unwavering.

"Phoenix?" I asked, looking up at him.

His violet eyes glanced down at me, and I immediately released him. Was he still Phoenix?

"Y-your eyes," I whispered while slowly backing away.

"I'm still me," he said in a deep voice.

I paused from distancing myself when I saw that the breeze still caught his blonde hair, causing it to fly wildly like it always did, and when I inspected his eyes more closely, they almost looked the same. Inside of the violet rings, his eyes were still the deepest shades of blue. There was a lot that reminded me of the "old" Phoenix, but there were a lot of differences, too. When he spoke, no matter what he said, it seemed as if there was rage riding on the tail end of each word. Phoenix seemed more tense than usual like he was ready for a fight and couldn't relax, even though no threats were nearby.

"Are you all right? D-do you feel okay?" I wondered, concerned for his wellbeing.

"We can talk more once we get you home," Phoenix said, which was a good idea.

Phoenix helped me lift my grandpa into the back of the van. Somehow, I managed to keep it together and not revert to the state I was in while holding Grandpa's dead body in my arms.

I closed the cargo door and was about to get into the driver's seat, but Phoenix stopped me.

"Maybe I should drive," he insisted.

I nodded, knowing it would be safer if Phoenix took the wheel. I was pretty shaken up, and when I reached for the door to the passenger side, I realized my hand was unsteady, tremoring uncontrollably.

"I should be asking *you* if you're okay," Phoenix mentioned before heading toward the house.

"I don't know. I think I'm still in a state of shock," I admitted.

"That's normal," he said.

I glanced over my shoulder to check on Ben, who still hadn't moved. "M-maybe we should— what if he's not—" I stammered, concerned about Ben.

"Don't worry, he's still breathing. His heart is beating normally," Phoenix said without emotion, his eyes forward, only focused on the road. "He's going to be fine. Might have a killer headache when he wakes, but he'll live."

"How do you know that?" I asked, confused.

"I can hear better now," Phoenix explained.

"Oh… right," I breathed heavily and sat silently the rest of the way home as I tried to sort out everything that happened—trying my best to cope with losing Grandpa.

When we returned home, it didn't feel the same without Grandpa. His chair would always be empty, and our home would never feel full without him. The basement was his sanctuary where I knew I would always find him, but now the space below the house was nothing but a reminder of what was taken away from my brother and me.

After putting Ben in his bed and taking the longest shower of my life, hoping to wash the pain away, I went into my room to see Phoenix sitting on the edge of my bed.

Once again, he was holding my notebook.

"I thought I told you that was private," I said more gently than expected.

He placed the book into the drawer. "I know, but I enjoy reading your poems. They deserve to be read."

How could I argue with such a sweet compliment? How could I tell Phoenix what to do after saving my life a second time? So, I didn't question what he read or scold him for invasion of privacy. I simply sat beside him, numb from the events that had unfolded.

"Thank you," I said softly.

"For what?" Phoenix asked, confused.

"For saving us… for saving *me*… again."

"I should've gotten to you sooner," he said, his voice just as tense, withdrawn, and without real emotion. "I should've been keeping a closer eye on you."

"What do you mean?"

"Ever since they gave me the injection, I— I guess you could say I've had a sense of urgency to make sure you're safe."

"You've been following me?" I wondered.

"I might've veered from the area I was assigned once or twice," he admitted, "maybe more…"

"So, you heard what was happening?"

Phoenix nodded.

"I didn't think you wanted anything to do with me, especially after the last time we saw each other. I thought you were mad at me and never wanted to see me again."

Phoenix stopped staring at his boots and looked up at me. "I didn't mean what I said. I should apologize. Pushing you away seemed like the only option, especially if— if…"

"If what?" I questioned, not understanding what Phoenix was trying to say.

He breathed deeply before speaking, "If… I can't have what I want."

"And what is it you want?"

"*You*," he said flatly. "After being injected, it's been harder to stay away from you. It's like I have an urge telling me to take what I want, what I *need*." I didn't understand how Phoenix's body could become more tense than it already was, and his fists were clenched tightly on his lap.

I scooted away from Phoenix, a bit frightened. "Sh-should I be worried?" I asked.

Then Phoenix realized he was scaring me and went through the process of taking deep breaths to relax. "I'm sorry," he apologized, doing his best to change his demeanor.

Surprisingly, it worked, and Phoenix no longer looked ready to maul somebody to death.

"I'm sorry," Phoenix repeated, his voice still deep, but I could tell he was embarrassed by his behavior. "I was aware of all the warnings they gave me before taking the injection, or so I thought. They didn't tell me about the side effects of controlling my desires. I will eventually learn to control them better. I didn't mean to frighten you. It-it's just that… I love you, Delilah."

"What?" I gasped, taken aback.

Phoenix smirked. "I've loved you for a while," he admitted.

"Y-you ha-have?" I stammered, wide-eyed in disbelief.

Phoenix let out a small chuckle. "Yeah. I did everything I could to deny my feelings for you, but the more you pulled away, or the more I told myself I didn't want to be around you, the more I realized I needed you."

"*Need*?" I whispered.

It still felt strange to feel wanted but stranger to be told I was needed.

Phoenix filled the room with angry-like laughter, and I didn't understand what was so funny.

"Why are you laughing?" I asked.

He held his stomach in his hands as he tried to control the laughter overtaking him. It took an entire minute before he was calm enough to speak. "I'm sorry," he said.

I was so confused. I didn't know what to say or ask. What could he possibly find so hilarious?

Phoenix sighed loudly. "I think that's the first time I've laughed like that since they gave me the injection."

My cheeks turned pink as peonies. "So, what was so funny?" I asked, annoyed and self-conscious.

"You're just so oblivious," Phoenix said.

My face became hot at the insults, and I bit the inside of my cheek, not wanting to say something I'd regret.

He continued as I fumed, his voice finally changing, reminding me of how he sounded before, "You're oblivious to how beautiful your soul is."

"H-huh?" I stuttered.

"It's so gentle and caring. You're oblivious to how you can balance the calming rage that's constantly brewing within me now. You're oblivious to how attractive you are, which makes you even more desirable."

My cheeks weren't pink anymore. They were bright red.

But Phoenix didn't stop, "You're oblivious to how much I truly care for you, and more so, you're oblivious to the fact that you love me too."

I was speechless, and I couldn't deny I had feelings for him, but I didn't dare allow myself to say how I felt out loud. And although I didn't speak, I stared as intently into Phoenix's eyes as he did mine. The longer I looked at him, the more I realized his eyes were more transcending than before. The beautiful blue sky was surrounded by glowing lilac which were sparks in the darkness of the room.

"I know you probably think the war is all I care about, but it's not," Phoenix explained.

"I know," I admitted. "I should apologize, too."

"Please, don't," Phoenix said.

"I didn't mean to hurt you. It-it's— people think you're dangerous, and I made promises, and…"

"Do *you* think I'm dangerous?" he asked, our eyes still connected.

I gulped loudly. "I… don't know."

"Are you willing to find out?" he whispered.

My heart beat wildly, and my palms were sweatier than on a hot summer's day. Did I want to find out? The emotions pulsing through my body overtook any logical thinking I might've had.

I nodded, and Phoenix placed his hand on the side of my neck to pull me in closer, his body tensing again. As soon as his lips touched mine, nothing else mattered. I didn't have to think about what happened to my family. I didn't have to worry about what the future held. All the pain I endured seemed to vanish.

Phoenix was right, and there was no denying it any longer…

I did love him.

# Chapter Twenty-six

## The Morning Of

Before it had gotten too late, Phoenix encouraged me to get some rest and promised he would stay the night. As passionate and animalistic as Phoenix was, he respected the boundaries. He held me until I'd fallen asleep in the most unselfish kind of way—he was there for me, and only me. It was comforting to have Phoenix beside me. I didn't want to be alone, especially since the next morning would be one of the most difficult mornings I would ever have to endure. I knew I would need to bury Grandpa and say my goodbyes.

Considering how exhausted I was, I assumed I would sleep the entire night without waking, but the rain beat hard on the rooftop. I rolled onto my side, searching for Phoenix, but I didn't feel his presence. I patted the space beside me for confirmation. He said he would stay with me. He promised…

I pulled back my covers when I noticed movement outside my window. The rain trailing down the windowpane made it hard to see what was going on, so I walked closer and pressed my nose against the cold glass. Phoenix was holding a shovel and digging a hole. He was still in his gear, which seemed waterproof, but his hair was drenched, and the droplets falling from the sky hit his face fiercely, which he seemed to ignore all too well.

The stars were still flickering in the sky, and the sun wouldn't be up for at least another few hours. I opened the window and yelled for Phoenix to come inside. He paused and brushed aside the wet hair that stuck to his brow. The rain stopped, and he glanced up at me, pausing from digging.

"I'm almost done," Phoenix said and thrust the shovel into the earth again.

I waited for Phoenix, awake in bed, until he came inside. I watched as Phoenix removed his weapons, unzipped his tactical vest, and set them on the chair. He dried his hair and the outside of his pants with a towel before lying beside me.

"Sorry I woke you," Phoenix apologized.

"It wasn't you. It was the rain," I explained.

"Yeah, it was raining pretty hard again."

"You didn't have to do that," I mentioned. "I could've prepared my grandpa's grave in the morning."

"I didn't want you to worry about that, not after everything you've been through."

"Aren't you tired?" I wondered.

"I don't need as much rest now," he explained.

"I see..."

"I was going to wait until the morning to ask," Phoenix began, "but since you're up, I ought to ask you now."

"What's that?"

"Your grandpa's hand was in his pocket, holding on to something."

I sat up, curious about what Phoenix was referring to, and he took a seat beside me.

"What was he holding?" I wondered.

"This," Phoenix said, pinching a metal ball between his fingers.

I took the ball from his hand and inspected the object, which was barely larger than a golf ball. It looked like it was made of silver and was completely smooth. I rolled it around in my fingertips, noticing a small cutout of a circle, which was the only etching on the ball.

"This is what he was telling Ben and me about. This is what he invented," I said, surprised by how simple it looked.

This tiny ball I was holding in my hand was supposed to be some type of deadly weapon?

"You know what it is?" Phoenix wondered.

I nodded. "He must've been trying to pull it out to use a-after… He was saying he had them locked away in the basement. I didn't think he had one in his pocket. Maybe he was trying to give it to me before he… you know."

"It's a weapon of some sort?" Phoenix asked.

"Yeah, it's supposed to produce UV rays that extend farther than a typical bulb. The way my grandpa was explaining it made it seem like it would create a huge burst of light… or something. Grandpa was saying it can wipe out multiple vampires at once."

"Like how many vampires exactly?" Phoenix asked, seriousness tainting his voice.

"I don't know. Hundreds? Thousands? This is the first time I've seen one. Grandpa was telling us about it for the first time when we were stuck on the road."

"An *entire hive*?" Phoenix wondered, hopeful.

"Yeah, maybe."

"This is amazing," Phoenix said, sitting straighter. "This could end the war. I wonder how you use it?"

I shrugged. "Supposedly, there are instructions on how to build them in the basement," I sighed, disappointed, knowing Phoenix would never be able to live his life until the war ended. But really, would any of us be able to truly live until someone took back nightfall?

"I didn't mean to make this such a big deal," Phoenix said. "Although I didn't know your grandpa had something that could change the course of the war. Do you mind if I take it back to the base?"

"Yeah, of course," I replied and handed the ball back to Phoenix. It was the least I could do for all he had done, and I knew Grandpa wanted the New Military to put his invention to good use.

Phoenix slid the metal ball into his pocket. It seemed to take everything he had to put the topic of Grandpa's invention on the back burner. "Let's get back to sleep. After we give your grandpa a proper burial, then we can talk about the weapon some more. That is, if it's okay with you?"

As much as I didn't want to admit it, my grandpa's death ignited something inside of me. It was a fiery thirst for revenge. Before Grandpa's death, I wanted nothing to do with the New Military or helping them defeat the vampires. Before, I wanted to ignore the fact that there could be a chance of saving nightfall. I wasn't willing to sacrifice much to make a difference, but after witnessing Grandpa die at the hands of a vampire, I was willing to let the fire burn within me.

I was finally ready to fight back.

# Chapter Twenty-seven

## It Isn't Goodbye

It didn't feel right to put Grandpa in the ground without Nick. Nick was full of grace, but if I excluded him from the burial, would he have forgiven me? One thing I assumed that Nick would *never* forgive me for was having Phoenix present when we said our goodbyes. But how was I supposed to shoo Phoenix away after saving me twice and helping dig Grandpa's grave?

Phoenix didn't protest when he heard me on the phone telling Nick what had happened after he drove away in his tractor. He didn't show an ounce of jealousy when I told Nick he should come and help put my grandpa to rest. So, even though I had doubts, I still hoped Nick would show Grandpa the same courtesy as Phoenix did and set personal preferences aside.

It must've been wishful thinking, though, because it was almost as if Nick and Phoenix traded personalities that morning. Nick never lost his temper. I wasn't sure he even had one until that day, but Nick's anger burned hotter than the Idaho's sun on a scorching afternoon.

And as for Phoenix, I didn't think he could fully control his emotions, especially after the injection. But the more time I spent around Phoenix, the less animalistic he seemed, like being around normal people helped soothe the change within him.

Nick slammed the door to his truck while the rest of us stood around the hole in the ground where Grandpa lay, wrapped in a blanket.

"Hey, Nick," Ben said with his hands in his pockets.

Nick ignored Ben and walked over to where I was so he could murmur into my ear through a clenched jaw, "You didn't tell me *he* was going to be here."

I should've given Nick a heads up, but in the back of my mind, I thought Nick might've opted to pass on the burial if I told him the person I promised to stay away from would be there, too. I didn't want Nick to have any regrets, or maybe, if I was being honest, I wanted both Phoenix and Nick there with me when I said goodbye.

"I'm sorry," I apologized to Nick. "I should've told you."

Thankfully, Phoenix continued to stand in the background without stirring things up.

Ben cleared his throat and spoke, breaking the silence, which I was thankful for. "I guess I'll start," he said, and we all waited patiently to hear what Ben had to say with our chins lowered because it seemed like the right thing to do. "Grandpa was a badass…"

"Ben!" I scoffed.

"What?" he replied as if he hadn't said anything offensive. "It's true and a good thing. Grandpa was a survivor and kept us safe. He kept others safe, too. We loved him, but what I'll remember the most is his love for others and the sacrifices he made to keep others alive. Not many people could have done what Grandpa did."

I nodded, agreeing as my eyes became watery. "Do you want to go next?" I asked Nick, glancing over at him.

Nick's shoulders were slouched, and his demeanor wasn't the same as when he arrived. The thought of never seeing Mr. Summers again sank in deep, creating a void in his chest, which I knew of all too well. The only difference was the sorrow inside of Nick would heal. Time would eradicate his pain. The hole would become smaller and eventually dissipate, unlike the darkness that would forever grow in my heart. I knew the only way to rid myself of the hurt was to do something—something rebellious, something I never thought I would do in a million years.

Nick removed his hat and held it to his chest before speaking, and he took another moment to kick the dirt with his boots, trying to think of the right words. "I'm going to miss the family lunches on the farm. It'll feel strange with one less chair at the table. Family is the most important thing on the planet, and we loved you like family, Mr. Summers. *You* loved me like family, like I was your own flesh and blood," Nick whispered. "I-I'm going to miss talking to you about shotguns and your time serving. I'll even miss listening to you chat about your record collection. It was nice getting to know you while I could."

Nick started to choke up, and I placed a gentle hand on the side of his shoulder. "He liked that you were a better listener than Ben and me… and also interested in guns," I chuckled lightly.

Nick didn't continue. Instead, he placed the hat back on his head to hide the tears trickling down his cheeks.

"Thank you," I said softly to Nick.

Nick nodded, still doing his best to suppress his emotions.

I glanced over my shoulder to see if Phoenix was still hanging out in the distance, but instead, he walked toward me and joined the circle around Grandpa's grave. I didn't expect Phoenix to say anything because he'd only met my grandpa one time, and that one time happened to be an uncomfortable circumstance, or more bluntly, when I was almost taken to the local hive. I didn't know what Phoenix could possibly say, but I was glad he decided to speak.

Phoenix subtly slid his hand into mine, and I looked into his eyes, which were still familiar even though they had changed. Phoenix's gaze was unwavering when he spoke, his words filled with confidence, "While we look not at the things which are seen, but at the things which are not seen; for the things which are seen are temporal, but the things which are not seen are eternal."

"Corinthians," I whispered.

Phoenix nodded.

"Now you should say something, Delilah," Ben interrupted, and I abruptly pulled my hand away, remembering Phoenix and I weren't the only ones standing there.

"Right," I said nervously.

Nervous partly because I knew I would have some explaining to do with Nick after all was said and done, but mostly, I was nervous because I didn't want to say the wrong thing. Anger and pain had begun to consume every logical thought in my mind as soon as Grandpa was gone. Revenge had been on my list since the vampire killed him, and I feared the new hate I had for vampires would send me down a path Grandpa didn't want me to venture to.

"We love you, Grandpa. Thank you for teaching us how to survive. We are going to miss you."

And with that, Ben and I grabbed the shovels to put the man who raised us into the earth, always remembering the sacrifices he made for us.

# Chapter Twenty-eight

## Forever Forgiving Me

Phoenix left to return to the base. Ben went inside to drown his sorrows by burying his head in video games, and Nick and I sat on the back of his tailgate. I was thankful we were at least facing away from the oak tree where Grandpa's body lay so I could focus on what I needed to tell Nick.

"So…" Nick trailed off as his head hung low.

"*So…*" I repeated, postponing the inevitable.

At least Nick didn't seem angry like when he arrived. He seemed calm and empathetic, but realistically, that always made the guilt inside of me grow more rapidly.

"I'm sorry," I said, my eyes searching for Nick's that were hidden underneath the brim of his hat. "I'm sorry for everything. I'm sorry for being a terrible girlfriend, for being a terrible friend."

"You lost your grandpa and all. You don't need to apologize," Nick said flatly.

"I did lose him," I paused, aware I didn't deserve Nick's kindness, "but that's no reason to break promises."

"I'm sure you intended to keep them," Nick added.

I hopped down from the back of Nick's truck, frustrated. How could he make endless excuses for my behavior? How could Nick have been everything I thought I wanted, everything I knew I needed, but all I wanted was to break things off with him? I didn't deserve him, and I couldn't allow myself to keep hurting him.

"You've been through a lot," Nick continued.

"Stop!" I screamed, which finally drew in Nick's gaze.

He sat in silence with wide eyes, surprised by my reaction.

I didn't expect the conversation to become so heated, but I was finding that "killing a person with kindness" was a real thing!

"Why are you being so nice?" I said hotly. "Why are you *always* so nice?"

"Uh… sorry?" Nick replied as if he wasn't sure if an apology would bring me down a notch.

"Why are *you* apologizing?" I questioned, annoyed.

Nick raised his voice, becoming offended by my criticism. "You act like my willingness to forgive is such a bad characteristic."

I scoffed, "That's not what I meant."

I was envious that Nick could forgive so easily.

"Then what do you mean?" he wondered.

"I-I… don't know," I said, my arms dropping to my sides in defeat.

"What do you want, Delilah?" Nick asked gently.

"What?" I asked, distracted by how much I was wishing I could be more like Nick.

"Do you want to be with me?" Nick clarified.

I inhaled deeply, stalling, unsure of how to answer his question. If Nick knew what was good for him, he would've left me months ago.

"Should I take that as a no?" Nick asked, tired of waiting for an answer.

I didn't know what I wanted, or rather *who* I wanted. All I knew was I needed to rid the town of vampires. I wanted to hurt them as much as they hurt my family.

"I want to be with you," I revealed.

"Do you want to be with Phoenix too?" Nick asked, catching me off guard.

"I-I, um…" I stammered.

"I guess I have my answer," Nick said disappointedly.

"N-no. I mean, I don't know!" I replied, panicking, aware I wasn't giving Nick the right answers.

I couldn't tell Nick what he wanted to hear without lying. I couldn't be the person Nick needed me to be!

"You can't have both, Delilah," Nick said, stating the obvious.

"I know that," I breathed heavily. "I know…"

"So, what do you want to do?" Nick asked.

As if I hadn't cried enough since Grandpa's death. I thought for sure my tears had dried up. I didn't think it was possible for me to feel more pain.

"I-I *want* to kill vampires! All the vampires that took everyone away from me, I want them to feel the pain I feel!" I shouted in anger.

Nick continued to speak calmly, "How would you manage that?"

"It's possible. My grandpa invented a weapon. I can tell Phoenix believes it's the key to winning the war," I stated passionately.

"So, all of a sudden, you're just going to suit up and fight vampires?" Nick wondered, skeptical. "Like, you're going to go into one of those hives or something?"

"I— maybe? I think I could do it—"

"You might not make it back alive. Revenge is never the best solution."

I didn't know if it was the best answer or not. All I knew was I wanted the hurt to end, and time wouldn't give me a solution.

"Sometimes you have to take matters into your own hands," I added fiercely.

Nick stood from sitting on the tailgate and sighed, "Sometimes, forgiveness is better. Sometimes, not blaming yourself is the best way to heal wounds."

"Well, not all of us can be as *perfect* as you," I said too harshly.

Nick's lips pursed, and he nodded in frustration. Without saying a word, he closed the tailgate to his truck.

"Wait," I said. "I-I didn't mean that."

Nick scoffed. "It's okay, Delilah. I know you're hurting. People say things they don't mean when they lose people they love. Maybe we should talk after you do what you need to do? If anything, I'm hoping we can still be friends."

I still couldn't believe Nick was being so understanding, even after everything I did… after everything I said. I knew he would continue loving me, always forgiving me. He was perfect, too perfect for me, and too perfect for this world.

# Chapter Twenty-nine

## Believe in Me

I studied the blueprints in Grandpa's basement. I found the stash of light bombs he had begun making, and I sat where he used to sit, determined to make a difference and bring down the monsters of the night.

"You have a visitor," Ben shouted from above.

"Okay," I replied, too preoccupied to ask who it was.

"Is it all right if I send him down?" Ben asked.

"Yeah…"

"Good morning," Phoenix greeted me as he joined me in the basement.

I didn't expect Ben to follow behind him, but maybe he was curious about what I had been doing for the past hour.

"Hi," I answered, still examining the blueprints.

Phoenix sat beside me, and Ben planted himself down on the last step of the stairs.

"How are things going?" Phoenix asked.

"Good," I responded, "I think I understand how to build a light bomb, but it might take all day to build just one."

"Are those them over there?" Ben wondered, pointing to the bucket on the floor next to me. "Can I see one?"

I pulled one of the light bombs out of the bucket and tossed it to Ben.

"Cool," he breathed excitedly as he examined the ball more closely. "Is this a button?" Ben's finger was drawn to the circular etching on the ball.

"No!" Phoenix and I shouted simultaneously.

Ben froze with panic in his eyes. "Uh…"

"Sorry, don't do that in here, at least not without these on," I explained while holding up a pair of goggles.

"What are those?" Ben wondered.

"They help to block out the harmful rays caused by the light bomb," I explained.

"Yeah, the Upper made the mistake of setting off the one I brought back to the base. She said it felt like she was sprayed in the eyeballs with acid. Probably was worse because of the injection, but I'm sure she'll see clearly sooner rather than later."

"Sorry, I would've warned you if I knew," I mentioned.

"Injection?" Ben asked curiously, out of the loop. "Does that have something to do with your eyes being all weird?"

"I'm surprised Delilah hasn't told you about it by now," Phoenix responded.

"She doesn't tell me much," Ben spat.

"The military guys inject themselves with vampire DNA," I explained, hoping to make a long story short. "Makes them better fighters."

Ben's jaw instantly dropped wide open.

"It's not as bad as it sounds," Phoenix added.

"S-so, you're like a… vampire?" Ben stammered.

"No, I'm nothing like those bloodsuckers," Phoenix replied.

"But now you're jacked, like, super jacked. I didn't notice before, not with everything going on, but wow, yeah. I bet you get all the ladies now, or even more so than you used to," Ben gawked, "and your voice. I wish I could—"

"Ben, can you please stop," I begged. He was so embarrassing.

"It's fine," Phoenix chuckled. "So, should we get started?"

"Uh… yeah," I answered. "Looks like my grandpa salvaged all the parts we need to get a good start."

Ben stood and began walking upstairs. "I'm going to grab another chair."

"Why?" I asked.

"I'm not going to sit around while you guys get all the credit for killing the vampires," Ben replied.

"That's unusual," I murmured, surprised.

"What is?" Phoenix wondered.

"Ben… he's never been the first to volunteer for work," I pointed out.

"Big events can change people's lives forever. I'm sure your brother will never be the same, and neither will you," Phoenix added.

He was right. I wouldn't ever be the same, at least not until I killed a few hundred vampires.

"You know," Phoenix began, "we can bring all this stuff to the base and get more hands involved. The faster the production, the faster we can make our second assault."

"Uh," I hesitated, "if you don't mind, I would rather do this here. I just— *I* want to do this. I want to make sure they are made correctly. I don't want to fail."

I wanted to be where Grandpa worked. I felt like he was beside me, still guiding me as I sat where he spent countless hours grinding away.

"I understand. So, then, are you saying you're all in?" Phoenix wondered, hopefulness tainting his voice.

"Yeah," I said unwavering. "I sure am."

Out of the corner of my eye, I could see a smirk forming on Phoenix's face.

"I'm going to help end this war," I confirmed.

"Me too!" Ben shouted as he struggled to drag the chair down the stairs.

"Let me help you with that," Phoenix suggested, standing from his seat.

"No!" Ben demanded as if he had something to prove. "Sit back down. I got this."

Phoenix did as he was told, and Ben sat beside Phoenix and me, eager to get to work.

"So, how many of these do we have to make?" Ben wondered.

"I'm not quite sure…" I replied. "Phoenix, do you know how many?"

"Uh, well, the Upper said she wanted at least a couple hundred by the end of the month," Phoenix said hesitantly.

"Why didn't you tell me sooner?" I asked in shock. "That'll take months, not weeks."

"I didn't want to say anything until I… I mean, *you* were positive you wanted to jump onto this moving train," Phoenix explained.

"We have enough parts here for a good start, but not hundreds of light bombs," I pointed out.

"Why don't I make a list of parts that we need, and we can give it to the New Military?" Ben suggested. "Then they can hunt them down or maybe just buy them… seeing as they don't seem to be hurting for money."

"That's a great idea, Ben," I said, becoming more positive about our situation.

"I have lots of good ideas," Ben added sarcastically. "You just don't ever listen."

I didn't have time to humor him with a counter remark. "But I still don't see how we can make that many. Why do we need to make so many anyway? What do you guys plan on doing with all of them?"

"The Upper wants to end it with one swipe. Yes, the bombs are concentrated and extend far, but the castle the hive resides in is large, with many rooms, and there are hundreds of vampires," Phoenix told us. "She had the idea of putting the light bombs into fishnets, dispersing them throughout the castle, and then setting them off all at once. The hive is expecting us now. We don't have the element of surprise, so we have to do this a different way… a smarter way."

"I-I don't see how that would work, though," I said, beginning to worry about how things would play out.

"What do you mean?" Phoenix wondered.

"Well, you have to push the button on each bomb, right?" Ben chimed in.

"Yeah, exactly," I answered. "I don't know how we'd be able to set them off all at once."

"You can just wire them somehow," Phoenix suggested. "Make a remote?"

"It's not that simple…" I explained. "I-I'm not my grandpa."

"We have a couple of techs at the base. Maybe they could help?" Phoenix added.

"I don't know. I-I…" I trailed off, any ounce of positivity leaving my body.

"You can do it, Delilah," Ben encouraged. "If anyone can do it, you can. You aren't Grandpa by any means, and Grandpa would agree, but he'd also say that you have an opportunity to be even better than him and…" A cocky grin formed on Ben's face. "You have me to help you."

"I agree with Ben," Phoenix mentioned.

Everyone was counting on me, and Ben was right—Grandpa always believed in me. So, it was about time I started to believe I could achieve something great, something that could help save nightfall.

"Okay, I'll try," I said.

"You sure you don't want to take me up on the offer to get more help?" Phoenix reminded me. "I'm sure I could get something sorted out to where we rotate in and out of your basement."

I had no other choice but to accept Phoenix's offer.

I nodded my head, "Let's get this done."

# Chapter Thirty

## Here's to Tonight

One night left until the deadline.

One more night until Phoenix would have to fight again.

One night left until I could get my revenge…

Sparks sprinkled over the worktable as I welded the last piece onto the last light bomb we needed to finish. I set the welding gun down and sighed with relief that we completed the task. Phoenix made his way over to me and removed the welding mask I'd been wearing the last hour.

"We did it," he whispered.

I wiped the beads of sweat above my brow, nodded, and hugged him. "I couldn't have done it without your help."

"Your grandpa would be proud of you," Phoenix mentioned.

"Thank you," I said softly, letting him go. "We should probably get the rest of the light bombs over to the base."

"Trey and Mac said they would take care of the transportation for us," Phoenix said as he glanced over at the soldiers who had joined us that night in the basement.

Trey gave a casual salute. "You got it, boss."

"But shouldn't we help and make sure everything gets where it needs to be?" I asked Phoenix. "Don't you think the Upper will want to go over the plans with me?"

"The bombs will be in capable hands, and the Upper has already gone over them with you a dozen times," Phoenix reminded me.

"One more time couldn't hurt," I said, worried about how tomorrow night would pan out.

"You're exhausted," Phoenix pointed out. "You've been working nonstop for the past few weeks. I want to take you somewhere. You deserve this one night. You've earned it."

"I-I don't know if that's a good idea," I went on anxiously. "Maybe we should go with—"

Phoenix placed his hands on my shoulders in hopes of calming my nerves. "Everything is going to be fine. Why don't you take some time to relax and take a shower?"

I looked down at my grimy hands. I couldn't remember the last time I had showered.

"Okay…" I replied, giving in. "I guess a hot shower would be nice."

I hopped on Phoenix's motorcycle, and he took me on a ride through the back roads. The wind rushed past us, but the chill in the air had disappeared with the cold season. The crescent moon and millions of stars were showing off, and it was as if all the worries in the world couldn't touch me while riding on the back of Phoenix's bike.

Phoenix pulled up next to the edge of the woods about an hour from my house. "Are we here?" I wondered, dismounting the bike after he cooled the engine.

"No, it's deeper in the woods," Phoenix explained.

"Do we need to worry about vampires?" I asked, skeptical.

"This is the opposite direction of where the hive is, and I've never seen any vampires over here."

"Okay, I trust you," I replied.

"I'd hope so," Phoenix responded playfully while setting his helmet on the seat. "Now, hop on."

"Huh?" I asked, confused.

Phoenix turned his back to me. "Get on."

"Y-you mean… like a piggyback ride?"

"Yeah, I guess so," he said, squatting lower for me to mount his back.

"But why?"

"The spot we're going to is about fifteen miles away, and you walk too slowly."

"Fif-fifteen miles?" I gasped in disbelief.

"Yeah," Phoenix shrugged, unfazed. "Approximately."

"That's, uh, really far."

"I know, but that's why I told you to get on," he reminded me.

"All right…" I agreed, even though I found it odd that Phoenix insisted on carrying me for such a long distance.

"You can get some rest on the way," Phoenix suggested.

"Yeah, right…" I replied, thinking he was joking, and climbed onto his back.

Phoenix quickly grabbed my legs and began to run at full speed. I rested my head on the back of his shoulder, which was comfier than I anticipated.

"You're not tired?" I asked.

"I'm good."

"Isn't fifteen miles a long run for even you?"

"*I'm good*," he gritted, annoyed I continued to doubt his abilities. "We'll be there before sunrise."

I quickly did the calculations in my head. "That's less than an hour and a half."

"Yup," Phoenix replied nonchalantly.

"How much sleep do you need exactly, you know, since the injection?" I wondered.

"An hour or two will get me through the night."

"That must be nice," I added as my eyes involuntarily began to close.

Phoenix's pace didn't let up, and although the terrain wasn't completely flat, the "ride" was smooth, and it made me even more sleepy. Phoenix's suggestion about getting some rest didn't seem like such a bad idea after all, and within less than a few minutes, I dozed off.

I dreamt of standing by the ocean with dozens of seagulls chirping overhead. I was swept off to another world where I nestled my toes in the sand. It was a place where waves endlessly folded over each other and crashed onto the shore. The sun sank lower into the horizon, finally, its turn to rest. I was somewhere safe, and I was free, no worries in sight—no war, only peace. So, I stayed there, enjoying the sunset because I knew I could stay there forever…

"We're here, Delilah," I heard Phoenix say.

"Huh?" I said groggily.

"Are you awake?"

I wiped the drool from the edge of my mouth. "Yeah, I'm awake."

I was startled when Phoenix gently set me down on my feet. My footing seemed unstable for a second, but Phoenix grabbed my waist to make sure I was steady.

"We're on top of a mountain," he explained.

I held onto Phoenix's hand. I had never been so high before. The clouds seemed inches away from my grasp. "B-but how— how did you," I breathed in awe. "How did I sleep through all of this?" I wondered, carefully glancing over the cliff.

Phoenix chuckled. "Guess you were more tired than we both thought."

"And what about you?" I asked again. "How are you? This has to be the tallest peak in Idaho. Seems like it was a steep climb."

"It's not the tallest," Phoenix clarified.

"Okay," I scoffed. "But still…"

"Got here just in time, like I said." Phoenix smiled, satisfied, while staring ahead into the horizon.

The sun began to rise, transforming the night sky.

"I thought we should share something different together," Phoenix mentioned.

I glanced over at Phoenix who was transfixed by the sun making its appearance. I had never felt so close to the Heavens. I could see everything. The forests went on for as far as the eye could see, and the endless rolling hills below us convinced me that we were the only two people on Earth.

"It's beautiful," I breathed in awe.

Phoenix turned his attention toward me. "I've been here a dozen times, but everything seems better when I'm with you."

I smiled at him. "How so?"

He exhaled deeply. "I don't know. I don't know what it is— how you do it and make me feel…"

"Hmm…" I hummed, flattered.

Phoenix continued, trying his best to put his emotions into words, "I just know that when I'm around you, everything feels right, like it's how things are supposed to be."

"Well, what's it like when I'm not around?" I asked, curious.

Phoenix pounded on his chest with a closed fist. "When you're not around, I feel empty, like something's missing. My past has damaged me, but you make me feel like I can be whole again."

"But I thought the New Military gave you what you needed," I pointed out.

"In a sense, yes, but the New Military can only give a person so much. I can pretend that all the fighting in the world will solve my problems, but realistically it won't. It's been more of a distraction, if anything. It's not a real solution, and I've come to realize what I really need is *you…*"

That morning, as we sat near the clouds, it wasn't the rage he was constantly containing that caught my attention, or the rings around his irises that seemed more subtle in the sunlight. It wasn't the change in his body or voice. It was his vulnerability that appeared when only I was around.

"It never mattered if I made it out alive from a fight. There was never anything… or anyone waiting for me," Phoenix said while gritting his teeth as if he was angry.

His eyes began to fill with water, and his gaze moved to his boots as if they were something interesting to look at.

"Are you worried something's going to happen tonight?" I wondered.

Phoenix's eyes met mine, and he stared at me for a minute in silence.

Before he spoke, he breathed a heavy sigh. "I'm worried I won't be able to be with you."

I wrapped my arms around Phoenix, understanding what he meant. I thought back to when I saw the picture in the newspaper of him lying on the cot. I remembered the overwhelming feelings of loss, thinking he was dead.

The task of making the light bombs had distracted me from what was coming. When night fell, I'd be safely guarded in the woods, waiting for the signal to set off the bombs, but Phoenix… he'd be with the other soldiers at the frontal assault. *He* would be the one in real danger. *He* was going to be the one who was fighting for his life.

"You're going to make it back to me," I told him without hesitation. "You have to."

Phoenix leaned away slightly and tilted my chin toward him so he could press his lips against mine, and when he kissed me, I felt like I was being swept away into the clouds. As his hands found their way to my waist again and Phoenix pulled me in closer, it was as if a tornado spun around us—dizzy in the best ways I could imagine. He kissed me wildly, wilder than the beast he kept caged inside.

# Chapter Thirty-one

## Get My Revenge

It took every bribe in the book to convince Ben he should stay at home where he'd be safe. Before Grandpa's death, Ben would've done anything to get as far away from a hive full of vampires. Determination and willingness to lend a hand were never mentioned in the same sentence as Ben, but something inside of him had changed for good.

In this type of fight, Ben had to have known that he would be nothing but a liability. Ben always believed he could protect me in one way or another, but this was different. Attacking a hive could mean he'd be joining Grandpa deep within the earth…

As I sat in the woods, my heart pounded as fiercely as a wild horse's hooves pounding the earth along the mountainside, running at full speed. To ease my nerves, I focused on the night sky. The moon had reached its peak nearly an hour ago. It was bright, full, and much too beautiful to be a witness to a night of bloodshed. I searched for the sparkling stars that always accompanied the darkened sky, but it was useless. The forest's branches were too dense and blocked most of the view.

"Copy," replied the soldier over the radio strapped to his shoulder.

The soldier's back was turned toward me, and he faced the direction of the hive. His mission was to ensure I was safe long enough to set off the bombs.

"I-is it almost time?" I wondered. I stood while brushing the dirt off the back of my jeans with one hand while the other held tightly onto the detonator.

"They're almost done clearing the perimeter," the soldier explained.

"Phoenix…" I whispered.

"What was that?" the soldier asked, turning his attention to me.

"Sorry, I-I…"

"It's ok," he replied, trying to comfort me. "I understand why you're anxious, but I can assure you, we're safe here."

I nodded.

"Name's Bernette," the soldier began to converse—a poor attempt to calm me.

"Delilah," I responded.

"I know," he half chuckled like I was somebody famous who didn't need an introduction.

The soldier's eyes weren't accompanied by rings of violet, and he seemed scrawnier than most of the other people in the New Military. He was most likely a recent recruit. It made sense to have the experienced fighters where it mattered the most—at the hive.

"How long have you been with the New Military?" I asked Bernette.

He thought for a moment, gripping his rifle tighter. When I looked closer, I noticed his arms were becoming exhausted from holding the weapon, shaking ever so slightly. He must've been dying to give his arms a rest and let the weapon dangle by his side, but maybe he was nervous too, or maybe his orders were to keep his guard up.

"Uh, exactly six weeks as of today," he answered.

"Oh…" I said, slightly disappointed my assumptions were correct.

"Don't worry," Bernette added. "I swore my life to protect you so you can get the others home safely, and that's what I plan to do. I may not look like it, but I've got a lot of fight inside me."

"Thank you," I said, acknowledging his bravery.

"So, how did you get all the light bombs set up with the detonator?" Bernette wondered. "Heard you weren't so sure things were going to work out with linking them."

"I had a lot of angels looking down on me," I half-heartedly joked. "Couldn't have done it without them."

We were interrupted by the Upper's voice over the radio, but I couldn't make out what she was telling Bernette.

"What is it?" I asked in anticipation.

"She wants confirmation that you'll be ready to go in a few minutes."

I glanced at the detonator in my hand to see I was shaking worse than Bernette's arms. I flipped the switch on, and the light flashed green, confirming we were in range.

"Yeah, we're good," I replied.

Bernette confirmed over the radio, and then he turned to me as if conversing would make the night go by faster. "I can't wait to get back to the base and celebrate. I can almost taste that chocolate cake on my lips," Bernette said optimistically.

"I love chocolate cake," I added, but more so out of politeness. There was nothing else on my mind besides how tonight would go.

"Hell yeah! Who doesn't? I'm going to eat a slice as big as—" Bernette paused, turning around in a circle with panic on his face.

"What's wrong?"

"Did you hear that?" he whispered cautiously, pointing his rifle in different directions, uncertain where to aim.

"I-I don't… I don't think so?" I replied, unsure.

"There," he said sternly, pointing his rifle just over my shoulder, pinpointing where the noise was coming from.

I thought I heard a branch snap behind me, and my heart thudded crazily.

"Get down!" Bernette shouted.

Without another thought, I purposely fell to the ground, slamming my stomach on the forest floor. I made sure to hold onto the detonator like it was more precious than anything on the planet.

Silver bullets flew above me as Bernette shot off at least a dozen rounds.

Then, suddenly, a blur leaped over me to Bernette. The vampire who was unscathed, grabbed Bernette's rifle, ripping it off its strap and detaching it from Bernette's shoulder. The vampire threw the rifle out of Bernette's reach as well as mine.

"Run, Delilah!" Bernette shouted as he reached for the knife that was strapped to his thigh.

But I couldn't run. I couldn't move. I was frozen as I watched the vampire wrap his hand around Bernette's neck and push him against a tree. "Run," Bernette screeched as his throat was being crushed.

"Too easy," the vampire smirked.

I thought Bernette was done for, but he continued to fight back. Bernette mentioned he had a lot of fight in him, and he was right. The brave soldier thrust the blade into the vampire's ribcage, like it was second nature to him, like he still had a chance of survival.

"Damn you!" the vampire's voice rumbled through the trees.

The monster released Bernette, removed the knife from his side, and bent down to look Bernette in the eyes. "This will be the last night you'll ever see," the vampire giggled to himself angrily.

Bernette's breathing was ragged like he was having difficulty filling his lungs with air. His bloodshot eyes were wide with terror. I watched Bernette slowly fumble for the button on his radio. His mouth opened, and he tried to speak, but nothing came out. Bernette held his hand to his neck, realizing the true damage the vampire had done.

The vampire smirked and gently removed the radio from Bernette's uniform. I could hear the Upper repeatedly asking for a response from Bernette. The vampire clenched the radio with his fist, easily crushing it into a ball. That's when Bernette's face turned a cold shade of blue. Life quickly left Bernette, and his entire body went limp.

"No…" I breathed in disbelief.

Since Bernette was out of the picture, the vampire turned his attention to me. I scurried to get off my stomach and sat up, my body realizing flight was no longer an option.

"Get the hell away from me," I growled.

"Hand over the detonator, my lovely," the vampire demanded, giggling again as he inched closer to me.

I eyed the rifle that was a couple of feet away from me. I knew there was a slim chance I'd be able to retrieve the weapon, but I had to do anything I could. My life wasn't the only one on the line. "Screw you!" I screamed while lunging for the gun.

Before I could get my hands on the weapon, I had been picked up and thrown across the woods. My head crashed on a rock, and the detonator went flying somewhere between the trees.

"Too slow," the vampire mocked. He took a minute to clap his hands, having the best night of his soulless life.

I scooted my back against a tree to brace myself and held my hand to the side of my head. I winced at the touch and glanced at my hand in horror, which was saturated in blood.

"Oh, dear," the vampire cooed. "Looks like you have a bit of a bloody wound there."

My head was foggy, and my sight was blurred. As the vampire approached again, it looked as if there were three of him.

He bent down, his sinister laughter ringing in my ears, and slid his finger just below the cut on my head. He must've placed a taste of my blood in his mouth because he squealed with ecstasy.

"Ooo, I could sit here, savoring you all night, my lovely," he said, and at that moment, I knew I was going to die. I prayed that it would be quick.

"Savor this!" I heard someone yell, and out of nowhere, a beam of light flashed, turning the predator of the night into ash.

I blinked a few more times to clear my vision, breathed in with relief, and looked up to see someone who I never thought in a million years would have saved me…

"Ben?" I gasped in disbelief.

"Bet you weren't expecting me, huh?" he said smugly.

I stood, yelling in frustration, "I told you to stay home!"

"Good thing I didn't listen," Ben replied, "or you'd be dead."

I sighed, realizing he was right. "True…"

Then I remembered how badly my head was throbbing. The trees surrounding me began to spin. I hunched over in pain while shutting my eyes, hoping I could ignore the pain and dizziness.

"Oh, dang," Ben said, realizing I'd been badly hurt. "Sit down."

I did as he said, and Ben knelt beside me, unzipping the fanny pack that was strapped around his waist.

"Goodness," I laughed weakly, "where did you get that?"

"In Grandpa's basement. It had all kinds of first aid stuff in it."

As my vision became less blurry, I could make out what Ben was wearing. "Is that Grandpa's old military outfit?"

"Yeah, looks good, doesn't it?" Ben asked, but it sounded more like a statement.

"Just get me something for my head," I pleaded. "Got any strong pain meds in that fanny pack of yours?"

Ben pulled out a bottle and read the label. "Yup, what do you know? Not sure how long it'll take to kick in, though."

"Don't care, I just need something… anything," I demanded.

Ben popped the pill bottle cap and poured two pills into his hand. "Hmm," he hesitated, "better make it three. Not sure how expired they are, and by the looks of it, you could use an extra."

I didn't argue and quickly snatched the pills from Ben's hand.

Ben grabbed a roll of gauze and wrapped it around my head. "This is a temporary fix until we get you to a hospital. Should stay on okay."

"Oh, no!" I shouted as I looked around frantically for the detonator. "The light bombs."

"What?" Ben wondered.

"I have to set off the light bombs," I told Ben as I crawled around on the ground.

"It's here," Ben said calmly, handing me the detonator.

I sighed with relief. "Thank God."

"All right, so set them off, and I will drive you to the hospital," Ben urged.

My heart plummeted to the pit of my stomach and exploded into a million pieces when I realized the green light had turned red.

"Everything okay?" Ben asked.

"No," I began to cry frantically. "No! No!"

"What is it?"

I stood as a rush of adrenaline pulsed through my veins. Thinking of all the lives that would be lost sent me into a frenzy. "It-it's— there's something wrong with the detonator," I wailed in horror.

"Hey, take it easy," Ben mentioned, placing a hand on my shoulder. "Your head is still bleeding, and you probably have a pretty bad concussion."

"I don't care about my head!" I screamed in frustration.

I didn't care about how much blood I lost. I didn't care how badly my entire body hurt. I didn't care whether I lived or died! I cared about the *soldiers* who were dying. I cared about whether Phoenix would make it out alive!

"I have to save them. I have to get closer. M-maybe it's just out of range," I said, still panicking.

"It's too dangerous, Delilah," Ben said gently. "Look at you, you're in no condition to—"

"They don't know what's going on. No one knows what's happening!" I continued. "The soldier who was with me… his radio is gone. I have to figure out something. I can't just stand around while people die. I have to do this."

Ben sighed, understanding how important it was that we set off the light bombs. "Okay… but I'm coming with you."

"No, you were supposed to be at home. You weren't supposed to be here."

Ben held up the light he had used to rescue me. "I'm coming with you," he insisted. "I can clear the path for you."

Ben was right. I could use his help. I had to remind myself he wasn't the same brother I had before Grandpa died, and we both knew we would be stronger together. If we stuck by each other's side, we were more likely to make it out alive, and the odds of saving more people would be better.

I nodded. "Let's go."

As we walked closer to the hive, through the dense woods, there wasn't another vampire in sight. Luckily for Ben and me, all of them were too busy protecting their queen and defending the castle. The entire time, I kept staring at the detonator, hoping the light would turn from red to green, but it never did.

Ben and I had trekked a quarter of a mile, as fast as we could, and ended up at the edge of the forest in front of the castle. "I-I don't know what's wrong with it. It's not going to work," I told Ben.

In the distance, I could see flashes of light from the extra flashlights we gave to the New Military. I could hear endless gunshots coming from inside the castle and, even worse, screams.

"What do we do?" Ben asked, worried.

"There's a light bomb coated in black paint that is linked to the detonator. That bomb is supposed to create a chain reaction and set off all the other ones. If we can get ahold of that one, then we can—"

"Yeah, I know, Delilah," Ben scoffed. "I've heard this a hundred times."

"Right… right…"

"So, I guess we're going in," Ben said anxiously and stood a bit straighter.

I inhaled deeply, "I guess we are…"

# Chapter Thirty-two

## Dust Myself Off

I thought back to a time when I was younger, a time when Grandpa was still alive. My dad hadn't come home for days, and I was sitting on a swing he had built for me that dangled from the oak tree in the front yard.

As I swung on the swing, I stared as far out onto the back road as I could, hoping that any minute my dad would pull up to the house. I always waited for him, whether on that swing or by the front porch window, and he'd always greet me with open arms, anticipating a welcome home hug. I waited for him because he always came home, *always*… except for that one time.

It would have been the perfect spring day if my dad had been there with me. The birds chirped joyfully, the sun was shining, and the fields were in bloom, but all I could focus on was the road leading to our house, anticipating my dad coming home, something that would never happen.

I didn't understand my feelings as I sat on the swing. It wasn't until I was older that I was able to decipher my emotions. It was rage and sadness entwined. I kicked my legs back and forth, swinging faster… higher and wondered why everyone was leaving me.

Dad always said God had a plan, but I didn't like how the writer wrote Mom's or Dad's story. Why was it ok for him to take them away? Didn't he care about me?

I continued to swing back and forth as fast and fiercely as I could. I didn't let my winded breathing or tired arms stop me. I ignored the cramp in my upper arm that was forming and kept allowing my emotions to run wildly, until… *snap*! The branch on the tree broke, and I fell to the ground, landing flat on my face.

Grandpa came rushing out the front door. He must've been watching me from inside the house. "Delilah, are you all right?" he asked, concerned.

I lay in the dirt, my tears creating small mud puddles as they violently trickled off my chin.

Grandpa came over and lifted me to my feet. "It's going to be ok," he insisted.

I stood whimpering like an injured dog with scrapes on both knees.

"Looks like you didn't hit your head," Grandpa pointed out.

I gave a couple of nods as blood began to run down my shins.

"Come on, let's get you cleaned up," Grandpa urged.

I followed him inside, where he cleaned the scrapes on my knees and put band-aids on them. As Grandpa took care of me, he said, "Delilah, it's important to know that over time, wounds will heal, and then we will eventually feel better, but the thing with deep scrapes is that they tend to leave scars. What's important is that we learn from our experiences, remembering the good and bad, because that's what molds us and makes us who we become later in life. I know you're a tough cookie, and you'll find a way to overcome the pain. Remember… pain is only temporary. It won't last forever."

I hugged Grandpa, tears still streaming down my cheeks because if it wasn't obvious, my heart hurt a million times more than the scrapes on my knees.

# Chapter Thirty-three

## Set It Off

Grandpa was right… he was always right, every life experience molded me into who I was. He taught me how to dust myself off during the hardest of times. He reminded me of how strong I could be, and the memory of falling off the swing showed me how far I'd come.

I looked at Ben who stood next to me. "You ready?"

Ben nodded firmly.

We took off, running the rest of the way to the castle, running from the forest's edge into the fight. Ben ran ahead of me, in better condition than I was. He knew he needed to get me to the light bomb, which would be in the foyer, and we were determined to do whatever it took to save as many lives as possible.

When we entered through the broken doors that had been breached by the New Military, there were hundreds of soldiers and vampires fighting each other, the majority in close combat. Knives and fangs were slashing flesh, causing the castle floor to be stained crimson. There was so much chaos that it was hard to tell which side had the upper hand.

"There!" Ben shouted over his shoulder while pointing to a group of training officers standing back-to-back in a circle, guarding the pile of light bombs. The soldiers were wearing specially made sunglasses, so at first, I didn't recognize Phoenix, not until we got closer to the circle.

"Watch out, Delilah! Behind you!" Phoenix shouted from a few feet away.

I quickly stopped and turned, but I had nothing to worry about. Ben flashed his light before I could get a good look at my attacker. There was nothing but a pile of ash behind me.

"Go, go!" Ben demanded, urging me to the circle of officers.

As I reached them, Phoenix growled at me, "What are you doing here? You are supposed to be in the woods!"

"Let me in," I told Phoenix and the other soldier beside him. "The detonator broke. I need to set the bombs off manually."

"Don't let her get to those!" a voice screeched from above. I looked up at the second story. There was a vampire whose skin was as dark as the forest floor. She was overseeing the fight. "You hear me? Don't let her near the bombs!"

It was strange to think such a thing, but she was beautiful for a soulless creature. Her head was absent of hair, her eyes were outlined thick with black, and her lips were as red as blood. She wore the most extravagant dress that seemed like it would be a burden to wear, too many jewels, too many precious metals, something that would weigh down a human like me.

"Get in there. Don't let us down," the soldier standing beside Pheonix told me as he stepped to the side to make an opening for me to pass through.

As I was about to step into the inner circle, I heard a loud thud. Ben had been hit so hard that he slid far across the concrete floor, damaging the light he was holding.

I didn't have time to react. I didn't have time to think of whether I should check on Ben or find the light bomb because, in an instant, I felt someone grab me from behind, wrapping their hand around the front of my throat.

"Hands off!" Phoenix yelled as he reached for my wrist, simultaneously tossing me from the vampire's grasp and into the pile of light bombs. I wailed in agony. Phoenix had yanked my wrist so hard that he dislocated it. The gaping wound on my head and the scratches on my neck from being pulled away from the vampire's grasp didn't compare to how badly my wrist felt.

"Get back in the circle!" the soldier who Phoenix had been standing beside commanded. "Don't break the circle!"

Phoenix quickly turned the vampire to ash and was ready to return to his designated position, but out of nowhere, there was a blur, and Phoenix stood frozen.

"Phoenix!" I screamed.

The vampire who was standing above us had made her way down and thrust a pointed gold rod into Phoenix's side, just below his ribcage.

I looked around, terrified I was going to lose everyone. Ben was dazed, but thankfully, Carmen, his "date" from the night at Chad's gas station, was playing bodyguard and kept the vampires away from him.

Phoenix wasn't as lucky as my brother, though. Phoenix fell limp… lifeless.

"Queen!" one of the soldiers yelled, directing the other officers' attention to the major threat.

A half dozen officers swarmed the queen, hoping they'd be the one to slay her, but she was too strong. Her reflexes were unmatchable, and effortlessly, she moved on from one soldier to the next like a person swatting pesky flies.

Then I heard a familiar voice. "Come on, Delilah. Do what you need to do, and get it done quickly!" Frankie said, filling Phoenix's spot in the circle. "Lives are counting on you. So, focus!"

But I couldn't focus. My breathing became rapid. My head began to pound as fiercely as my heart, and I was worried I was on the verge of a panic attack.

Frankie knelt beside me, his violet eyes inches from mine. "If you want to save Phoenix and your brother, you do it by setting off the bombs. That's the only way! So, don't give up on us now, Summers."

I took a second I didn't have to spare, but I took that moment anyway to gather myself. Remembering… remembering my dad, my grandpa, and the mother I never had the chance to meet. I was going to do this one way or another for the people I loved, for the people I cared for… for the people who loved me and believed in me. I wasn't going to lose anyone else. I refused to.

I attempted to untie the fish net with one hand since the other with the dislocated wrist was useless, but after a few seconds of struggling, I knew it would be impossible. I realized Frankie had a knife strapped to the side of his leg, so I grabbed it and used it to cut the net. As I did so, many of the light bombs rolled out of the circle of soldiers in all directions, including the one I needed to detonate the rest.

"Shit!" I screamed in frustration.

"Well done," Frankie added, annoyed.

"I need to get the one that's painted— over there!" I pointed and began to crawl out of the circle.

The soldiers who stood around the bombs dispersed as soon as they realized what had happened. Frankie tried to follow beside me as best he could, but there were too many vampires to fight off.

I stayed low, crawling on my elbows. I hoped I would go unnoticed, but how could I have been so naive to believe I could stay invisible in a room full of bloodsucking demons?

I felt a hand around my ankle, and I glanced over my shoulder as the queen pulled me across the room in the opposite direction from where the black light bomb was. The knife I had borrowed from Frankie slipped from my grasp.

Then the queen paused from dragging me like a ragdoll, and I flipped over onto my back as if confronting my attacker face-to-face would give me a better chance of survival. She bent over me with her back hunched like a wild animal, ready to devour her prey.

The queen didn't say a word. It was straight to business. She displayed her fangs as she lifted her pointed golden spear to thrust into me, just like she did to Phoenix.

My only thoughts were of how I couldn't let everyone down. I needed to help win the war, and that was what I intended to do. I held up both my arms, crossing them in front of me, a desperate attempt to shield myself from being stabbed, but the queen's unwavering strength was undeniable…

It was useless to try and stop her, but at least I was able to avoid getting struck in the chest. My attempt to block the queen's attack made her miss her target, and the spear slid into my shoulder rather than my heart.

As she went to retrieve her weapon, I gripped the spear with what strength I had and sat up—a poor attempt to make it more difficult for the queen to remove the spear from my shoulder. But instead of pulling the spear from my flesh, which she could've done with ease, she thrust it deeper, and my screams of agony rang throughout the castle. Her mouth opened widely, and I knew what would happen next. Her fangs would tear through my flesh, and she would suck me dry in an instant.

Suddenly, she paused and stood tall, sensing a threat behind her. In a blur, the queen quickly spun around, but since she had been distracted by me, she let her guard down for a second too long.

Phoenix had his blades deep in both of her shoulders as soon as she stood. She countered by flexing her fingers and plunging her nails into the sides of Phoenix's torso.

I wailed in utter pain as I yanked out the spear that was lodged in my shoulder and stabbed the queen in the back of her leg.

She quickly removed her nails from Phoenix's sides and turned toward me, screeching in frustration, "You little pest!"

Phoenix wrapped his arm around the queen's neck, trapping her in a chokehold. "Go, Delilah," Phoenix said breathlessly.

I crawled to the black light bomb as fast as I could, weaving between vampires and soldiers fighting.

I could hear my grandpa's voice in my head, "*You're a tough cookie. Pain is only temporary.*"

It felt like I had crawled a mile when it had only been a few yards. Eventually, I reached the light bomb, but as I held the ball in my hand, I realized, without my tools, there was no way of opening it up to get to the wires.

"Summers!" Frankie shouted.

My gaze shot over to Frankie, who retrieved the knife I had dropped. He tossed it across the blood-stained castle floor. It was as if the knife slid toward me in slow motion through the legs of soldiers and vampires. I wasn't optimistic the knife would reach me with all the obstacles in its way, but by some miracle, the knife bumped against the side of my foot.

I placed the light bomb between my thighs to hold it in place, picked up the knife, and inserted the tip of the blade into the etching on the light bomb. The button released, allowing me access to the wires.

Within seconds, light as bright as the sun shone everywhere, and the sweetest of sounds rang through the castle. A hundred vampire screams radiated throughout the rooms, and cheers of joy emanated from every soldier who still breathed life.

I collapsed to the ground. My sight was hazy from the light, and I didn't have anything left to give. Relief washed over me, knowing I did my best.

"Delilah!" a familiar voice yelled.

I saw a fuzzy image of Ben rushing toward me. When Ben came closer, he put pressure on my shoulder where I had been stabbed.

"Delilah," Ben continued. "Are you all right?"

I couldn't understand what Ben was asking me. I felt light-headed. Maybe I'd lost too much blood.

"Stay with me," Ben said, but I couldn't respond. I couldn't keep my eyes open any longer…

# Chapter Thirty-four

## Resurrection for One

So also you have sorrow now, but I will see you again, and your hearts will rejoice, and no one will take your joy from you. John 16:22

If I died there in the castle, it would've been okay. If it meant others lived because I gave my life, it was a sacrifice I was willing to make. If giving my last breath meant others could bask under the moonlight and spend an entire night counting the stars, then everything was worth it.

I wouldn't have to endure the sorrows found on Earth. I could experience endless bliss alongside my parents and Grandpa. I could be at peace.

But what about Ben? How would he be able to move forward without me? Would he change again? Would his heart turn completely to ice and become a different person entirely, to the point I wouldn't recognize him? I would miss him. I would miss Phoenix…

I opened my eyes but not to see a world I stared at from above. I awoke but not to see Heaven. I felt different, but not because I was dead.

Phoenix was sitting beside me, reading the newspaper. When he heard me sit up on the cot, he set down the reading material on a small table beside him.

Phoenix smirked like I had done something to amuse him. "Well, hello there, sunshine."

I examined my surroundings, confused. Every cot in the infirmary was empty except the one I was using.

"What's going on? Where am— what happened?" I wondered.

"You're back at the base."

"Where is everyone else? Is Ben at home?"

"Ben is at home," Phoenix confirmed, "and everyone else is packing up the supplies, getting ready to head out."

"Is— was Ben hurt?" I asked, worried.

"He's fine. No serious injuries, just a couple of bruised ribs."

"So, he's safe?"

Phoenix's expression changed, empathy radiating from him. "Everyone is safe… because of *you*. Your sacrifice allowed many people to go on living."

"But why aren't there any injured?" I questioned.

"The, uh… injection," Phoenix explained hesitantly. "We gave it to the soldiers who hadn't already received it. The injection helped save a lot of lives. We couldn't afford to lose anyone else."

I jumped off the cot, which seemed easier than I'd expected, and threw my arms around Phoenix. "I thought I was going to lose you," I breathed, relieved everything was over.

"Ouch!" Phoenix winced.

I released my grip. "Oh, sorry. Are you still hurt?"

Phoenix chuckled nervously, and his words were shaky, "I-I hope you don't get upset, b-but the only way we were going to save you was… The doctor said there wasn't another way. She said you lost too much blood and…"

I tugged at the collar of my shirt to see the stab wound on my shoulder had healed. I felt for a bandage that should've been wrapped around my head, but there wasn't one. I rolled the wrist that should've been in pain even if it was set back in place. It was as if I had never been injured.

I held up the glass of water that was beside the cot, and a pair of violet eyes stared back at me.

To be continued…

Made in the USA
Monee, IL
27 June 2025

19925485R00208